SCORCHED

SCORCHED

MARI MANCUSI

SCHOLASTIC INC.

ISBN 978-0-545-77331-7

12 11 10 9 8 7 6 5 4 3 2 1   14 15 16 17 18 19/0

Printed in the U.S.A.   40

First Scholastic printing, September 2014

*To my parents, who instilled a love of fantasy and imagination at
an early age by reading me the Narnia series, Lord of the Rings,
and countless Choose Your Own Adventure novels.
I promise to pay it forward with Avalon someday.*

They came at noon, black shadows dancing across the sky, drowning out the sun. Their cries echoed through chambers and courtyards. Their fire blazed down narrow streets.

Some dropped to their knees in prayer. Others tried to flee. But in the end, they all fell down—ashes choking their lungs, flames singeing their flesh.

There was no place to run. No place to hide.

They *would* find you.

And when they did…you would surely burn.

—*The Scorch*
by Julian Bachman, year 54 PS

PART 1:

ICE

Chapter One

SCREECH!

Connor's eyes flew open. Blinding white lights barreled toward him at breakneck speed. No time to think, he hurled himself to the side, adrenaline igniting the reflexes he'd honed in boot camp. A bright blue metal monstrosity shot past him, wailing an angry protest in its wake.

That was close. Too close. Sucking in a breath, he crawled up onto a nearby platform, trying to gain his bearings. Shiny hunks of metal machinery—like the one that had nearly crushed him—lined the road, dark and silent, while others cruised by, determined white lights chasing brilliant red tails. They reminded him of something he'd once seen on the Surface Lands. *Cars,* his father had called them. Of course they looked a lot different when living, breathing, and not caked with rust.

But that meant…A smile crept to his lips.

It had worked. It had actually worked.

"Well, what do you know," he murmured, drawing in a lungful of the freshest air he'd ever breathed in all his seventeen years, with zero smoky aftertaste. It was crisp. Colder than they'd predicted for August in Texas. So cold, in fact, he could see his breath reflected in puffy clouds as he exhaled.

Shivering a little—his travel jumper was definitely not made for this kind of weather—he found himself gazing up into an open sky littered with stars and anchored by a bright, full moon. The vastness of the universe unabashedly spread out before him made him a little dizzy.

Maybe I should make a wish, he considered, remembering the old rhyme his mother used to sing. *Star light, star bright…*

Wish my supplies would arrive all right, the soldier in him finished, reminding him he wasn't on some pleasant stargazing holiday. His eyes reluctantly left the sky, scanning the ground below, searching for his canister. One couldn't travel with one's belongings, they'd told him in the debriefing, except for specially designed clothing. Something about splitting up different types of molecules. The essential items they'd sent to aid his mission would be arriving separately. In a titanium pod. Right about—

A large metal cylinder shot through the sky, almost knocking him out before bouncing harmlessly to the ground.

—now.

"What in God's good name was that?"

Connor whirled around to find the largest woman he'd ever seen exiting one of the nearby apartment buildings. He tried not to gape at her immense frame, wrapped securely in a black, puffy coat. What rations must these people be allotted in order to gain such girth? As three equally well-fed and well-dressed young boys filed out behind her, his mind flashed to the orphans of Strata-D. Their rail-thin frames, their hollow, hungry eyes…

He set his jaw. Just another reminder of how important this mission truly was.

As he watched, the three boys scrambled past their mother, eagerly circling the titanium capsule, eyes shining with interest. One reached down, daring to touch it…

Connor swept in, neatly scooping up his belongings. As the children squawked in protest, he held up his free hand. "It's okay," he tried to assure them. "It's just my—"

"Get away from my kids, you freak!" Mom was now on the scene, waving one hand threateningly at Connor, the other fumbling at her coat pocket. For a split second, he feared she was reaching for a weapon. Instead, she pulled out a small, black plastic device. Some kind of primitive transcriber?

"See something, say something," she muttered to her children, waving them behind her, as she frantically started pressing at the screen. "That's what they say to do. Can't let the terrorists win."

"Please," Connor pleaded, taking a few steps backward, his mind desperately searching for a rational explanation for the canister falling from the sky. Preferably one that didn't require prior knowledge of quantum physics. He was supposed to be blending in, not making a scene. He wasn't exactly off to an auspicious start.

His eyes lit upon an open window, two stories up, red-checkered curtains fluttering in the night sky. "My…girlfriend," he stammered, his mind reaching for the proper terminology as he waved his arm in the direction of the window. "She tossed me out." He gave the woman his best sheepish smile, then held up the canister. "Told me to take my gear and never come back." The woman narrowed her eyes, staring at him for a moment, then up at the open window. Connor realized belatedly that she could very well know the girl who lived in the apartment above or know that there was no girl to begin with. This wasn't like back home; people here knew their neighbors, shared cups of sugar—that sort of thing. Had he just made a huge mistake?

Believe me, he pushed, in a feeble attempt to try to bend her will. *Believe me and walk away.*

But it was no use. The trip had left him completely depleted. And he had no idea how long it would take to regenerate his spark. He'd be forced to do things the old-fashioned way—at least for the foreseeable future.

"What's her name?"

Connor startled. "What?"

"Her name," the woman repeated. "Your girlfriend who threw you out. Does she have a name?" She gave him a pointed stare, as if daring him to answer, her fingers still hovering dangerously close to her transcriber.

"Oh right. Her name is…"

His mind went blank. Completely blank. *Come on, Connor. A name! Any name!* He could feel her eyes upon him, sharp, assessing, as they took in his strange clothes with growing suspicion. He had to do something—say something—and fast. Before it was too late. "Her name is…"

With one fluid movement, he ripped open the capsule, his fingers diving for his gun. Before the woman could even grasp his intentions, he had the weapon trained on her face. "Her name is *get the hell back*!" he growled. "And I suggest you do as she says."

The woman's eyes bulged and a small squeak escaped her lips. Staggering back, she held up her hands in surrender, her transcriber falling from her meaty grasp and clattering to the pavement below. Her children screamed, latching on to their mother, their innocent little faces mirroring her terror as Connor narrowed his eyes, doing his best to look desperate and dangerous. As if he were the type of guy who shot down mothers and children in cold blood every day before breakfast.

"Please, mister," the woman begged, fat tears streaming down her cheeks. "You can have everything. Just let us go." She shrugged her bag off her shoulder, allowing it to fall to the ground. "There's plenty of cash in there. Take it all. Just don't hurt my kids."

Connor sighed, lowering his gun. And…so much for blending in.

"It's okay," he tried to assure her, guilt gnawing at his insides. He'd meant to stop her from making her call, not scare her and her family half to death. "I promise I'm not going to hurt you."

I'm the good guy, he wanted to add. *The one they sent to save your world.*

But of course he couldn't tell her that. It would just bring up too many unanswerable questions. And he had to get a move on anyway—catalog his gear, get changed, locate the museum. Do a little preliminary scouting before introducing himself to the girl. He had a lot to accomplish in the next four months—before the Reckoning day—and, as his father would say, there was no time like the present.

Or the past, in this particular case.

He gestured to the woman's bag with an apologetic look. "Take your stuff. Just walk away and pretend you never saw me, okay?"

Yeah, like that was going to happen. He could tell from the

look in her eyes she'd remember this incident till her dying day. Her children too. But it couldn't be helped, he reminded himself. And they would thank him if they knew the truth. They would get down on their very knees.

The woman's face crumpled in relief. "Thank you, sir!" she babbled. "Thank you, thank you so much." She scurried to grab her bag, then collected her cracked transcriber. "Merry Christmas," she babbled as she gathered up her children and turned to leave. "Merry Christmas to you and yours."

Connor had started to walk away. But the woman's words made him pause. "Wait, what? What did you just say?" He turned back to her questioningly.

The woman whimpered, holding her hands in front of her face, as if she was afraid he was going to hit her. "Um, I just said merry Christmas," she stammered. "Or, you know, whatever holiday you celebrate—Happy Hanukkah? Kwanza?"

"But…" Connor protested, his mind racing with sudden confusion. "It's August."

The woman stared at him, as if he'd lost his mind.

"It has to be August," he repeated, panic welling up inside of him. "They told me it would be August. Four months before the Reckoning."

"Um, I don't know what that is," the woman sputtered. "But it is Christmas. I promise you, it's Christmas Eve. In fact, I was just about to take the boys over to see the tree. They've never seen it lit up and—"

She kept babbling, but Connor was no longer listening. He dug into the capsule again, heart pounding wildly in his chest as he searched for his transcriber. There had to be some mistake. The woman had to be lying. Because there was no way…

His hands closed around the device and he pulled it from the pod with shaking fingers. He flicked it on, waiting anxiously for the screen to illuminate, scarcely able to breathe.

December 24th, the device read. *7 p.m.*

"No," he whispered in horror. "That can't be right."

But it was, he realized. The signs had been there from the start. August in Texas—it should have been a hundred degrees out—not cold enough to snow.

Something must have gone wrong back at the base. Someone must have pressed the wrong button, turned the wrong dial.

"I was supposed to have four months!" he cried, looking up at the woman with wild eyes. She gave him a helpless shrug, then turned and fled down the street as fast as her thick legs could carry her, her kids scrambling to catch up. Connor watched them go, suddenly feeling as frightened as they must feel. But for a very different reason.

"I was promised four months," he whispered to no one.

With four months, he could have secured a strong link with the girl. He could have made sure the egg never fell into her hands. He could have gotten a jump on the government…

…and saved his father's life.

Now he had exactly fifteen minutes. Fifteen minutes to find the museum. Fifteen minutes to retrieve the egg and the girl. Fifteen minutes to figure out a way to make this all turn out right.

Or the apocalypse that ripped apart his world would begin…all over again.

Chapter Two

"If I get one more snot-nosed kid asking me if the *T. rex* used to dine on people, I'm going to close up the museum and become a history teacher. I mean, really! What are they teaching kids in schools these days?"

Sixteen-year-old Trinity Foxx looked up from her laptop in time to see her grandpa come barreling into the museum's main office, rounding the corner too quickly and slamming into a table of fish fossils by the door. She winced as he scrambled to stop a four-hundred-million-year-old cephalopod from crashing to the floor.

"Hey! Watch the ancient artifacts," she protested, logging out of the museum's Facebook page and rising to her feet. "Some of them are even older than you are. And almost as brittle."

"Thanks." Grandpa shot her a smirk as he limped over to his desk, rubbing his knee. "Your concern is truly heartwarming, as always."

She snorted. "Why are you giving tours anyway? What happened to Gene?"

Grandpa dumped a stack of mail onto his desk, then nearly knocked it off as he shrugged out of his suit jacket. Trinity had to dive to save it from landing in a nearby trashcan, which may or may not have been her grandfather's intention in the first place.

"Quit right after his last paycheck bounced," he muttered. "But really, it's for the best. The idiot couldn't even keep his Triassic and Jurassic time periods straight. How could he be expected to educate and inspire America's youth?"

"Right." Trinity sighed as she walked back over to her desk, ripping open the red-marked "Urgent" envelope at the top of the stack. This one was from the electric company, who'd been threatening to shut off power to the museum for the last three months. She didn't know why companies bothered wasting paper on fourth and fifth notices. Just because they couldn't afford to pay the first one didn't mean they needed a new copy. "Well, I hope you charged the group full price, at least."

Grandpa walked around to sit behind his desk, avoiding her eyes. "They were from a poor district in Stocktown. Mostly migrant farmer kids and illegals."

"Of course they were." Her grandpa's kind heart was one of his best qualities—but it was also going to be the death of them. "And what about that history museum in Kentucky?" she asked. "The one you loaned the Ornithischian dinosaur exhibit to six months ago?" She flipped through the stack of envelopes, praying for something that resembled a check.

Grandpa waved her off. "Next week. They promised to pay me next week."

Trinity gave up, plopping the stack of bills onto her desk. It was always next week, next month, next year. Except what Grandpa couldn't seem to grasp was there wouldn't be a next week, month, or year if they didn't start finding a way to pay the bills.

Back in the day, Foxx's Fantastical Fossils had been a famous West Texas attraction, luring tourists off the highway with exhibits that promised to rival all but the most top-tier institutions. Her grandfather's collection of dinosaur bones from the Jurassic period alone was well worth the trip off the interstate.

But five years ago the main highway had been rerouted and traffic thinned to a crawl, the roadside attraction now too far a detour for all but the most determined of tourists. And though the money stopped flowing, the bills kept piling up, and much of the collection had to be sold off or loaned to wealthier museums just to keep the lights on and the doors open.

To make matters worse, her grandpa had started replacing some of his former exhibits with what some might call... *questionable* stand-ins, hoping to draw back the crowds. From a mangy Chupacabra corpse to a rack of jackalope horns, Trinity knew it was not for nothing the townspeople had started whispering about "Crazy Old Foxx's Fossilized Freak Show." It was only a matter of time, she knew, before they'd be shuttered for good.

And where would that leave her?

"Grandpa..." she started to plead, then closed her mouth. What good would it do? Her guardian, much as she adored him, was the quintessential nutty professor—too wrapped up in his own spectacular inner world to comprehend even the most basic of money matters.

Which left it all up to her.

Since she'd moved in after her mother's death, she'd done what she could, from taking over the museum's publicity and custodial duties after school so they could cut back on staff, to cleaning houses and mucking out barns on weekends to earn extra cash. But try as she might, it never seemed like enough. And her carefully constructed world was feeling more and more like a house of cards each day. Every time the phone rang or someone knocked on their door, she'd freeze in panic—convinced it was social services, come to take her away. Her caseworkers had never been truly convinced that her grandpa was capable of taking on the responsibility of an orphaned teenage girl. And they'd be more than happy for an excuse to throw her back into foster care.

But Trin was not going back. Not now that she finally found a family to call her own. And whether that meant hiding their financial situation from neighbors and teachers or begging debt collectors for "just one more extension," she did what she had to do to keep the two of them together. Last week she'd even pawned her mother's emerald ring to pay their overdue property taxes.

She involuntarily glanced down at her finger, still sporting a tan line from where the ring had been—before she'd been forced to hand it over to the shady-looking man behind the bulletproof glass. It had been the only treasure she'd been allowed to keep after her mother's death and her finger felt naked without it.

But it was worth it to see her grandpa's face, she reminded herself, when she presented him with the stack of bills. Enough money to pay their property tax and even a little left over to celebrate Christmas. Knowing their home was safe and their family intact was worth more than the Crown Jewels.

She sighed. Some days she felt much older than sixteen.

"Hey, hey!" her grandfather protested, catching her face. "Chin up, young girl! It's Christmas Eve after all! And I've got a surprise for you."

"A surprise?" she repeated, looking up with curiosity despite herself. "Are you actually going to let me open a gift early for once?" Grandpa had strict rules about waiting until after breakfast on Christmas morning for any unwrapping, and usually Trin was cool with that, enjoying the anticipation and all. But this year she already knew what she'd find under the tree—the expansion pack for her favorite RPG video game, *Fields of Fantasy*—and it was killing her to wait.

Sure, she knew it was a shameful indulgence—and the money it cost would have been better spent on paying their bills. But Grandpa had insisted, saying everyone deserved something frivolous at Christmas, and, for once, she'd been too excited to put up much of a fight. Video games were her kryptonite, after all. Her escape when real life got too tough.

"Absolutely not!" Grandpa shot back. "You know the rules." He wagged his finger at her. She sighed. Maybe after he went to bed she could unwrap the box and download the CD onto her computer, then carefully wrap it up again and place it back under the tree. Terrible, she knew. But otherwise, how was she even going to sleep, knowing it was just sitting there under the tree waiting for her?

"Okay, not a present. Did we win the lottery then?" That would be a surprise she could certainly get behind.

Grandpa smiled mysteriously. "In a sense," he said. "It's a new exhibit. Arrived this morning when you were at school, from my guys in Antarctica."

Last year, when times had been a little better, Grandpa

had partially sponsored a small eco-archeological study on the effects of global warming on penguins. But for all the data the team had sent back so far, Trinity had been convinced they were just sitting up there, sucking down glacier-made frozen margaritas and running dollar bills through a paper shredder.

"Well, all right," she said approvingly. "What did they find?"

"An egg," Grandpa pronounced. "Perfectly preserved too. Evidently the team was out measuring one of the melting glaciers when they came across it, still half embedded in the ice. They believe it's been just sitting there, frozen, for millions of years."

Trinity felt her heart beat a little faster. "And what do they think it is?" she asked, trying not to get her hopes up. She had to admit, a new exhibit like this—if it could be verified—could be sold to pay off some bills. To keep the lights on. Maybe even get her mother's ring back. "Some kind of bird? A dinosaur egg?"

Please let it be a dinosaur egg. They could loan it out to a bigger museum and collect a fee that would pay their electricity bill and—

"Even better."

Trinity pursed her lips, enthusiasm deflating as she caught the gleam in Grandpa's eyes. It was a look she knew all too well—the same he'd worn last summer when he'd presented her with fossilized Sasquatch dung he'd purchased off eBay. It had even, to her chagrin, come with a certificate of authenticity.

She sighed. Maybe they could advertise candlelit tours as romantic…

"Come on!" Grandpa urged. "You're going to love this. I promise!"

She reluctantly followed him out of the office, heading

down what had once been a gorgeous marble hallway, a majestic showcase filled with treasures from around the world. Sadly, today that showcase seemed as extinct as the dinosaurs themselves. The marble floors were cracked and stained and the treasures long gone, with only a few dinky exhibits remaining behind—those that no one had wanted to borrow or buy. It made her heart ache to see the halls that had once teemed with life and history reduced to a cavernous graveyard of broken dreams and empty display cases.

"Here we are," Grandpa announced, stopping in front of the Millennium Chamber. Trinity raised an eyebrow in surprise. The chamber had lain empty for the last two years, with none of the remaining exhibits deemed worthy of Grandpa's favorite room. For him to put the egg here—well, he must truly believe it to be something special. She bit her lower lip, her heart thudding in anticipation as she watched him unlock the door and gesture for her to enter.

She did, trying to prepare herself for inevitable disappointment and—

She stopped in her tracks, staring in disbelief at the egg perched in a glass case at the center of the room. It was beautiful. No—that wasn't enough. It was breathtaking—the size of a basketball and the color of pure gold, its surface intricately etched with what looked like feathers. Or maybe scales…?

"Oh my God," she murmured, approaching slowly. Maybe her grandpa really *had* stumbled on something big for once. After all, she'd devoured every book in his research library over the last two years and had never come across anything remotely like this. "It has this sheen. Almost—I don't know— like it's not even real."

She found herself reaching out, her hand pressing against the glass. This wasn't just some fossil. This was a real egg—perfectly preserved as her grandpa had said. Had it really been frozen in a glacier for millions of years?

"Isn't she beautiful?" Grandpa asked in a reverential whisper. "I've spent my entire life searching for something like this. People will come from around the world to see it—once they hear what we've found." He turned to her, his eyes glistening.

"But what is it?" she asked, reluctantly turning away from the egg and back to her guardian, her eyes filled with questions. "What could it possibly be?"

"Why, isn't it obvious?" He stepped toward the case, a slow smile spreading across his whiskered face. "It's the world's last dragon egg."

Chapter Three

*D*amn, this helmet itched like a flecking bond'ura flea.

    Caleb Jacks forced himself to sit straight and tall on the hard wooden bench, staring directly ahead at the other soldiers in his unit. It had been a bumpy two-hour trip to Old Oak Grove, Texas, with no windows or fresh air in the truck, and by the time they pulled up to the museum, Caleb was about ready to vomit in his helmet. But he couldn't let his discomfort show, couldn't afford to stick out in any way—not after he'd spent months securing a spot on this elite, black-ops team.

It hadn't been easy, especially getting placed on this particular mission. But the Dracken had done an excellent job at forging his paperwork, and his years of experience living on the streets down in Strata-D had made him strong and smart. He just channeled his twin brother Connor—the true soldier in the family—kept his head down, followed orders, and didn't complain. He was, as his commander complimented, a natural choice for the mission.

Caleb swallowed back a chuckle. If only the old bastard knew how right he was.

Cold air flooded the truck, and he forced back a shiver as

the rear door opened. All eyes turned to watch their superior heave himself up onto the truck bed, his heavy frame shaking the vehicle as his boots hit the floor one by one. He was dressed in the same standard-issue bulletproof vests as the rest of them, with only a shiny American flag pin to set him apart as the leader of the team. It still amused Caleb to see these people have so much pride in a country that would soon be accused of burning the entire world to the ground.

Just before the back door closed again, Caleb observed two men standing outside. Dressed in black suits and wearing mirrored sunglasses, they whispered urgently to one another. They were the brains of the operation, he noted grimly. The only ones who had any clue what this mission was really about. The rest of them were simply dumb muscle, obeying orders without question. They couldn't be blamed for what these two men planned to unleash on the world.

"Okay, ladies," the leader sneered. "You've all been briefed on your mission. Anderson," he barked at the burly, dark-skinned man at the end of the row, "you work to disable the security system and video surveillance. Burn any tapes you find. I do not want to see any of your ugly mugs on the nightly news."

"Yessir."

"The rest of you, seek out the objective and secure it by any means necessary. But please, for the love of Christmas, be careful with it. You scramble this sucker and the Pentagon will have my ass." He leered at his men. "And then I'll have yours."

The men tittered nervously while Caleb resisted the urge to roll his eyes. If only they knew how durable their precious "objective" actually was. Hell, you could take a sledgehammer to the egg and you'd be hard pressed to make even the slightest dent. There was a reason, after all, why it'd survived for millions of years.

The captain kept talking, but Caleb stopped bothering to listen. He had his own mission to think about, after all. One far more important than these duffers could ever imagine. His heart thudded in anticipation just thinking about it as he stared down at his hands.

Two long years he'd been here, waiting for this night. Two long years he'd spent alongside his Dracken brothers and sisters—preparing for the Reckoning. Two long years and now the hour was finally here. *He* was here. The one Darius had chosen—out of everyone else—to carry out the most important mission the world would ever know. Sure, partially it was because of his age—he blended in with the rest of the operatives better than the older Dracken would. But still, he had been chosen. He had been entrusted with the future of the world. The street rat criminal of Strata-D. The guy everyone had dismissed as worthless. He would change the world forever.

And he would finally meet *her*.

His heart hammered foolishly at the idea. The legend. The Fire Kissed. The girl who would fly. Was she inside the museum even now, unknowingly waiting for her destiny to unfold? He tried to imagine the look on her face when he told her who she really was, what she would do. Right now, she probably thought herself a normal girl. He used to think he was normal too. She would have no idea of her role in changing the shape of the world.

He couldn't wait to tell her.

Are you in there, Trinity? he asked silently as the truck door creaked open again. *Because, ready or not, here I come.*

Chapter Four

A dragon egg?

Trinity let out a slow breath. She could feel her grandpa regarding her with eager eyes, as if anticipating praise for a job well done. She hated to hurt his feelings—on Christmas Eve nonetheless—but she couldn't risk him going off half-cocked, spilling the ridiculous story to anyone who would listen. Their museum's reputation was already in too much jeopardy as it was. And if social services caught wind that her grandpa had lost his mind as well as his bank account, they'd be sure to take her away.

Time for some tough love.

"Come on, Grandpa, we've been through this," she tried, as kindly as she could. "A dozen times at least. There are no such things as dragons."

"Of course there aren't *now*," he came back, in a *duh* voice that would rival any six-year-old's. "They've been extinct for millions of years. Probably wiped out by an ice age. But somehow, some way, this egg was preserved. The very last of its kind."

She sighed. "But if dragons had been real," she tried to rationalize, not sure why she bothered, "we'd have found other remains before now. Fossils. Bones. Just like we have with the dinosaurs and a hundred other extinct species."

"Perhaps," Grandpa replied with a shrug. "Or perhaps their bone structure was different from other reptiles of their time. Maybe it wasn't meant to withstand extreme temperatures. For all we know, maybe their bones completely dissolved, leaving no trace behind. Except…" His eyes gleamed again. "This egg." He grinned widely. "Thankfully those researchers had no idea how valuable their find really was. Or else I never would have gotten it so cheap."

She stopped short. "Cheap?" she repeated slowly. "Define cheap." She'd assumed since Grandpa had partially sponsored the expedition, he'd have some claim on the egg. She should have known better. Those so-called researchers had been nothing but money-grubbers from the very start.

"Well, cheap for the world's last dragon egg," he clarified. "But well worth it. Just think, Trin, of the throngs that will come once we announce our legendary find. The media, the scientists, people from around the world."

"How much?" she repeated, nerves tensing. And where had he gotten the money? She'd cut up his credit cards six months ago, after the whole Nigerian unicorn horn incident. And their bank accounts typically hovered at less than zero status. In fact, the only real cash they'd seen in the last few months was the money she'd given him after selling her mother's ring…

Oh God.

He couldn't have. Could he?

"You didn't. I mean, you didn't use…" She trailed off, unable to even voice the accusation. But the look on his face told her all she needed to know. And her house of cards officially came crashing down on top of her.

"Oh God," she whispered. "How could you?"

If they didn't pay their property tax, their house would be seized. It would go on the auction block and be sold to the highest bidder. They'd end up homeless…

…they'd take her away.

"I had to!" Grandpa sputtered, his face flushed and his eyes flashing. "They were going to sell it to someone else."

"You mean someone who could afford it?"

"Yes…I mean, no…I mean…" He gave her a tortured look. "You don't understand. I've waited my entire life for this kind of discovery. Something special. Something extraordinary. Something that will shake up the very foundations of paleontology as we know it! How could I let something like that slip through my fingers?"

How indeed? By habit, she reached to twist her mother's ring around her own finger, only to be reminded it wasn't there anymore. Because she'd sold it. To keep her family together. Instead, it had paid for some kind of freakish mythical monster spawn. She wondered if the egg was even real. Had even come from a glacier. She imagined the researchers laughing to themselves as they boxed up some arts and crafts project and wrote out the bill. *He'll buy it,* they'd probably sniggered. *The gullible fool will buy anything.*

She glared at the egg, tears welling in her eyes. It was all she could do not to unlock the case and smash the thing to smithereens. She thought about how hard she'd worked. How tired she was. And how none of it mattered in the end. Her grandpa cared more about his precious exhibits than he did about their family.

"Hey, hey!" She felt a hand on her shoulder and turned to see her grandpa gazing at her with concern in his eyes. "What's wrong? I thought you'd be excited. I mean, a dragon egg, Trinity! We're going to be famous."

"We're going to be homeless."

"We'll buy a new house—a hundred houses with the money we make. We'll go down in history."

"Not before we go down in flames."

He stared at her, disappointment clear in his watery blue eyes. "You used to love my discoveries," he said softly. "You used to get so excited. What happened to you, Trin? When did you stop believing?"

She shrugged her shoulders, the lump in her throat making it impossible to speak. She remembered all the times her grandpa had come home from his many trips overseas with treasures from around the world. Real treasures—the kind scientists and journalists were chomping at the bit to see. But Grandpa would always make them wait—so she could see them first. It had made her feel so special—to spend hours with him, poring over the discoveries, imagining aloud what the creatures must have looked like when they still roamed the earth. Like some kind of magic—shared just between the two of them.

But then she'd grown up and realized magic didn't pay the bills. Didn't keep families together. And certainly didn't guarantee the happily ever after the storybooks claimed. Which made it, in her opinion, pretty darn useless.

"Just go home," she said in a gruff voice, wrestling to control her upset. "I'll lock up. We'll figure out what to do with this…this…thing…on Monday." Maybe the guys who sold it to him had some kind of return policy…

"Don't you want me to help—?"

"I think you've done enough," she snapped.

Grandpa's face crumpled, and her heart broke as she caught the hurt in his eyes. But her anger burned too hot for her to back down now. He had to know that what he'd done wasn't okay. It wasn't funny or kooky or cute this time. He was supposed to be the adult, the one who took care of her. And like every other adult in her life, he'd let her down.

"Okay," he said in a soft, desperate voice. "I'll pick up the Chinese food on the way home. Extra duck sauce, just as you like it."

"Sure. Whatever." As if she could eat. As if it would taste like anything but cardboard.

"And maybe you can open up just one present…"

She scowled, turning away, staring hard at the wall, willing the tears not to fall. She could feel her grandpa's eyes burning into her back but refused to acknowledge them—refused to let him off the hook that easy.

After what felt like an eternity, she heard his deep sigh followed by fading footsteps. Only after the door clanked shut did she allow herself to cry, sinking to the floor, head in her hands, violent sobs choking from her throat as tears rained down her cheeks. The kind of ugly cry she only allowed herself to have when she was sure no one was around to see.

Trinity…

Her head shot up. Oh God, was someone here?

Don't cry, Trinity.

Her face flushed crimson. Who had caught her in such a mess? But the room was empty. The door remained closed. Had she simply imagined the voice?

She shook herself, feeling stupid, then rose to her feet, swiping away the tears with her sleeve. She was just stressed. Stressed and exhausted. She needed to lock up and go home and lose herself in a marathon session of *Fields of Fantasy*— pre-expansion pack. Slay a bunch of virtual dragons and get this real-life nightmare out of her head.

Why would you want to hurt a dragon?

What? She stopped in her tracks. "Who's there?" she demanded angrily, her voice echoing through the chamber. Was this some kind of joke?

No answer.

"Grandpa? Is that you?" she tried again. But even as she asked, she knew it couldn't have been her guardian. The voice was too high-pitched, too plaintive—the voice of a young child, not an old man. Maybe one of the kids from the earlier tour? Her eyes darted around the chamber, searching for some kind of corner or crevice where a child could hide. But she came up empty. The only ones here were her...

...and the egg.

She found herself glancing fearfully at the glass case, heart racing in her chest. But the golden sphere only gleamed back at her, still and silent as the grave. She grimaced. What was she thinking? That the exhibits were coming to life and crying out her name? God, that was the kind of fantasy her mother would have concocted near the end. She reached for her missing ring again, then gave up and started back toward the exit.

Don't go, Trinity. Don't leave me here alone.

"Stop it—it isn't funny!" she cried, fear throttling her now. "Seriously, show yourself or I'm going to call the cops." But no mysterious child stepped forward to claim the voice. It was almost as if it had come from thin air…

Or from her own head.

Like mother like daughter, something inside of her jeered. She pushed it angrily away.

It's just this damned place, she tried to assure herself as she stalked out of the room, grabbing her jacket from the office and heading toward the exit, her steps reverberating through the cavernous hall. A glorified graveyard of fossilized ghosts—it would have anyone hearing things. Hell, maybe she could transform it into a haunted house next Halloween. That would be one way to bring in some cash at least.

Because the alternative explanation…

I'm nothing like Mom. Nothing like Mom.

A squeal outside caused her to pause at the front door. It was a welcoming sound—a real sound, existing outside her head. She peered out the front window and, to her surprise, saw a large, black truck idling just beyond the front parking lot, the rear door rolled open. She watched, curious, as a group of men dressed in black and armed with heavy artillery started spilling out the back, heading straight across the parking lot and toward the museum.

"What the…?" she whispered.

On impulse, she clicked the deadbolt into place. As if that was going to stop some kind of impending invasion. The place had never exactly been Fort Knox when it came to security, even when it *was* holding treasures that might be worth stealing. She glanced out the window again, panic raging through her. Were they really planning to break into the museum?

Well, they're probably not here for the guided tour.

She decided not to wait to find out. Turning on her heel, she bolted from the door, back into the museum, her mind racing and her pulse pounding out her fear. Should she call Grandpa? The police? Should she try to escape out the back door or would they have the place surrounded? And what would she be escaping from anyway? Who were they? What did they want? And why would they be here in the first place? It wasn't like they had anything left worth—

The egg.

She stopped short. What if it *was* valuable after all? What if someone had gotten wind of its arrival and had come to steal it? Or what if it was stolen to begin with—if the researchers hadn't found it in a glacier after all? The authorities could have tracked it down here and come to take it back to its rightful owners. It seemed crazy, but it was the only explanation that made any sense.

She looked around, realizing she'd stopped directly in front of the Millennium Chamber. She also realized that the door, which she was sure she'd left open, was now securely closed. Was there someone inside? Were they taking back the egg? She imagined her grandpa's face when she was forced to tell him his golden treasure had been ripped away before he'd ever gotten a chance to share it with the world. It would kill him. Absolutely kill him. And any hope she had to recoup what he'd spent would be gone forever.

She hesitated at the door. Maybe she could reason with them. Or at least let them know it wasn't her grandpa's fault. He'd never willingly purchase stolen property. He might be gullible. He might deluded. But he wasn't a criminal. She drew in a breath and approached slowly, apprehension coursing through her. Wrapping her hand around the doorknob, she gingerly pushed it open, peering inside.

The Millennium Chamber was no longer empty.

The boy inside was tall and broad shouldered, around her age, and dressed in a strange jumpsuit of shimmering metallic material—very unlike the men in black she'd seen outside. He had a sharp-angled face, messy brown hair, and serious blue eyes. But what was truly startling was his skin. So pale it was almost translucent.

Closing in on the display case, the boy reached into his bag. With one fluid movement, he pulled out what appeared to be a small pistol, though unlike any Trin had ever seen. She gasped as he raised the weapon and smashed it down on the glass with surprising force.

What the hell was he trying to do?

Chapter Five

"Damn you, blasted thing," Connor swore under his breath as he slammed his laser pistol against the case a second time. But it was no use; the glass remained intact and the egg inside only gleamed back at him, as if mocking his efforts. He needed something heavier—a bat maybe or some kind of crowbar. The kinds of tools he could have easily acquired had he been given the four months he'd been promised.

He raised the gun again, started to swing—

"Get the hell away from that!"

Startled, he lost his grip. The pistol bounced harmlessly off the case and skittered across the floor to the opposite side of the room. He spun around, his jaw dropping as his eyes fell upon none other than Trinity Foxx herself, standing in the doorway.

Holy shiny dragon scales.

She was younger, of course, than any of the grainy photos or videos he'd seen on his reader. They'd all been taken years later. She was smaller than he'd pictured her too. In the photos, she'd always seemed larger than life. Her hair was darker and longer, tumbling down her back in untamed waves, and her skin was freckled and tanned from a life spent on the Surface Lands.

And yet, he realized, for all those differences, her eyes were exactly the same—midnight black, almost too large for her face, framed with a sweeping curtain of lash. He swallowed hard, heart racing. How many nights had he spent at the academy, under a blanket, reader in hand, studying that face? Wondering how a girl with eyes like that could bring about the end of the world?

Now he finally had a chance to find out. And, more importantly, a chance to stop her.

He bit his lower lip as he turned back to the display. His plan had called for getting her as far away from the egg as possible before the Reckoning took place. That way she'd never be close enough to hear the fiend's call. But it was too late for that now. And maybe she could help him. With the government agents running through the halls, he didn't have much time left.

"Look, do you have a key or something?" he asked, gesturing to the case. It felt strange to be addressing someone so notorious, and he wondered if she could hear the slight tremble in his voice. "We need to get this egg out of here. Now!"

She stared at him, disbelief clear on her face. Then her brows furrowed and her frown deepened. Not surprising, he supposed. She had no idea he was the only person who could save the world. And he had no time to explain.

"Are you kidding me? Look, I've called the cops. They're on their way. So I suggest you get out of here now, before it's too late." He could hear the thread of hysteria winding through her bold-faced lie as she worked overtime to keep her terror masked from his view. He found himself admiring her tenacity even though it was at odds with his mission.

"You don't understand," he tried, his mind whirling, trying to figure out the best way to explain the situation in the shortest amount of time. *If only he'd had those four months!* "My name is Connor. I'm here to help you. The men breaking into the museum—they'll do whatever it takes to get this egg. We have to get it out of here before they find it."

"*We?*" she repeated, her dark eyes impaling him. "There is no *we*. Now get the hell away from there." She reached into her bag and pulled out a strange metal canister from her purse. He squinted at it; was it some kind of weapon? A grenade of some sort? He was really getting sick of all these surprises.

Holding up his hands in surrender, he stepped back from the case, glancing longingly at his pistol, still out of reach on the other side of the room. But maybe it was best this way. Let her unlock the case, then jump in and grab the egg before she could put her hands on it.

"Just don't touch it," he warned, as she fumbled with a set of brass keys. He realized her hands were shaking furiously, at odds with her defiant expression. "I'm serious."

"What, is it going to bite me?" she retorted, finding the proper key and sliding it into the lock. The case popped open. Connor's eyes zeroed in on the egg.

Now! He made his move, lunging toward the prize. But Trinity was too quick, turning on him and blasting him in the face with a hot stream of liquid from her canister. Connor staggered, blinded, his eyes burning as if on fire. He rubbed them with his fists, trying to clear them, but only managed to increase the sting.

"Please!" he begged. "Whatever you do, don't touch the egg!"

She didn't answer. And when his vision finally cleared, she was gone.

And so was the egg.

"Damn it!" he cried, grabbing his pistol and bag, and running out of the room. He couldn't lose her or the egg. The future of the world depended on it. He raced down the hallway, following the sounds of her footsteps slapping against the marble floors some distance ahead. He glanced behind him, half expecting the operatives to be hot on his heels. But thankfully the corridor was empty.

I could have saved her, he thought wildly, as he cut through the dinosaur exhibit. *I could have gotten her out of this whole mess unharmed. She could have lived a normal life, had a happily ever after.*

But now it was too late.

A scream echoed through the hallway. Her scream—coming from right around the corner. He skittered to a stop, swinging a hard right into the sea-life installation. Ducking behind a giant turtle fossil, he located Trinity, in the grip of a burly man dressed in black. She was still clutching the egg with white-knuckled fingers as the man pressed a pistol to her temple.

"Let me go!" she screamed, fighting him with all her might. But the man outweighed her by at least a hundred pounds and, by the looks of it, had a killer grip.

"I've got some girl," he reported into a black metal device attached to his shoulder. "She was trying to escape with the egg."

"Don't let her go," a voice crackled over the airwaves. "I'll be right there."

Connor froze, his heart in his throat. *That voice.* He'd

recognize it anywhere. As if it were his own. But that was impossible. There was no way *he* could be here. Unless…

Oh God. Had the Dracken come after the egg too?

He'd have to figure it out later. Right now, all that mattered was freeing Trinity and retrieving the egg—before either the government or the Dracken showed up. Forcing his hands to stay steady, he attempted to line up his target. But Trinity was in the way—a human shield—and he couldn't find a clear shot. And if he cried out to her, he'd give his position away.

Could he send to her? While he couldn't direct her thoughts thanks to his current lack of spark, he could probably muster up a helpful suggestion or two and pray she thought it was a good idea.

He squared his shoulders. It was a weak plan, at best. But he had no other options. And he was running out of time. Squeezing his eyes shut, he lobbed a command as hard as he could in her general direction, praying she'd hear and obey.

Duck! Now!

He opened his eyes and focused back on her. Her gaze darted around the room, as if trying to locate something. Someone. Had she heard him? Would she understand what he needed her to do? Would she obey his order even if she did?

Trust me, he tried. *It's the only way to save you now.*

She heard him that time—he saw it in her eyes—giving him an almost imperceptible nod before purposely shifting her weight, slumping to the ground, and catching her captor off guard. As the man struggled to retain his grip, Connor made his shot. The laser from his pistol sang true and a moment later the man's head exploded in a burst of green plasma. The egg fell from Trinity's grasp and started rolling across the room.

Good girl, he sent with a grin. It was the first thing that had gone right all day.

Diving for the egg, Connor locked it into his arms before turning to Trinity, who was staring at the now-headless man, mouth gaping. "Come on," he commanded, shifting the egg and offering his free hand to help her to her feet. "We have to go. Now!"

She hesitated at first, then reached up, her fingers brushing his, connecting the two of them for the first time and sending a shock straight to his core.

For a moment, time stopped—simply stopped—and all he could feel was her. Pure, unbridled emotion. White hot fury warring with icy cold fear. It was all he could do not to jerk his hand away.

"It really is you," he whispered, fascination mixing with horror.

She was as powerful as the legends had said. Maybe even more so. All that raw energy, that spark burning inside of her. To bind that to a dragon…Connor shuddered.

Thank fleck he'd gotten to her first.

Chapter Six

Outside the museum, Trinity turned to her rescuer, adrenaline pumping wildly through her veins. "Thank you," she whispered, her fingers fluttering involuntarily to her neck, where she could still feel the burning of her captor's rough hand. She had been so sure she was dead—that he'd pull the trigger and it would all be over in a flash of light. Until this stranger had charged in and saved the day—like a caped crusader with a *Star Trek* gun. "I'm sorry I Maced you," she added guiltily. "I just thought—"

"Come on," Connor interrupted, glancing at the door they'd exited from. Under the glow of the streetlights, she caught a ghost of fear flicker across his otherwise impassive face. "We need to keep moving."

She hesitated, her feet feeling glued to the pavement. Should she follow him? He'd saved her life. But could she trust him? Or was he just another one of the thieves after the egg? Of course, he already had the egg. If that was all he was after, he would have already left her to fend for herself.

"Come on!" he repeated, his voice rasping with urgency. "I can't fight them all at once!"

And she couldn't let him just take off with her grandpa's egg. "Okay," she declared, making up her mind. "Let's get out of here."

Connor turned and ran, the egg cradled under his arm like a football, gun holstered to his side. As she followed, sprinting down the street alongside the museum, she could hear the emergency door bang open again, men's voices cutting into the night air.

"Don't let her get away!"

Dashing down the street, dodging trashcans and debris, Connor was quick and nimble as he spun a quick left, then right, passing the local Arby's before turning into an empty parking lot. Trin did her best to follow, trying to ignore the shouting and banging behind her—the sounds of their pursuers gaining ground. Her heart sped up, spiking her adrenaline as her feet pounded the pavement—one by one by one. As she turned the corner, she nearly plowed into her rescuer, who had, for some reason, stopped short. She opened her mouth to beg him to keep going, then realized he couldn't.

The parking lot dead-ended at a tall, barbed-wire fence.

Trin looked up at the chain links, nerves tensing. Long ropes of barbed wire gleamed back with sharp-toothed smiles. She glanced around the parking lot, desperate for an alternate escape route, but came up blank. There was no alternative.

Gesturing to Connor, she dove toward the fence, ripping off her jacket on approach.

"What are you doing?" he demanded.

She gave him a grim look. "Up and over. It's the only way." She shoved a toe into the chain link and prepared to throw her jacket over the top while trying to ignore her rising fear.

She hated heights. But she hated the idea of being shot in the back even more.

"Wait."

Frustrated, she turned back around. "We don't have time to—" she started, but trailed off as she caught Connor pulling a small silver disc from his bag and placing it on the ground. Once it was secure, he looked up at her.

"Use the Bouncer," he instructed.

She stared down at the device, perplexed. "Wait, what—?"

"Just step on it!"

"Um, okay…" Confused, she tentatively pressed a foot against the disc—the Bouncer—whatever it was—no idea what it was supposed to do. No sooner did her foot connect than she literally bounced—impossibly high into the air— clearing the top of the fence by at least a foot. It was like something out of *Fields of Fantasy*—impossible in real life.

For a split second, she seemed to hang, motionless in thin air. Then gravity wrestled back control, sending her crashing down onto the ground, unfortunately still on the wrong side of the fence. She stared down at the Bouncer, then up at Connor. The voices in the alley grew louder. They were running out of time.

Connor yanked her to her feet. "When you're in the air, jump forward," he instructed. "So you'll land on the other side."

She nodded, forcing her gazillion questions back while clenching her jaw and stepping hard on the disc. Once again her body shot upward, this time giving her at least a two-foot clearance.

"Now!" Connor cried.

She threw herself forward, clearing the fence and tumbling

to the ground, a hard shock rocking her core as her tennis shoes connected with pavement. Not a perfect ten landing, by any means, but it did the trick. Scrambling to her feet, she turned to watch Connor step on the disc himself, shooting into the air as she had, though not half as high. In fact, he barely cleared the barbed wire, skimming his knee along the razor's edge before crashing back to Earth.

"Go! Now!" he cried.

Trinity didn't need a second invitation. She dashed down the alleyway. From behind, she heard a strange whirring sound. She glanced back just in time to see the Bouncer fly through the air and land in Connor's hand. He stuffed the amazing device into his bag and hurried to join her, just as three men in black swarmed the empty lot behind him. The men screamed furiously as they all tried to scale the enclosure at once, succeeding only in knocking one another down.

"That should buy us a little time," Connor told her, running up alongside her. She noticed the barbed wire had torn his jumpsuit at the knee, the blood soaking through the silver fabric. She considered suggesting a tetanus shot, but realized future infection was probably the least of his worries right about now. "But we have to keep moving. Find someplace safe to hide so we can regroup and figure out a plan. Come on." He picked up the pace.

"Wait!" Trinity called after him, leaning over, hands on her knees, trying to catch her breath. "We have to find my grandpa first."

Connor stopped, turning around, an impatient look on his face. "What?"

"My grandpa," she repeated, rising to full height. "He's

expecting me to come straight home. He'll worry if I don't show up."

"He'll have more reason to worry if you do," her rescuer shot back. "Those men? They'll figure out where you live. They'll come for you there. And if they find you with the egg—well, let's just say they're not in the habit of asking questions first." He frowned. "You can call him from the road. Let him know you're okay." His voice left no room for argument.

But Trinity stood her ground, crossing her arms over her chest. "No," she said. "If what you say is true, that means he's in danger too. And there's no way I'm going to let him risk his life over some stupid museum exhibit."

Connor squeezed his eyes shut, looking exasperated. Then he sighed, dropping his shoulders. "You're right," he said. "Let's go grab him. But then we have to get out of there. Find someplace safe. Okay, Trinity?"

She nodded, relieved, then started racing home, tearing down Main Street, lungs burning as if on fire. If only she hadn't been forced to give up track last year to work at the museum—she might have been in better shape for a quick getaway. Connor barely seemed winded, still clutching the egg protectively against his chest. The golden shell seemed to catch the moonlight, gleaming teasingly at Trinity, and she found herself itching to touch it again—to see if it would still feel like it had back in the museum.

She'd expected it to be cold; it'd been locked in ice for millions of years, after all. But to her surprise, the egg had been warm to the touch, as if it had been simmering on a stove. For a split second she actually wondered if her grandpa had created some kind of special heating device to incubate his rare find, believing he could actually hatch a baby dragon. But in her heart she knew even he wasn't *that* deluded.

You probably imagined it, she scolded herself. *Like the voices you thought you heard. It's just an egg. A very old egg. Nothing else.*

Though, she had to admit, there had to be *something* special about this egg. Otherwise, all these people wouldn't be after it. She stole a glance at Connor. Once they'd collected her grandpa, she would have to demand some answers from this mysterious stranger. Like—who were those men? Why were they after the egg? How had he gotten there in the nick of time? And—

She stopped short as she turned onto her street, her heart lurching.

How did he know my name?

Chapter Seven

"Grandpa! Grandpa! Are you here?"

Trinity burst into the house, scanning the cozy living room the two of them shared. Her eyes darted from the threadbare couch pushed up against one wall to the ancient rabbit-eared TV propped against the other. Their cracked IKEA coffee table still sat in the center of the room, littered with dinosaur-shaped coasters. And the old bookshelf in the corner remained overflowing with dog-eared paleontology journals and video game guide books.

She breathed a sigh of relief. It was all there. Nothing out of place, no sign of a struggle. After Connor's warning, she'd pictured the place ransacked and destroyed. But no, their Charlie Brown special of a Christmas tree still stood tall and gangly by the couch, strangled by multicolored lights and video-game-themed ornaments. And the pile of newspaper-wrapped presents still waited patiently under her grandpa's scrawled cardboard sign: *Do not open before Christmas…Or else.*

But her grandfather was nowhere to be found.

Just to make sure, she checked the two bedrooms and bathrooms, while Connor paced the living room, his steps eating up the narrow distance between walls. But the rooms were all vacant. No sign he'd been here at all.

Until she reached the kitchen.

"What the…?" She trailed off. "Connor! Get in here."

He was at her side in an instant, gun locked and loaded. She pointed a shaky finger at the boxes of Chinese food, overturned on the counter, noodles spilling out onto the floor.

"He was here," she whispered, trying to stop her brain from jumping to a million conclusions. None of which she wanted to face. "He brought home the takeout, just like he said. But where did he go?"

Connor didn't answer. He walked purposely to the side door, checking the deadbolt. Then he started examining the windows one by one. They were all closed. They were all locked. Just as the front door had been. That had to be a good sign, right? But then…?

"Maybe he just went back for duck sauce," Trin found herself rationalizing. "They're always forgetting to throw it in the bag and he knows it's my favorite. And…and the cat probably knocked over the food. She does it all the time, no matter how we much we scold her for jumping on counters." She nodded her head vigorously, as if agreeing with herself. "Yeah, that's got to be it. Makes total sense." She grabbed a roll of paper towels off the table and dropped to her knees, busying herself with the mess, trying to reset her sanity to a workable level—to push the nagging doubts far from her mind.

"Trinity…"

"In fact, I'm sure he'll be back any second now," she assured Connor, refusing to look up. She knew what he was going to say and she didn't want to hear it. They couldn't leave. Not now. Not when Grandpa was probably right around the corner. "We just have to hang here a few more minutes. No big deal."

"Trinity, you have to look at this."

She squeezed her eyes shut, then opened them, forcing herself back to her feet, turning to Connor questioningly. With a grim face, he pointed to the counter.

Or, more precisely, the pocket knife that lay on the counter, speckled with what could only be blood.

"Oh God," she whispered, her world spinning out from under her. "Oh God, no."

She staggered back, stumbling against the stove, her knees buckling, her lungs refusing to take in air. For a moment she couldn't move—couldn't take her eyes off the knife. Ghosts from a Christmas past swam through her head and her stomach lurched.

Please God. Not again. He's all I have left.

Strong hands grabbed her forearms, jolting her back to reality. She looked up to find Connor, staring down at her with a hard look in his eyes, as if willing her not to fall apart. She swallowed hard, trying to regain her composure, as she waited for the comforting rationalizations to spill from his lips. That it was all a mistake. It probably wasn't his blood. That everything would be okay.

"I told you we shouldn't have come here," he ground out instead.

She stared at him for a moment, unable to move, unable to speak. Then the rage came—a volcano erupting inside of her and setting her ablaze. She reached up, her fist finding his face with all the force she could muster. Then she shoved him away.

"Are you kidding me?" she cried. "That's all you have to say?" It was all she could do not to reach out and strangle him. To punish him somehow for dragging her into this mess to begin with.

He told you not to touch the egg, something inside her nagged. *Maybe you should have listened.*

Connor's face darkened, his cheek branded crimson from where she'd struck him. "Look, I don't think you understand the seriousness of what's going on here. The egg cannot fall into enemy hands. The future of the world depends on it."

Trinity stared at him in disbelief. He was crazy. She'd dragged a crazy person into her house. She scowled at him. "You want the egg so badly, just take it," she spit out. "Take it and get out and leave us alone." She no longer cared that it might be valuable. They could find another way to save their house. One that didn't involve crazy boys and men with machine guns and near-death escapes over barbed-wire fences. She glared at the egg out in the living room, sitting innocently on the coffee table, where Connor had left it. Once again she had the nearly overwhelming urge to grab it and smash it to smithereens. The stupid thing was nothing but trouble.

Don't let him, Trinity. Don't let him take me away.

She froze, fear throttling her and rendering her immobile. *That voice.* The same one from back in the museum. The one she'd convinced herself was all in her head. Had it really just addressed her again—from inside her own living room?

I'm nothing like Mom. Nothing like—

"What's wrong?" Connor demanded, peering at her with alarm on his face. "You're pale as a ghost."

She waved him off, not wanting him to recognize her fear; he already had too much advantage over her already. "I'm fine," she informed him with as much scorn as she could muster. Anyway, *he* was the one who was crazy. Not her. "Now, weren't you leaving?"

"I'm not leaving without you."

"Well, *I'm* not leaving without my grandpa."

Their eyes met, Connor's gaze bearing down on her—dark blue irises shimmering with fire. For a fleeting moment, she wondered if they would glow in the dark, then berated herself for the ridiculous notion. Who gave a crap if he had beautiful eyes? He had an ugly, uncaring soul underneath. One that cared more about expensive relics than real-life people.

She matched his eyes with her own, wrestling him into a stalemate, daring him to look away first.

And then…he did.

"Fine," he muttered, turning his back on her. "Have it your way." He started out into the living room and toward the front door. She stared after him, a gnawing uneasiness tugging at her insides as he extended the distance between them. He was leaving. Just like she'd told him to. Just like she'd thought she'd wanted.

And in a moment, she'd be totally alone.

She stood there, shifting from foot to foot as she fought the urge to stop him. She hated how much she didn't want him to leave and tried to tell herself it was for the best. She didn't need him. She didn't need the egg. The sooner he left, the better for everyone. Right?

She heard a deadbolt click into place.

"Wait, what are you doing?" she asked, following him into the living room, surprise and relief washing over her as she realized he was still on the same side of the front door. The now securely locked front door.

He gave her a weary look before heading over to the big, front picture window and studying it with critical eyes. "If we're going to be waiting here, I'd like to reinforce things a bit. Is that all right with you?"

Her heart stuttered. He was staying? He was choosing to wait? Even though he said it could be dangerous? Even though he needed to protect the egg? That was, as he said, his number-one priority. His so-called mission to save the world. So why on Earth would he choose to stay? To keep himself and the egg in danger?

She bit her lower lip. There was only one explanation. For her.

Guilt writhed through her as she watched him attempt to shove the bookshelf in front of the window, straining with the effort. Maybe she'd judged him too quickly. Maybe he was being cautious, not coldhearted. And maybe her stubbornness was stupid, not strong. After all, what would she have wanted her grandpa to do if he were in this situation, waiting for her instead? Certainly nothing that would put him in danger.

Still, she couldn't just take off...

Mind racing, she glanced out the window, her eyes settling on the dark silhouette of the ramshackle barn behind her best friend Caitlin's house. Her heart clenched as she gazed longingly at the familiar haven. How many times had the two of them escaped there, late at night, while everyone else was fast asleep? They'd curl up in the hay-filled loft, streaming gory horror movies on Caitlin's iPad or gagging down cheap whiskey, pilfered from Grandpa's stash, while drunk texting cute boys from school. For the past two years, the barn had been Trin's sanctuary when times got tough.

And things didn't get much tougher than this.

"Wait," she told Connor, making up her mind.

He stopped and turned to her, wiping a sheen of sweat from his brow. "What?"

"See that barn?" she asked, pointing out the back window. "My neighbors left two days ago—they were going to Disney World for Christmas. The barn will be empty—they only use it to store bikes and stuff anyway. We could hide out there and watch the house to see if he comes back. You can see everything perfectly from there."

Connor's eyes swept the barn's exterior, assessing it quickly. Then he nodded in agreement. "Good idea," he said in a clipped voice. But she caught a flicker of relief cross his face and was glad she'd decided to speak up. "Let's go."

They burst out the back door, sprinting toward the barn. No sooner had they reached its entrance than a pair of head-lights turned in, illuminating the dead-end street. Hurrying, they dove through the front doors, just as the all-too-familiar black truck screeched to a halt outside Trinity's house. As they watched, the team of armed men spilled out once again, surrounding the cottage in seconds. There were a few indeci-pherable shouts followed by a loud crash as they kicked in the front door—the same door Trinity had been standing behind only moments prior.

"Oh God," she whispered, horrified but unable to turn

away. If they had been there. If they had just waited one minute longer to leave…

A strong hand clasped her shoulder and she turned in surprise. Connor stood behind her, tall and straight, his jaw tense and his gaze never faltering from the window. The moonlight gave his pale skin an almost unearthly pallor and his eyes did indeed seem to glow with faint luminescence. She drew in a breath, waiting for another "I told you so"—one in this case she totally deserved—but it didn't come, and she was grateful for that.

They stood for a moment. Silent and watchful. Alone yet together. Trinity hyperaware of Connor standing strong and steady behind her, his hand still securely clamped on her shoulder as they waited to see what the men would do.

They didn't have to wait long. Soon the sounds of crashing and banging and breaking glass assaulted their ears, soundtracking the search-and-destroy going on inside. Trin cringed, glad that she couldn't see through the walls, couldn't watch her beloved home being torn apart. She imagined the invaders shredding couch cushions, knocking over the TV, ripping her precious books from their shelves and tossing them away like rubbish. She pictured her Christmas tree toppling over, ornaments shattering, candy canes splitting in two, presents being stomped on and torn to shreds—one present in particular.

"Great. Now I'm never going to get to play the *Fields of Fantasy* expansion pack," she muttered. When Connor gave her a questioning look, she sighed. "Yeah, priorities, I know. But still…"

Her only relief was catching sight of her cat fleeing the house unharmed. Baby Puss was a resourceful one. She'd been a stray, just like Trin—one of the reasons they'd bonded from the start. She could rest assured the cat, at least, could take care of herself.

Her grandpa, however, was another story. Where could he be? If only he wasn't so stubborn about cell phones. She glanced fearfully down the street, half expecting him to be strolling down the lane, straight into their clutches. Would she be able to intercept him before he reached the front door?

But her grandpa didn't appear. And eventually the soldiers streamed out her broken-down front door and loaded back into the truck. Trinity let out a sigh of relief while Connor continued to watch, eagle-eyed, until they pulled away, disappearing into the night.

"They left one guard inside," he informed her, and she was grateful he had thought to count them. "We'll wait here a little longer," he added. "In case your grandpa comes back, we can grab him before he tries to go inside."

He said it casually, as if he truly believed that at any moment the elderly man could waltz up the street, oblivious and unaffected by all that had transpired. She appreciated the sentiment, even though she knew he probably didn't believe it. She was beginning to have her own doubts as well.

"Thank you," she said, her voice a little choked. "I'm sorry I was being stupid before."

He cleared his throat. "Not a problem. And understandable under the circumstances."

"And I'm—I'm sorry I hit you," she added, hoping he couldn't catch the blush spreading across her cheeks as she turned to him.

Connor threw her a half smile. "You hit pretty good," he

remarked, reaching up to touch his cheek, which still glowed a faint red in the moonlight. "I'm glad you're on my side."

He said it casually, a joke maybe. But the words sent a shiver tripping up her spine all the same. *His side.* That sounded good somehow—even though she had no idea what side he was really on. She wanted to believe it was with the good guys. But how could she be sure?

"Anyway, I'm the one who should be apologizing," he added, dropping his hand and giving her a rueful look. "If things had gone to plan, you and your grandpa would be miles away by now. Living happily ever after, the egg all but forgotten."

The egg. Her eyes traveled back to the object in question, still cradled under Connor's arm. Even now she could feel its strange pull, gnawing at her insides, and she had to fight the urge not to reach out and touch it. To take it into her arms, run her hands across its intricate surface. To feel its unearthly warmth under her fingertips.

"So what's the deal with the egg, anyway?" she asked, shoving her hands into her pockets instead. "Why is everyone after it?"

He looked at her curiously. "Didn't your grandpa tell you?"

She dropped her gaze, her cheeks burning now as she remembered what her grandpa had claimed.

"He told you, didn't he?" Connor pressed. "He told you something about the egg."

She paused, her mind racing with lies. But in the end, the truth spilled from her lips. "He said…" she whispered. "He said it was a dragon egg."

She waited for the snorts of laughter, the rolling of eyes,

the snide comments, and maybe an offer of a bridge in Brooklyn up for sale.

Instead, Connor gave her a regretful smile. "It's a dragon egg, all right," he confirmed. "Trust me, they're pretty distinctive. No other creature on Earth—now or ever—lays this kind of egg."

"Come on," she protested, hardly believing she was going to have to have this argument for the second time in one day. "Let's be real. We all know there's no such thing as dragons outside of movies and video games."

"Not anymore," Connor agreed, "seeing as they all died out in the Ice Age. And since their skeletal structure was made up of a mixture of silica and gelatin, their bones decomposed into sand. That's why you never find any dragon bones—any proof they ever existed at all."

He said it so matter-of-factly. Like he was giving a science lecture. And while one part of her wanted to protest that it was impossible, another part, deep inside, was starting to wonder. Strange things *had* been uncovered over the years. And she admittedly had never come across anything as strange as this egg. Could her grandpa really have finally stumbled upon something real after all these years? Only to have it ripped away? Guilt gnawed at her insides as she remembered how quickly she'd dismissed his claims without even giving him the benefit of the doubt. When she found him again, she realized, she might just owe him an apology.

"Those men," she tried, unable to keep the tremble from her voice as she thought back to the man gripping her by the neck, gun pressed to her temple. "From the museum. Do they think it's a dragon egg too?"

Connor shrugged. "From what we understand, someone from Customs tipped off your government, letting them know an unidentified object had crossed the border. But whether they know exactly what it is at this point…" He made a helpless gesture.

She mulled this over, her brain snagging on the fact he'd used the word "your" when mentioning the government. Was he from another country? That would, at least, explain the strange lilting accent and odd clothing. And possibly the paleness of his skin. But what country? And how had he known about the egg?

"In any case, they're the least of our worries," Connor added in an uncomfortable voice, "now that I know the Dracken are here too. They're a much greater threat than your government could ever be."

"The Dracken?" The term sounded familiar for some reason, though she had no idea why.

"A group of dragon sympathizers," he replied, without missing a beat, "like an animal rights group, but for dragons."

She raised an eyebrow. "Are you for real?"

"Absolutely," he shot back, giving her a grim look. "And, unfortunately, so are they. I'm not sure why they're here. I guess they must have caught wind of my mission somehow— and sent my twin brother, Caleb, to stop me." He scowled. "Unlike your government, Caleb knows exactly what the egg is. And what it can do."

Trinity had no response. Absolutely no response. Dragon animal rights groups, evil twins. She felt as if she had been dropped into the middle of some game without being taught how to play. Half of her wanted to tell Connor to get out all over again, to take his crazy stories and never come back. But at the same time, he'd been right about the men invading her house. And if she hadn't listened to him…

"I'm sorry, Trinity," he added, giving her an apologetic look. "You were never supposed to be involved in any of this. If all had gone to plan, I would have gotten you and your grandpa away from here months ago. Instead, I barely had enough time to get you out of the museum."

Trinity finally found her voice. "Connor, you're not making any sense," she protested. "No one even knew this egg existed until a few days ago—when researchers dug it from the ice. And according to my grandpa, they shipped it straight to the museum." She peered at him. "So how could you or the Dracken people know it would be here? Or that the government would try to break in and take it?"

Connor suddenly looked nervous, as if he'd said too much.

"Tell me," she pressed. "What are you leaving out? How did you learn about the egg?"

He leaned against the wall, staring out the window. At first she thought he wasn't going to answer. But finally, he opened his mouth to speak.

"Where I come from, everyone knows the story of the first egg."

"Where you come from?" Trinity repeated, a clamminess washing over her. As if somehow, some way, she knew his next words would change her life forever. "And where is it, may I ask, that you come from?"

He gave her a hard look. "About two hundred years in the future."

Chapter Eight

At first, Trinity wasn't sure she heard him right. Two hundred years in the future? Was this some sort of joke? "That's not funny," she said hoarsely.

He blinked. "Do you see me laughing?"

She took a step back, trying to will her brain to think, to cling to some sort of rationality in a conversation gone mad. And to think she almost believed him about the dragon egg. Even though that was completely ridiculous as well. Everyone knew there was no such thing as dragons. And as far as time travel...

Her confusion veered sharply to anger. How dare he try to play her like this? She needed to get away, call the cops, find out what was really going on. And, most importantly, locate her grandpa and make sure he was okay.

"I've got to go," she stammered, realizing too late Connor had effectively barricaded the barn's front door. Would he try to stop her if she pushed past him? And what about the egg? Was she willing to leave it behind?

What an idiot she'd been! Hiding away from the government agents, allowing them to ransack her house. Maybe they had a good reason to be after the egg. Maybe it was a matter of national security. Or that the thing was contaminated—or carried some nasty disease. Maybe she should have turned it over from the start, instead of aiding and abetting a crazy person to steal it away.

Connor stepped forward, his expression anguished, beseeching. "Please, Trin," he begged. "I know it sounds crazy. But I can explain."

"Explain?" she sputtered. "Explain what? That you've come back from the future to steal a freaking dragon egg?"

"That's oversimplifying things a bit. But yes, that's the idea."

"And you'd do that, why?"

He gave her a sheepish look. "To stop the dragon apocalypse?"

She narrowed her eyes, fury winding up inside her. She was right to have punched him—she only wished now that she'd hit him harder. Instead, she'd somehow gone and convinced herself that he was some kind of self-sacrificing hero with her best interests at heart. When all along, he'd been playing her like a fool.

At the end of the day, she was as a gullible as Grandpa.

What could she do? She could try to scream, to alert the last guard in the house to her presence. But Connor had a gun. He could shoot her before help could arrive and he'd still have the egg. She bit her lower lip, mind racing. There was no way she could overpower him on her own. And the barn wasn't exactly a stocked arsenal.

Then she remembered her cell phone, stuffed in her pocket. Could she reach in and dial 911 without him seeing her? Maybe if she kept him talking…

"Prove it to me," she blurted, forcing her voice to stay strong as she slowly inched her hand down to her side.

Connor nodded tersely, though he looked slightly relieved. He dropped to his knees, ripping open his black bag and rummaging through. She took her opportunity, slipping her hand into her pocket and gripping her phone, seeking the three buttons she needed for help to arrive. Once she'd pressed them, she let out a small sigh of relief. Now she just had to keep him occupied until the cavalry came.

"You already saw my laser pistol," he reminded her, looking up from his bag. "Not exactly your everyday handgun."

She frowned, thinking back to her captor's head, exploding in a mass of green goo. Growing up in Texas, she'd seen a lot of guns—but never anything like that. Still, she wasn't about to give him the satisfaction of admitting it.

"Sorry. I let my *Weird Weapons Monthly* subscription expire last year," she retorted, willing herself not to glance down at her jeans. She could hear the tinny "911, what's your emergency?" coming from the receiver and took a step back, to make sure Connor was out of hearing range. Hopefully when they didn't receive a reply, they'd track her by GPS and send help.

"What about the Bouncer, then?" Connor asked, pulling out the strange disc they'd used earlier to escape over the fence. As he held it in his hand, the sphere twisted and turned, hovering an inch above his palm. She turned away, ignoring the niggling at the back of her brain. He really did have a lot of strange stuff. But still!

"I'm sure they sell those by the dozen at sci-fi cons across the country," she managed to say, though her voice had definitely lost some of its confidence.

"Right." Connor pressed his lips together, then went back

into his bag of tricks, this time pulling out a shiny, egg-shaped object, encased in silver. He set the bag aside and rose to his feet, pushing it into her hands. "What about my transcriber then?" he asked, his voice starting to take on a desperate tone. "Tell me this technology exists here."

Against her better judgment, she closed her hands around the object, studying it with careful eyes. Her fingers brushed against a small button on one side and, to her surprise, a three-dimensional hologram popped up in her palm. A woman, who looked to be in her late forties, seemed to stare up at her.

"Connor, on your way home could you pick up—"

She shrieked, the device tumbling from her hand. Connor caught it midair, running his thumb across the smooth side. The image vanished.

"My mom's holomail," he explained, looking a little wistful. "It's all I have left of her now."

Trinity knew she was gawking, but found she couldn't help it. As much as she didn't want to admit it, Connor was right; that thing definitely didn't belong in her world. In fact, none of it did. Nor did Connor himself, with his strange accent and strange timing, appearing at the exact moment she needed him to help save the egg. She let out a frustrated breath. Why was the most impossible explanation suddenly the one making the most sense?

"There's one more thing," Connor said. "This one I think you'll recognize."

He reached into his bag and, to Trinity's surprise, pulled out a small, red velvet box. A ring box, she realized.

"Um, don't you think you should at least buy me dinner first?"

Connor sighed, then pulled open the lid. Trinity gasped,

her eyes bulging from their sockets as she realized what was nestled inside.

Her mom's ring. The one she'd pawned to pay the taxes. The one that inadvertently brought the egg into her life to begin with. She looked at Connor in amazement. He pushed the box in her direction. With trembling fingers, she somehow managed to pull it out and hold it in unsteady hands.

"How did you get this?" she stammered as she examined the all-too-familiar piece of jewelry, cataloging its beloved imperfections: the scratch on the left side, the missing pave diamond on the top right. It was exactly the same—and yet somehow different too. Older looking, more worn. As if it had been antiqued.

Like two hundred years antiqued.

With shaky breath, she turned it over, her eyes searching for the inscription she knew she'd find inside.

To Emberlyn, my love.

"Your father gave this ring to your mother," Connor stated quietly. "He told her to never take it off her finger. After she died, you vowed to do the same. At night, you would twist it around your finger exactly five times while staring up at the ceiling, praying for courage to face the next day."

She looked up from the ring, feeling the color drain from her face. "I never told anyone that," she whispered.

"Not yet," he replied smoothly, his blue eyes piercing her own. "But you will."

She didn't know what to say.

"According to our histories, you wore this ring until the day you died," Connor continued. "It became a symbol to many people. After your death, the Dracken took it and claimed it as their own. It took a lot of work for us to get it back. Many men died in the effort. But the Council knew they could never convince you to help us unless I could prove I was telling the truth."

Trin stared down at the ring. Then she slowly slid it onto her finger. It fit perfectly, of course, and for the first time all week, her hand felt whole again. *Oh, Mom.* She blinked back the tears, looking up at Connor, a million questions whirling through her brain, each warring to be asked first.

But before she could speak, car headlights flashed through the window, freezing the words in her throat. She cringed. The cavalry had finally arrived—just in time for her to realize they may not be the men in white hats she'd assumed they'd be.

Connor caught her guilty face, then glanced out the window. The car had pulled up just outside the barn's front door and the driver's side door popped open.

"Oh, fleck," he whispered. "Trinity, what have you done?"

Chapter Nine

What *had* she done? Only what she thought was the right thing at the time. But now she wasn't so sure. She stared down at the ring, her stomach churning. What if Connor was telling the truth? What if he really was from the future—sent to stop the government from stealing the world's last dragon egg and thus sparking a worldwide apocalypse? Had her 911 call led the bad guys directly to the prize?

"Trinity? Honey? Where are you? Can you hear me?"

She let out a sigh of relief as she recognized the voice outside. Not the scary men in black she'd feared—or even Connor's so-called evil twin. Just good old Sheriff Bob, the portly, senior law man who spent more time out fishing with her grandpa than preventing any crimes. Trinity had known the old sheriff her entire life, and he'd always had a kind word to say and a piece of mint gum to share. There was no way he'd be mixed up in some dragon conspiracy.

She started for the door. Connor grabbed her arm, yanking her back. "Don't go out there!" he hissed.

"It's okay," she assured him. "It's just Sheriff Bob. He's responding to my call—he probably recognized the cell number. I'll tell him I'm looking for my grandpa. For all I know maybe he's been at the police station the whole time, reporting the break-in or something." Even as she said the words, hope stirred within her. If only it could be true! Everything could still turn out okay.

The barn door groaned as Sheriff Bob attempted to pry it open. "Trinity? Are you in there?"

She opened her mouth to reply. But Connor was too quick, grabbing her hands and yanking her hard against him. His eyes found her own, piercing her with their intensity.

You can't trust anyone. Even people you think you know.

She gasped as his words blazed through her brain, followed by a jolt of terror and urgency. *His* terror and urgency, she realized with shock.

Please believe me, Trinity. Everything depends on it.

She stumbled back, breaking their connection, shaken to the core. She stared at him wildly, finding it impossible to still her erratic pulse. How had he done that? Connected their minds with a simple touch. Magic? Some kind of psychic link? A weird futuristic technology?

However he'd done it, the effect remained the same. And she knew now, without a shadow of a doubt, that he believed everything he'd told her. The time travel, the dragons, the apocalypse—it was all real. All true. And his fear was now hers as well.

"What do we do?" she whispered, her voice hoarse. "He's not going to leave until he knows I'm okay. And there's no back door to sneak out of."

Connor considered this. "I'll hide in the loft," he told her. "With the egg. You try to get rid of him as quickly as possible.

If you run into trouble, I'll back you up." He patted the gun he'd holstered to his side.

Trinity bit her lower lip, wanting to argue. Sheriff Bob was her grandpa's best friend. She couldn't let Connor hurt him, no matter what. But there was no time to come up with another plan.

"Okay." She drew in a breath. "But keep your finger off the trigger unless this becomes an epic fail. Upping the body count is not exactly going to help our cause at this point."

"Agreed." Connor saluted her, tucking the egg under his arm and starting his climb. Once he disappeared from view, she approached the front door, pulling it open with shaky hands.

"Hey, Bob," she greeted in her most cheerful, unbothered voice. "What are you doing working Christmas Eve—?"

Her words died in her throat as two men wielding powerful flashlights stepped out from the backseat of the sheriff's car, where they'd evidently been waiting, purposely out of view. They were dressed identically, in sharp, custom-fitted black suits, their eyes shaded by mirrored sunglasses, even though the sun had set long ago. Trinity's eyes darted from one to the other, apprehension coursing through her veins. This did not seem good.

The two men didn't wait for an invitation to enter. They pushed into the barn as if they owned the place, overturning bikes and opening storage chests. Trinity turned to Sheriff Bob, begging for an explanation, but the small-town sheriff just gave her a helpless shrug. He would be no help, she realized. It was all up to her.

"What are you doing?" she demanded of the men. "This is my neighbor's barn."

"Homeland Security, ma'am," one of the men interrupted. He flashed her a badge so quickly she had no idea whether it was legit or had come from a Cracker Jack box. "Perhaps a better question would be what are *you* doing here?"

Her mind raced to come up with a reasonable explanation on short notice. Then she realized honesty might be the best policy—at least partial honesty. "There were men," she said at last. "They barged into my house. I freaked out and ran here to hide before calling 911. I think one of them might still be in the house."

The men looked unsurprised. "No need to be afraid," the first one said in a voice that told her otherwise. "Those were government agents. We have reason to believe your grandfather may have come into possession of some stolen property. Do you know anything about that?" He gave her a pointed stare.

His insinuation infuriated her. She met his gaze, her eyes fierce. "My grandpa would never take anything that didn't belong to him," she retorted. Then she shot a look over at Sheriff Bob. "Tell him," she demanded. "Tell him he'd never do something like that."

"Well, yes, the girl's right about that," Sheriff Bob blustered, looking nervous and unsure. "I've known Charlie Foxx for fifty years. He's good people. He'd never intentionally—"

"Search the barn," the first agent interrupted, evidently bored by the glowing tribute for the man he'd been sent to hunt down. He pointed to the ladder. "You check the loft. I'll finish up here."

Trinity sucked in a breath, watching the suited man start toward the ladder. In a moment, he'd be up there and Connor had nowhere to hide. He had his gun, but if he shot it, he'd give his position away to agent #2. The barn would erupt into a war zone, with she, most likely, the first civilian casualty.

She had to do something and fast.

Her eyes fell to the sheriff's revolver, dangling from its holster. Her grandpa was always teasing him about forgetting to secure it. "Someday you'll shoot yourself in the foot," he'd say. And suddenly she knew exactly what she had to do.

She started to stagger, waving her arms wildly around her. "Oh God," she moaned in an overloud voice, attracting the attention of the agents. "I feel dizzy! I think I'm going to—ohhh!"

She threw herself backward, with as much drama as she could muster. As predicted, the chivalrous Sheriff Bob dove to catch her. Not an easy move for a man of sixty-five, clocking in at more than three hundred pounds, but the sheriff, to his credit, gave the rescue his all.

Sorry, Bob, she thought, as she allowed herself to collapse into his meaty grip, letting her arms flop to the side like limp spaghetti.

"Never mind her," the first agent instructed. "Get moving."

But Trinity's fingers had already wrapped around the sheriff's gun, yanking it from its holster. She leapt to her feet, flicking off the safety, aiming the firearm at the two men.

"Drop your weapons. Now!" she cried.

The agents froze, looking at one another doubtfully. Trinity waved the gun, hoping they couldn't detect the fact that her hands were shaking like crazy.

"Do you even know how to use one of those?" the first agent asked, evidently not quite buying her "I'm a crazy killer and you should be scared of me" routine. Which wasn't all that surprising, she supposed, seeing as she'd never actually shot at anything but the zombies in her video games.

"She certainly does."

Trin looked up in surprise as Connor dropped down off the ladder with an easy grace.

He trained his own gun on the agents and gave them a cocky grin. "In fact, you might have seen her handiwork, back at the museum. Man in black? Head blown to smithereens?" He snorted. "The girl's completely cracked. If I were you, I'd do as she says."

The agents exchanged unhappy glances but reluctantly obeyed, gingerly lowering their weapons to the floor before straightening up again. Trin shot Connor a grateful look, a rush of adrenaline surging through her. He gave her a curt nod as he deftly kicked the surrendered guns across the barn and out of reach.

Now get the sheriff's handcuffs, she heard his voice in her head. She still didn't know how he was doing that, but now wasn't the time to ask.

"Bob, I need your handcuffs," she said in a terse voice, turning to the white-faced sheriff. She held out her hand.

"You don't want to do this, Trinity," Bob blurted, sounding as if he were still in shock. Not surprising, she supposed. After all, the last two minutes had probably contained more action than the poor guy had seen since taking office forty years ago. "Please. For your grandpa's sake, just put down the gun."

"Handcuffs, Bob," she repeated apologetically. She felt bad to freak him out like this, but what choice did she have at this point? "And then turn around and walk out the door. Get back in your car and drive back to the station. Pretend you never saw us."

She could feel Connor's hard stare at her back—he obviously disapproved of letting the sheriff just walk away. But for Trin, this was nonnegotiable. She looked at Bob with beseeching eyes. "Please. Just go," she begged. "Find my grandpa. Make sure he's okay."

Please believe me, she begged silently. *I don't want you to get hurt.*

For a moment the sheriff didn't move. Then, with a heaving sigh, he handed over the cuffs and walked out the door. A moment later, she heard the engine roar to life and the car pull away. She knew he could be calling for backup, that they had to act fast. She approached the agents, cuffs in hand.

"You're going to be in a lot of trouble," the first agent said.

"Really? And here I thought you were going to give me a medal," she muttered as she worked to cuff him to a nearby post. Connor followed suit, commandeering some old rope from the back of the barn to secure his buddy to the ladder. Trin had to admit, his knots looked good. Futuristic Boy Scout, perhaps?

Once both men were secure, she turned to her partner-in-crime, drawing in a breath. "Now let's get out of here."

Chapter Ten

"Walk slowly," Connor instructed. "As if nothing's wrong."
Trinity forced her steps to slow, trying to still her racing heart as they walked down Old Oak Grove's Main Street as if on a casual Christmas Eve stroll. She even managed to force out a "Merry Christmas" to Mr. Jenkins as he hurried home to meet his wife and daughter. She imagined her neighbor stepping into his warm, cozy house, probably with a fire in the fireplace and a hot meal on the stove. Baby Ava crying "Dada!" and holding up her little arms for him to scoop her up and give her a welcome home hug. A normal, family Christmas that Trinity had always wanted so badly—and seemed destined never to have.

A lump formed in her throat.

Walk, she scolded herself. *As if nothing's wrong.*

But *everything* was wrong, and the enormity of what she'd just done hit her hard and fast. Had she really just stolen a policeman's gun, then turned it on two Homeland Security agents before taking off with stolen property? How many laws had she broken in just that five-minute stretch alone? How much jail time would she face for those crimes if caught? She imagined herself on trial, up on the stand, telling the jury a wild story about a boy from the future, trying to stop the dragon apocalypse. At least she'd probably end up in Shady Brook rather than prison given that story, along with her mom's history. Though the thought didn't make her feel much better.

"So what now?" she demanded, turning to Connor and allowing the anger to well up inside her, displacing her fear. It was the only thing she could do to force herself to keep moving, to not curl up into a ball and pray the nightmare would just go away.

"We have to find someplace safe," he told her, shifting the pack he wore to keep the egg from plain view. "So we can regroup and figure out a plan."

A plan. Right. "You didn't think to make one of those already?" she replied bitterly. "You know, before you decided to travel two hundred years into the past to save the world?"

He cringed, and she regretted her words immediately. It wasn't his fault things had gotten so out of control. *She* had been the one who insisted they go to her house, the one who'd called 911. In fact, the majority of the mess they were in now was directly her fault. Not Connor's. All he'd done was save her life and protect the egg. She should probably be a little more grateful.

She opened her mouth to apologize, but he cut her off. "You're right," he said slowly. "You're completely right. A true soldier is prepared for all possibilities. I wasn't and I've put you in danger because of it. I'm sorry." He gave her a rueful smile. "Is it too much to ask for a second chance? I'd like to make things right."

A chance. In other words, he was asking her to trust him.

After all they'd been through, that was a pretty tall order. But what were the alternatives? She could walk away, a fugitive from the law. Turn herself in to the authorities and hope for the best. Or take her chances with this boy from the future—and at the very least have a partner in crime.

"I suppose I can do that," she said with a sigh. "And I know where we can go too. A safe place where we can regroup." After all, if she was going to join forces with him, he had to know she was an equal partner, not just along for the ride.

He gave her a grateful look. "Where's that?"

"My mother's old house," she told him. "It was foreclosed on about a year ago, but with all the other bank-owned houses in the neighborhood, they haven't gotten around to putting it back up for sale. There's no electricity or running water, but I'm sure we could dig up some candles and flashlights. We'd be safe there—at least for tonight. Until we figured out what to do next."

Connor seemed to consider this for a moment. Then he pulled out his transcriber, pressing at the screen. "What's the address?" he asked.

"Twenty-three Elm Street," she replied automatically, trying to ignore the sudden pang as she recited the address she had once proudly called home. She didn't want to go back there. In fact, she'd promised herself a thousand times she'd *never* go back there. But what other choice did they have? As Connor said, they couldn't trust anyone. And there was nowhere else to go.

Connor looked up from his transcriber. "There's no record of that address in your personal file," he told her. "Which means my brother Caleb likely won't know it exists. Should be safe enough to spend the night at least. Regroup and figure out what to do next." He gave her a curt nod, soldierlike again. "Lead the way."

So she did, leading him out of town, cutting through an old, abandoned ranch, down an unpaved street, across the Old Town bridge until they reached the former interstate, very much a road less traveled. It wasn't the most direct route to her mother's house by any means, but it seemed safer to stay off the main roads.

As they stepped onto the old highway, now cracked and overgrown with weeds, Trinity couldn't help but remember what it had once been—a bustling thoroughfare of cars and trucks, rushing past as fast as they could in an effort to get someplace better than here. How many times had she stared longingly down this road, wishing she could leave her stressful life behind? And yet now, she found herself looking longingly back instead.

From here, she could just make out the sparkling Christmas tree illuminated in the center of town. Had it been just last week she and Caitlin had gone down there to watch the lighting ceremony? Scarfing down slices of pizza from Caitlin's dad's shop while checking out the cute guys stringing up the lights?

A choking sob escaped her.

"Are you okay?" A warm hand slipped into her own and she realized that while she'd been lost in her thoughts, Connor had upped his pace, falling to her side. He squeezed her freezing hand, a comforting gesture that somehow managed to soothe her raging fear. At least she wasn't alone in this. At least she had someone on her team.

"I'm fine," she replied quickly, trying to downplay her

fear. Still, she couldn't help a nervous glance around her, half expecting to come face-to-face with the machine-gun wielding soldier from the museum. Or maybe the two men in black, escaped from their bindings and ready for revenge. But the highway was empty. Silent as the grave. "I'll feel better when we're not so exposed."

"So will I," Connor agreed. "Being aboveground like this, with all this open sky—well, it winds me up." He glanced uneasily at the starscape spread above them like a glittery portrait. "I keep expecting…well, you know." He shuffled his pack to one shoulder.

"Are you saying you live underground in the future?" she asked.

He nodded. "Only a few of the elite Dracken live on the Surface Lands in specially made sky houses. The rest of us are simply moles, scrounging in the dirt." He snorted bitterly. "Though I suppose it's better than the alternative."

"Which is…?"

He gave her a steely look. "Being eaten by a dragon."

Oh. Right. She paused, not sure what to say. It still seemed so unreal, like something out of a movie. Her eyes traveled to the pack on his back, containing the egg. Could something so small and fragile-looking really spark a worldwide apocalypse?

"It was called the Scorch," Connor told her, as if overhearing her thoughts. "The year the dragons decimated the surface of our world. They burned through every forest and every field. From the smallest town to the largest city. Homes, businesses, theme parks—it didn't matter. Nothing could withstand the dragons' fire."

Trinity shivered, trying to imagine a world like that—where

monsters ruled the skies and flames fell like rain. Where there were no football stadiums, no movie theaters, no Disney World even. What would it be like to live in such a place? To be forced underground, never seeing the sun. No wonder Connor was so pale. "When does this happen?" she asked curiously, though she wasn't entirely sure she wanted to know. "This…Scorch?"

"About ten years from now."

She stopped in her tracks. "Wait, what?" she cried. "But that's so soon!" For some reason, she'd had it in her mind that this terrible holocaust was a far off event—two hundred years in the future, like her new friend. But ten years? Could this nightmare really be right around the corner? She found herself looking fearfully at the trees dancing in the breeze. The twinkling lights of Old Oak Grove shining in the distance. Could her entire world really be taken down by dragons within the next decade?

"It didn't take long," Connor replied. "Once your government managed to hatch this one egg and realized what they'd stumbled upon, it was only a matter of time before they figured out how to extract its DNA and start the cloning process." He grimaced. "They probably thought they were doing great work, bringing extinct creatures back to life." His voice betrayed his disapproval. "Little did they know. It wasn't long before the creatures had broken free and started flying wild."

She shuddered. "Couldn't anyone stop them?"

"No one knew how. Dragons are pretty much immune to traditional weaponry. Guns, missiles—everything your government tried to throw at them. And by the time people did start figuring out other methods to bring them down, the world was overrun."

"That's awful," she murmured, trying to grasp the implications of his words. Suddenly her earlier money concerns seemed pretty weak. She had been so worried about them losing their house. Yet in ten years, there would be no houses left to lose. Kind of put things in perspective. "I can't even imagine…" A chill wound through her and she found herself unable to continue.

Connor stopped short, taking her other hand and pulling her around to face him. Even in the darkness, his eyes seemed to glow as they found hers, locking on and refusing to let go. As he clung to her, she could feel the passion and strength streaming from his fingertips, electrifying her entire being as his emotions tangled with her own. The sensation was both exhilarating…and terrifying.

"That's not going to happen this time around," he told her in a thick voice, squeezing her hands so tightly she was half afraid he'd break her bones. "I may have gotten off to a rough start. I may have arrived late. But I have the egg. And I have you. And I promise you, Trinity, I will stop the dragon apocalypse. I will stop the Dracken." He paused, then added, "No matter what I have to do."

Chapter Eleven

"Here we are. Home sweet home," Trinity announced as she pulled the torn screen door open. The bank had changed the locks when they'd foreclosed on her former home, but they evidently hadn't bothered to check all the windows. She wasn't surprised, not really. After all, there was nothing inside worth stealing. Just dusty furniture and even dustier memories.

She drew in a breath. The last time she'd stepped inside this house, she'd stumbled upon a nightmare, her worst fears coming true. This time things were decidedly less dramatic. The house felt more like an ancient crypt than a fresh grave. Caked with dust and draped with intricate spider webs, it was an empty husk of what had once been a home.

She could feel its emptiness hammering at her bones. But Connor said he wanted to make sure. He cased the house, first and second floor, gun raised and ready, as she waited by the back door for his okay. After determining that it was, indeed, as abandoned and vacant as she promised, he set down his gun and allowed his shoulders to relax. Trinity rummaged about to find a few candles and matches, and even scored an industrial-strength flashlight from the garage that amazingly still held some battery power. She spread the candles around the living room and removed the plastic covering from the faded flowery couch.

Connor watched her at her tasks, still looking a little uneasy. He'd changed out of his strange silver jumpsuit and now wore slouchy dark-rinse jeans, riding low on his narrow hips, and a tight navy T-shirt, stretching across his broad chest and bringing out the blue in his ever-glowing eyes. Trin had to admit, for a guy from the future, he was pretty hot. If only she could snap a quick pic and text it to Caitlin. Of course, explaining how she met him might prove a bit difficult.

She shook her head. *Get your mind out of the gutter, girl,* she scolded herself. After all, he was here on a mission to save the world—not hook up with the locals.

That said, the guy from *Terminator* did manage to find the time…

"So you used to live here?" Connor asked, completely oblivious to her ridiculous thoughts, thank God. "It's strange we have no record of that."

"I wasn't here long," she admitted, sobered by the question. "My mom bought the place to convince the judge I'd have a quote—" she made rabbit ears with her fingers "—stable home environment." She screwed up her face. "What a joke that was. Didn't last long enough for the first mortgage check to cash."

Connor regarded her solemnly. "Is that when she died?"

"When she blew her head off, you mean?"

He winced. "I'm sorry."

She waved him off, not wanting to deal with the pity she knew she'd find in his eyes. It was bad enough to be back here in the first place. Everywhere she looked—everything she saw—a bitter reminder of that other Christmas Eve two years ago today. That fateful afternoon when she'd danced home from school with light steps and a happy heart. Eager to get the party started. To celebrate her first real Christmas in her first real home.

From now on, things are going to be different, her mother had promised. *From now on, we'll be a family.*

But that, it had turned out, had been just another one of Mom's fantasies.

"It's amazing they managed to get all the brains out of the carpet," she muttered, kicking the obviously bleached-out rug with her toe. The shotgun had made quite a mess—in fact, if it wasn't for her mother's bloodstained bunny slippers still stuffed on her feet and the emerald ring on her finger, she probably wouldn't have even recognized the corpse sprawled out on the living room floor.

Out of the corner of her eye, she caught Connor's cringe and immediately wished she could take back the vulgar words. After all, it had been her idea to come here—not his. And there was no reason to lash out and punish him for what her mother had done to her. Over the last two years, she'd tried to forget it altogether, to block out the memories and move forward with her life best she could. But being back here, at the scene of the unforgivable crime, was proving too much, especially with her nerves already stretched so tight.

"She was sick," she found herself saying, surprising herself as the words spilled from her lips. She never talked about what had happened with her mother. Not to Caitlin. Not even to her grandpa. He'd tried to get her to talk about it, of course, even sent her to shrinks they couldn't afford to help her release what she'd bottled up inside. But it had been no use. She'd never been able to voice the betrayal and hurt she'd experienced on that devastating day—the day she'd realized that all the promises in the world meant nothing and the only person she could truly trust was herself.

"Not physically sick," she continued in a rush, twisting the ring on her finger forcefully. "I mean, she heard…voices… in her head. Sometimes they were so loud she couldn't hear anything else." She pressed her palm against the wall, hanging her head as she remembered. "They told her to do things. Things she never would have done otherwise."

Like abandon her only daughter without even saying good-bye.

She trailed off, uncomfortably reminded of her own voices—the ones she'd heard back in the museum and at her grandpa's house. Was it just a coincidence? Her mind playing tricks? Or had her mother's illness been lurking inside of her all along? Waiting for just the right moment to dig its sharp talons into her consciousness and rip out her sense of reality?

I'm nothing like Mom. I'm nothing like Mom. I'm NOTHING like Mom.

She shoved off the wall, plopping down on the couch and scrubbing her face with her hands. "Anyway, that's when my grandpa took me in. He didn't have to. But he knew how miserable I'd been in foster care over the years when my mom was in and out of hospitals, and so he somehow convinced the judge to award him custody." She gave Connor a sad smile. "And we became a family. Just the two of us."

And then I yelled at him, she added to herself. *I basically called him a fool for wasting our money on some useless artifact.*

But it wasn't useless. And *she* was the one who'd been a fool.

She glanced out the window, unease knotting her stomach. Where was he? Why hadn't he called? Had the blood on the knife been his? The fact that the agents were looking for him meant, at least, they didn't have him. But what about these Dracken people? Could they have captured him somehow? And if so, what would they do to him? Would they hold him captive until she agreed to turn over the egg?

"I just hope he's okay," she said quietly. "I can't stand thinking about him out there somewhere, all alone, maybe in trouble. It just makes me feel so helpless." Her voice cracked on the last part as she fought back a sob.

For a moment she just sat there, staring out the window, not knowing what to do, what to say. Then, to her surprise, she felt a hand on her shoulder. Connor reaching out, without a word, gathering her into his arms.

Her first instinct was to resist, to pull away. To put distance between herself and this stranger. After all, she wasn't the type of girl who just fell into a guy's arms at a moment's notice, no matter how hot they might be.

Yet she was so stressed, so frayed, so at her wits' end. And his arms were so warm. So gentle and comforting. An embrace for her tired soul to melt into. She found herself relaxing, resting her head against his chest, breathing in his warm, rich scent. As he stroked her head with careful fingers, she could feel his heartbeat, strong and steady against her ear.

"I'm sorry, Trinity," he said so softly she could barely make out the words. "No one should have to go through something like that."

She gave a choking laugh and pushed herself off the couch, out of Connor's reach, stalking to the other side of the room, trying to ignore her pounding heart. Seriously, what was wrong with her? She paced the room, her nervous steps eating up the distance between walls, feeling embarrassed and awkward and not knowing what to say. Here Connor was, trying to save the world from a dragon apocalypse, and all she could do was babble on and on about her pitiful life story. As if it would matter to him in the least. So her mother died. Big deal. His whole freaking world had died. Hell, he probably only hugged her in an effort to get her to shut up for three seconds, so he could get back to the mission at hand.

She turned back to him, crossing her arms over her chest, trying to pull herself together. To appear strong and in control. "I'm sorry. I didn't mean to unload on you like that. Trust me, it's not something I normally do. Even with people I know." She scanned the room, her nose wrinkling in distaste. "I guess it's just this place—filled with empty promises and broken dreams."

Connor was silent for a moment, regarding her with serious eyes. At last he spoke. "The Surface Lands can be like that for me."

"The Surface Lands?" she repeated, cocking her head in question, more than grateful for the sudden subject change. "What are the Surface Lands?"

"That's what we call the world aboveground where I come from," he clarified, waving an arm around the room. "You know, where the dragons rule. Every time I head up there—on mission or whatever—I feel like I'm stepping into a graveyard."

"You mean because of all the people who died in the apocalypse?"

"*Because* of my father."

His voice was gruff. Brittle. As if it hurt to say the words out loud. And they sent a startling revelation straight to her core. He'd lost someone too. Someone he loved. His family had shattered, just like her own. Suddenly she didn't feel quite so pathetic for spilling her secrets, for accepting his comforting hug. Because, she realized, he wasn't looking at her with pitying eyes like the rest of them did. He was looking at her with understanding.

"Was he…?" she started to ask, then trailed off, not knowing how to voice the question.

"Burned alive by dragon fire?" Connor finished for her. Bitterness flashed across his face. "Yes. It's a common way to go in my world."

She waited for him to continue, but he fell silent instead, probably as uncomfortable as she'd been sharing such intimate details with a practical stranger. She wanted to tell him that it was okay, that she'd never betray his secrets or mock his pain. But she stayed silent, thinking perhaps it was too much, too soon. The near-death experience and mad escape for their lives had stretched her emotions taut as piano wires. But that didn't mean he felt the same.

"He was a Hunter," Connor said at last. "A Dragon Hunter, just like me. He was good too. Maybe the best ever. Until…" He trailed off again, silent for a moment, then shook himself. "In any case, that's the kind of senseless death I've come back to prevent. If I succeed in my mission—and I don't intend to fail," he added, giving her a fierce look, "the Scorch will never take place. And dragons will be gone for good."

The fire in his eyes and the fervor in his voice sent a chill down to her bones. He was so passionate, so determined—especially for someone so young. Completely unlike any of the boys she knew from school. They were all too wrapped up in sports or video games or the latest viral something-or-other to hit the interwebs to concern themselves with the atrocities of the world. Never mind muster up the energy to do something about them.

But Connor was different. The travesties he'd witnessed had made him strong, not scared. Determined, not demoralized.

"Tell me about this Scorch," she requested, wanting to hear him talk more, to unravel the secrets of his strange, futuristic world—and maybe a few about himself. "What was it like? I'm trying to picture it, but all I can think of was this really bad movie I saw once."

Connor seemed to consider this for a moment. "If you want, I can show you," he said at last.

"Show me?" She squinted at him, confused. "What do you mean?"

At first he didn't answer. Outside she could hear the wind whistling through the trees, announcing the encroaching storm. A coyote howled mournfully across the plain, echoed by a few neighborhood dogs. But inside the house, the silence was thick and suffocating as she waited, on the edge of her seat, for what he was going to say.

Finally, he nodded. "Yes," he said. "I think it's the only way to do this. Otherwise, it'll be just words. You'll never truly understand what it was like. Why this is all so important." He gazed at her, his eyes darkening with emotion. "But I warn you, it's not an easy thing to see."

She squared her shoulders, not sure what she was agreeing to. But she'd come this far already—and she wanted him to know that she could be brave too.

"Nothing has been easy since I met you," she declared, drawing on all her remaining bravado. "Why start now?"

"Right." Connor gave her a wry look. "Well, don't say I didn't warn you."

He reached out, taking her hands in his own. She felt something hard and cold between them and realized he'd placed a sapphire-colored gem into her palm. She stared down at it, wondering what it was for. Before she could ask, Connor closed his eyes, his face glowing with concentration as he squeezed her hands tightly in his.

A moment later the gem began to heat in her hand, hotter and hotter, until she was sure it would catch fire and singe her skin. Panicked, she glanced up at Connor, but his eyes remained closed and lips pressed firmly together—as if nothing was wrong. And so she forced herself to ignore the burn, closing her eyes and readying herself for anything.

But nothing could prepare her for what she saw next.

Chapter Twelve

The world was on fire.

At least that was Trinity's first thought as she opened her eyes. No longer safe and sound in her mother's old house, she found herself standing in the center of Old Oak Grove's town square, an inferno raging all around her, as far as her eyes could see. White-hot flames licked at shops and restaurants while bright orange fire devoured the trees. Smoke, thick as pea soup, flooded the streets, as desperate, human-shaped shadows flew past her, stumbling in a frantic attempt to reach safe ground. Sobs echoed through the air, competing with children's screams, and the marble fountain in the center of the square violently boiled over.

"Connor?" she cried, trying to peer through the smoke. "Are you there?" Her voice was raw and hoarse, and her lungs burned in protest as she waited for his reply.

But there was no reply. No answer to her calls. No sign of the time traveler who'd sent her to this hell on earth.

She was alone.

How could he do this to her? Just dump her here at the end of the world—with no explanation as to what she was supposed to do? Where she was supposed to go? Was this simply a vision of an event that had already taken place? Or had he actually sent her forward in time? Was she safe and sound in her former home, still gripping Connor's hands? Or was she really here, her life in danger?

An inhuman screech ripped through the air, shattering her questions and rendering her immobile. At the same moment, the smoke seemed to sweep away in a gust of sudden wind. Gathering all her courage, she dared to look up, just in time to see the shadow of a giant serpent swimming through the sky, its wingspan so vast that, for a moment, it blotted out the sun.

A dragon. A giant dragon. Whirling above her, beating the skies with its leathery wings, its tail snapping back and forth behind it. From where she stood, she could just make out the thick red scales, the impossibly long claws, the razor-sharp teeth, the black, vacant eyes. It was both impossibly beautiful and exquisitely terrifying, and Trinity found she couldn't look away.

The beast turned on a dime—shockingly graceful for its gigantean size—and landed on a nearby church steeple. As Trin watched, breath in her throat, it slowly pulled back its massive head, opening its mouth with a long, loud hiss. A blast of fire shot out and she leapt back, just in time, as it rained down onto the town square, only inches from where she'd stood. Heat slashed at her skin, drenching her in sweat.

Get out of there, Trinity! Now!

She started to run—down the street, through the alley, over the bridge. Screams assaulted her ears as she leapt over charred lumps she didn't want to identify as human and her nose was assaulted by the smell of burnt flesh. It was all she could do not to stop and puke her guts out. But to stop was to die. So she kept moving.

Bursting into a vacant lot, she heard a cracking sound above. She looked up, her eyes locking on a burning roof, reaching the point of collapse. She leapt back, but found she couldn't dodge the fiery chunk of wood flying at her face. Instinctively she put up her arm as a shield. As the wood hit her hand, she shrieked as the flames seared her skin.

Cradling her burnt hand, she bit back the pain, reassessing her surroundings. The collapsed roof prevented her from going any further forward. And the way she came was no longer an option. As she desperately tried a few doors—all of them locked—her eyes fell upon a small hole—a drainage ditch, large enough to crawl into. It looked dark and dank, the kind of place filled with rats and snakes, but she dove in anyway, splashing through the murky water, ignoring the putrid smell, thankful to be out of the fire's path.

As she pushed on, literally seeking the light at the end of the tunnel, the space tightened, stealing her breath. Sweat dripped down her neck and her legs cramped as panic rose inside of her. What if she got stuck in there?

She paused, willing her pulse to steady as she watched the frantic feet of those still running for their lives outside. She didn't know what was worse—hearing the screams of terror or hearing those screams fall silent. When this was over, there would be nothing left. No one left.

A thundering outside the tunnel made her draw in a breath. A moment later, the circle of light eclipsed and she found herself engulfed in darkness. It wasn't until her eyes adjusted that she caught movement in the blackness. A single eye, peering back at her—large, blue, with a gold-crescent pupil.

A dragon's eye.

She squeezed her own eyes shut, trying to prevent her body from shaking with terror and giving her position away. The dragon was too large to enter the tunnel and eat her raw, but it could always choose to serve her up as flambé. Neither scenario sounded like a good way to go.

Open your eyes, Trinity.

She startled. That voice again! From back at the museum. And at her grandpa's house. Could it be…?

Can you hear me, Trinity? Open your eyes.

She found herself obeying, reluctantly opening one eye, then another. Sudden bright light forced her to squint and she realized the dragon had stepped away from the entrance and was now standing a few feet away. Calm, fireless, observing her with a curious expression on its face.

Come on out. I won't let them hurt you.

What else could she do? With effort, she began to crawl again, squeezing her way through the tunnel until she was able to emerge on the other side. Relief flooded her as she scrambled to her feet, stretching her cramped muscles. For a moment she was so happy to be free of the confined space, she forgot she was still face-to-face with a dragon. A talking dragon, nonetheless.

"Who are you? And how do you know my name?" she found herself blurting out, probably the most ridiculous, insignificant questions possible at a time like this. But what else did one say to a dragon? *Eat any good people lately?*

The dragon seemed to chuckle, as if she could hear Trinity's thoughts. Maybe she could. *My name is Emberlyn,* the voice in her head informed her.

Trinity's heart stuttered.

"That's my mother's name," she rasped.

The dragon nodded her massive head, not looking surprised. *You named me after her,* she explained. *To honor your mother's memory. But you usually call me Emmy.*

"But that doesn't make any sense." Why would she name a world-destroying monster after her mother? For that matter, why would she name a world-destroying monster at all?

Because you're the Fire Kissed, Emmy replied, once again reading her mind. *And we are destined...*

Chapter Thirteen

"NO!" Trinity leapt to her feet, screaming at the top of her lungs. Connor grabbed her, locking her into a protective embrace, his hands gripping her back until she stopped fighting him, realizing where she was. No longer in the midst of a raging inferno. No longer face-to-face with a dragon that had her mother's name. She was back at her old home, safe and sound, with Connor by her side. Had it all been some kind of dream? But no, a searing pain shot up her arm. She looked down to find blackened skin, blistering from where the wood had hit it.

She jerked away from Connor, staring down at her burnt hand, then up at him, fury and fear surging through her. "How could you do that?" she cried. "How could you send me there without even warning me first?"

It had been real. All of it. She could have died! She could have been burnt alive. How could he just stand there, knowing he'd put her life in danger like that?

Connor looked down at her hand, his face awash with confusion. "Wha—how did you get that?" he stammered.

"You tell me. You're the one who sent me smack dab into the middle of Armageddon world," she retorted, trying not to focus on her throbbing hand. If a little burn hurt this badly, what would it have been like to be engulfed in a sea of flames like the others? She held her stomach, this close to throwing up as her hand continued to pulse in pain.

"But it was just a vision," Connor protested. "A recording of a past event. Not even first hand—it came from my history reader. It shouldn't have been able to hurt you…"

"Tell that to my hand."

Connor regarded her burn, looking confused and frightened. Then he squared his jaw, seeming to recover his inner soldier. "Hang on," he said at last. "I have something that will help."

Trinity watched as he reached into his bag and pulled out a small tin, prying open the top and scooping out a glob of grease. She obediently held out her hand and he smeared the stuff over her burn. The heat cooled immediately and she found herself able to breathe normally again.

"What is that stuff?" she asked.

"Burn salve," he replied. "It's a big seller where I'm from, as you can imagine. It'll knock out your pain and prevent infection. Unfortunately, it may also make you a bit sleepy."

Connor scooped out more goop and continued to apply it to her wound. His touch was warm, gentle. His strokes even and clean. Against her better judgment, Trinity felt herself start to relax, the apocalyptic nightmare fading from her consciousness. She was exhausted, she realized suddenly, and her head was pounding. Side effects from her trip through time and space?

Once he had finished, he led her back over to the couch. She collapsed in relief, leaning her head against a pillow, trying to will away the creeping nausea. "Tell me everything you saw," he instructed, his voice filled with concern. "I need to figure out what's going on here. Something's got to be wrong. There's no way you should have gotten hurt from a memory."

And so she told him, starting with the burning town and the dying people, and ending with the small green dragon coming in for a landing.

"She said her name was Emberlyn—Emmy, just like my mother—and that I was the one to name her that. Which is ridiculous, right? I mean why on Earth would I be going around naming dragons? Naming dragons after my dead mother, I might add? And then she said something else weird. She said I was..." She trailed off, catching Connor's grim expression. "What?"

"This is worse than I thought," he declared. "The dragon is gaining strength and reaching out to you through your bond. She must have yanked you out of the vision I sent you—and dragged you into the Nether so she could talk to you."

"The Nether?"

Connor bit his lower lip. "It's a place beyond space and time, existing in the collective unconsciousness of all dragons." He raked a frustrated hand through his hair. "This is all my fault—I should have never opened you up like that to receive my send. But I never imagined she would already be powerful enough to intervene."

Trinity stared at him, more confused than ever. "So wait," she said. "You're saying that this dragon here, inside this egg, somehow hijacked your vision and dragged me into some magical dragon world so she and I could have a little meet and greet?"

"It's a bit more complicated than that, but that's the idea."

"But why would she do that? What does she want with me?" She thought back to Emmy's words and shivered.

We are destined...

"Most dragon eggs can hatch on their own without the aid of humans," Connor explained. "But certain dragons—queen dragons, often—attempt to bond with a selected human before they're born. It gives them an added level of protection from Hunters like me." He looked down at his hands. "Your bond with Emmy began back at the museum, when you first pulled her from the exhibit case."

She stared at him, unease crawling across her skin. "So that's why you told me not to touch the egg."

"I thought maybe I could save you from it all. Let you live a normal life. But now it's too late. Emmy has touched you and the bond between you will only grow. She'll use that bond to convince you to help her. To save her life."

Trinity stared at the bag containing the egg, remembering how tempted she'd been to touch it. To hold it in her arms. To trace it with her fingertips. Had the dragon been silently luring her under its spell all along, hoping to convince her to help it hatch and destroy the world? The thought was revolting.

"Well, don't worry," she declared. "I'm not about to play mother to a dragon. Not after I saw what the beasts are capable of." Her mind flashed to the town square, engulfed in flames. The children's screams. The burning flesh. So much senseless death. The end of the world itself—all sparked by this one egg. There was absolutely no bond on Earth that was going to convince her to save this disgusting thing.

She turned to Connor. "I want to help," she declared. "Whatever needs to be done to keep dragons extinct—I'm your girl."

Connor didn't answer, pulling the egg from his bag and turning it in his hands. Trin flexed her fingers uneasily, the compulsion to touch it once again burning through her like a fever. She wondered if she should mention the urge to Connor but decided against it. He might decide she was too far gone to help him and she didn't want to be left out.

"Judging from its transparency, I'd say we have about a week before it hatches," he told her. "We'll need to find a way to destroy it by then. The sooner the better."

She gave the egg a dubious look. "Couldn't we just…I don't know…smash it?"

"It's not that simple. Dragon eggs are pretty much unbreakable," he informed her. "Harder than diamonds. But we can try to burn it." He looked up at her hopefully. "I don't suppose you have any spare plutonium?"

"Um, no. Sorry. Not exactly something they stock at the local Wal-Mart."

"Right." He pressed his lips together. "Well, then we're going to have to go with the alternative."

"Which is?"

He seemed to consider this. "A volcano perhaps. If we can drop the egg into an active volcano, the lava should be hot enough to destroy it."

"Oh-kay." She considered this for a moment. "But wait," she said, a thought coming to her.

Connor looked at her questioningly.

"If we destroy the egg," she said, "won't that…I don't

know… cancel out your own world? I mean I saw *Back to the Future*. If we succeed, will you start to disappear?"

She meant the question as a kind of half joke and was surprised at the uneasiness she felt after she voiced it. What if he *did* just disappear? Vanished into thin air, never to be seen again? The thought disturbed her more than she wanted to admit.

Thankfully, Connor shook his head. "It doesn't work like that. My timeline has already been established. There's no way to alter that. But by destroying the egg, we can set your world on an alternate timeline. One that doesn't end in apocalypse."

She furrowed her brow. The quantum mechanics were making her head hurt. "So you can't go back then," she realized aloud, "because in the new alternate future, you wouldn't exist."

He nodded.

"Dude, that's rough," she blurted out before she could stop herself.

He chuckled. "Don't worry. I knew what I was getting myself into when I accepted the mission," he assured her. "We have to do whatever we can to save the human race. Even if it means sacrificing ourselves." He paused, then added in a whisper, "Sacrifice one to save the world," as if it were some kind of mantra.

Trinity opened her mouth to reply but was interrupted by her phone. She jerked, glancing at Connor. Pulling the phone from her pocket, her eyes widened as she read the unfamiliar telephone number on the caller ID.

"Hello?" she answered hesitantly after putting the phone to her ear. After all, it could be anyone. The government agents. Sheriff Bob…

"Trinity! Where are you?"

"Grandpa!" She leapt from her seat, gripping the receiver tightly in her hand. "Where are you? Are you okay?"

"I'm fine," he assured her. "I was worried about *you*. I only left the house for a short time—I was opening up a package with my pocket knife when your damn cat jumped out at me, knocking over the Chinese food. I managed to slice up my hand pretty good and decided to head over to the clinic to make sure I didn't need stitches. I'm sorry I didn't leave a note. I figured I'd still beat you home."

Trinity swallowed hard, remembering the bloody knife. What she'd imagined…

"Unfortunately they took forever—evidently Christmas Eve is one of their busiest nights. When I finally got out, I swung back to the museum to see if you needed a ride, but the whole place was barricaded by police tape. They told me there was a break-in and someone had been shot and killed." His voice trembled. "My first thought was it had been you."

Trinity closed her eyes. It certainly could have been, had it not been for Connor. "Where are you now?" she asked.

"I'm still at the Denny's across the street. The police told me to stay put so they could send someone over. Evidently there are some government agents in town who want to question me about the break-in. The police are trying to get a hold of them now but they're not answering their phones."

No. They were a little tied up at the moment, Trinity thought grimly. "Listen to me, Grandpa," she said in a tight voice. "Something's happened. I can't explain over the phone, but I need you to get out of there. Use the back door if you have to. Pretend you're going to the bathroom or something. Whatever you have to do—just leave."

There was silence on the other end of the line. "Trinity... you're scaring me. What's going on? Where are you? Why shouldn't I wait for the agents?"

"Just trust me, okay?" she begged. "I'll meet you by exit 13 off the old interstate. When you get there, I'll explain everything."

There was another pause. She could almost hear his objecting thoughts over the phone and waited impatiently for him to voice them. But instead, he said at last, "Okay, fine. I'll be there in ten minutes."

She let out a sigh of relief, then hung up the phone, turning back to Connor. "He's okay," she breathed, relating her grandpa's story. "But we have to go meet him."

"I'll go," he said, scrambling up from the couch and grabbing his coat. "You stay here."

"I should come too," she protested. But as she attempted to rise to her feet, a strange weakness overtook her and she found herself falling back onto the couch, her head spinning and her stomach churning all over again. She looked up at Connor in confusion.

"The Nether," he explained grimly. "It'll kick the fleck out of you every time. You'll need a couple hours to feel like yourself again." He paused, then added, "It's probably better if you wait here anyway. We can't afford for you to be recognized, and someone needs to stay here and guard the egg. It'll be quicker and safer for me to go grab him and bring him back here. No one knows who I am."

"But—" she protested weakly. "I should—"

"Listen to me, Trinity," he commanded, cutting off her

protests. "This is the kind of thing I've trained for. What I was sent here to do. I promise you I will take care of your grandpa. I won't let anything happen to him." He patted the gun to his side. "No matter what."

She chewed her lower lip, wanting to argue. But in her heart she knew he was right. He was the soldier, the professional. He'd proven himself an ally and she had to trust him now.

"Okay," she relented. "But be careful. I don't want anything to happen to…" she drew in a breath, "…either of you."

Their eyes met, his steady and glowing, hers anxious, hesitant, but full of sudden longing. As her heart hammered in her ears, he leaned down, closing the gap between them.

His kiss was soft, gentle—a wisp of a butterfly's wings against her lips. And yet it left a trail of blazing fire in its wake. And, more importantly, a promise.

"I'll bring him back," he declared as he pulled away, piercing her with his glowing eyes. "I swear to you I'll bring him back safe and sound. No matter what."

"Please do," she murmured, as she watched him walk out the door. "He's all I have left."

Not anymore, corrected the now all-too-familiar voice, tripping across her consciousness like a whisper. *I'm here now. And we are destined…*

Chapter Fourteen

Connor headed out the front door, preparing for the trip back to the interstate. As he plodded down the front steps, he found himself glancing back at the house, a pleasant ache settling in his stomach as he thought of Trin, waiting inside. He could still feel the ghost of her lips against his own and it made him smile like a first-year academy student.

Then he frowned. *What the hell was he doing?* Only jeopardizing his entire mission. After all, what was the one thing the Council had warned him about—above everything else?

Do not get attached.

Of course, that order had seemed much simpler when given back in the sterile, cold debriefing room, deep underground, two hundred years in the future. After all, why would anyone want to get attached to *her*—the girl destined to bring dragons back into the world? The one who had set in motion the Scorch that had led to the deaths of millions of innocent people? People like his father. He should want Trinity Foxx dead.

And yet, somehow, at that moment, all he could think of was running his hands through her glossy black hair, fingering each and every strand. Pulling her into his arms, breathing in her baby powder scent...

What is wrong with you? You're a Dragon Hunter. Get a grip!

He shook his head, firming his resolve. She was a weakness. And he couldn't afford weaknesses. His mission was too important. The entire world was depending on him to succeed. Not to mention his father.

He'd let his father down once. He wasn't about to do it again. When the time came, he would do what he had come here to do. No excuses, end of story. They were his orders after all. And Connor always followed orders.

PART 2:

SMOKE

Chapter Fifteen

"Trinity! Wake up! Wake up!"

Trinity shrieked as rough hands grabbed her, shaking her shoulders, forcing her awake. Her eyes flew open. Connor stood above her, a strained expression on his face. "They've found us," he said in a tight voice. "We have to get out of here."

The jolt of terror was a better wake-up call than any shot of espresso, and Trinity was up in an instant, stuffing her feet into her shoes. As she looked around, eyes still bleary, her foggy brain tried to piece together the night. Connor had left to get her grandfather. She'd gone upstairs, drained from her trip to the Nether, and collapsed onto her old bed, hoping to rest her eyes for just a moment before they returned.

"Where's Grandpa?" she asked. "Did you get him?"

He shook his head grimly. "There was…a complication," he told her, shoving a coat, then a backpack into her hands. The dragon egg was inside, she realized, feeling the warm, smooth shell under the canvas, even now tempting her to pull it from its sheath and cradle it in her arms. Pushing the urge from her mind, she slipped the straps over her shoulders instead. Then she turned to Connor. He put a finger to his lips.

"They're downstairs," he hissed. "We need to go out the window."

Who was downstairs? The government? Or worse…the Dracken? Panic surged through her as she watched Connor force open a creaky window at the other end of the room. A complication. What did that mean? Was her grandpa all right? Or had they gotten him after all? A cold knot formed in her stomach as nightmarish possibilities whirled through her brain.

"Go!" Connor instructed, gesturing to the now-open window. "I'll be right behind you."

Forcing down her fear, Trin managed to climb out through the window frame onto the sloped roof. The temperature had dropped and the wind rushed in her ears. Thank goodness Connor had thought to give her a coat. Gingerly, she slid her way down to the edge of the slick roof, peering over the side. Oh God. She bit her lower lip, terror racing through her. They were still up so high!

"You've got to jump!" Connor commanded, his voice suddenly in her ear, startling her and almost causing her to slip. She hadn't heard him come up behind her. "I've jammed the window, but it won't take them long to break it."

She stared down at the ground below, which seemed to weave in and out of focus. Her stomach roiled. "I'm…I'm afraid of heights," she confessed, a sudden dizziness overwhelming her.

Connor looked at her as if she were crazy. "But you're Fire Kissed!" he protested.

"What?"

He waved her off. "Never mind," he said. "I'll go first."

Without pausing, he proceeded to push himself off the roof, landing hard on the ground with an *omph*. After righting himself, he looked back up at her, holding out his arms. "I'll catch you," he shouted. "But you have to jump now!"

The ground loomed, seeming a thousand miles away. Above, she could hear a banging sound, footsteps entering the bedroom.

"Come on!" Connor begged from below. "Hurry!"

The window began to creak.

Trinity sucked in a breath, realizing she had no choice. She closed her eyes and slipped off the roof. Air whooshed in her ears like thunder as she flailed to the ground, her mind spinning with visions of cracked ankles and smashed wrists—

Strong arms seized her, breaking her fall. She opened her eyes. Connor's face was inches away, his mouth locked into a self-satisfied smirk. "See?" he said, setting her down onto the ground. "I told you." He motioned to a motorcycle leaning against a dilapidated fence. "Get on behind me," he instructed as he threw a leg over the bike.

She stared at him, her still half-asleep brain torn with confusion. "Where did you get a motorcycle?"

He shook his head. "It doesn't matter. Just come on! We've got to go, now!"

She reluctantly complied, climbing on behind him and holding on tight. Above them, the window shattered and a voice called out into the night.

"Trinity! Wait!"

She tried to look up, but the motorcycle took off, flying across her former front yard at way too fast a speed. Down the road, up the off ramp, and back onto the abandoned interstate without slowing down. She tightened her grip, cling-ing on for dear life as icy wind blasted her already frozen ears and the potholes from the abandoned highway caused the bike to bounce and weave dangerously.

As they passed old exit 13 without slowing down, Trinity bit her lower lip, worry worming through her insides. What had happened with her grandpa? Connor had promised her he'd get him. Did he now mean to leave him behind?

"Where are we going?" she tried to ask, her pulse kicking up in alarm.

But he either couldn't hear her or chose not to answer.

Chapter Sixteen

C onnor! Could we *please* stop for a moment? I'm about to fall off the bike."

The sun was rising, bruising the horizon with blues and pinks, as Trinity squirmed in her seat. They'd been riding for hours and she was sore and frozen, not to mention confused and scared. All she wanted to do was stop for two seconds and get some answers. Like why had they had to make such a quick escape? Who had come after them at her mother's house? And, most importantly, what had happened with her grandpa and where was he now?

To her relief, Connor pulled the bike up to a stop sign, then dropped his feet to the ground. "Sorry," he said, allowing her to dismount before parking the bike a few feet off the road. "I just wanted to make sure we put enough distance between us and them. We can rest here a few minutes."

As he knelt down to check the bike, Trinity assessed their surroundings. They'd left the highway hours before, Connor choosing back roads over main thoroughfares in an apparent attempt to keep a low profile. Which was smart, she supposed, even though she found the desolation more than a bit creepy. From what she'd been able to tell, they'd crossed into

New Mexico over an hour ago, and since then there'd been nothing but brown, empty desert, stretching out on both sides of the road, as far as the eye could see. The only signs of life were the beady-eyed vultures, circling the roadkill, and they hadn't passed another car in hours. And here she'd thought Old Oak Grove was in the middle of nowhere. Her hometown was a bustling metropolis compared to this

Except…she squinted her eyes, peering south. Was that a small town out there, far in the distance? From here she could just make out the shadows of a few one-story buildings, scattered across the landscape. Some tiny, nothing town the rest of the world had forgotten, she supposed, just waking up, ready to face the day.

To celebrate Christmas, she realized dully. Because it was indeed Christmas morning, as much as it didn't feel like it. She sighed. What was it about this particular holiday that seemed determined to make everything in her life go to hell? Next year—if they survived all this—she should just cancel the whole event.

The thought made her cringe. What was she doing here? All alone, in the middle of the desert, a fugitive from the law, with nothing more than the clothes on her back and a mythical dragon egg in her pouch. And her grandpa still MIA.

She fumbled for her phone. Maybe he'd left her a message…

"No!"

The phone was knocked from her hand. It skittered to the ground, the screen cracking on impact. Trinity turned to Connor in shock. "What are you—?" she started, but the words died in her throat as she caught the look in his eyes.

She dove for her phone. But he was too quick, grabbing

it and slamming it down on the pavement. Trinity watched, horrified, as her only link to her grandpa smashed into a thousand useless pieces.

"What the hell did you do that for?" she demanded furiously.

Connor stared at her, his blue eyes wild. "You can't let anyone know where we are!" He grabbed her roughly by the hand, his fingernails digging into her burn. She screeched in surprise and pain. "Now get back on the bike. We need to keep moving."

She yanked her arm away, staring at him in disbelief and fury. What was going on here? This was not the same Connor from the night before. The one who'd held her close and comforted her—the one who'd kissed her softly and promised to keep her grandpa safe. It was as if he'd transformed into another person altogether.

"Connor, what's wrong with you?" she demanded, the hurt in her voice impossible to hide. "You're scaring me!"

Connor let out a frustrated breath, squeezing his hands into fists, then loosening them. "Look, I'm sorry," he muttered. "It's just…I don't think you understand how much danger you're in here. I'm only trying to protect you."

"I know you're trying to protect me," she tried to reason. "But I also need some answers. Like where are we going, for one?"

He frowned. "To see some friends who can help us."

Friends? Trinity cocked her head in confusion. He'd never mentioned any friends. In fact, it was pretty clear he'd been on a solo mission. She stared at him, warning bells going off in her head.

"What about the volcano?" she asked slowly.

A shadow of confusion flickered across his face before he was able to mask it with a reassuring smile. But it was enough. Fear cut her to the core. Oh God. She'd been such a fool.

"You're not Connor," she realized aloud. "You're Caleb. His twin."

He looked at her for a moment, as if trying to decide something. Then his mouth quirked to a grin. "At your service, m'lady," he quipped, dropping to an exaggerated bow. He actually had the nerve to look pleased with himself. She squeezed her hands into fists.

"How dare you?" she cried, furious beyond belief—at him for tricking her, at herself for falling for such a stupid trick. "You can't kidnap me!"

He raised an eyebrow. "Um, I think the word you're looking for is 'rescue.' I *rescued* you."

"Oh really? Since when is dragging someone out of their bed in the middle of the night considered a rescue?"

"Simple. When that *someone* is in the clutches of a guy who plans to kill her."

She stared at him. Stunned. He gave her a smug smile, followed by an impish shrug. It was all she could do not to punch his lights out.

"You're crazy," she growled. "There's no way Connor would…" She trailed off, doubtfully. Was she really so sure of that? After all, she'd only met the guy yesterday…

No. That was crazy. Connor had saved her life. More than once, in fact. If he'd wanted to kill her, he could have easily done it. He'd had a million opportunities.

"Look, I'm sorry I had to trick you, but trust me, it was for your own good. If you'd just get back on the damned bike, I'll explain everything." He made a step toward her.

"Get the hell away from me!" she hissed. "I'm not going anywhere with you."

Caleb regarded her, a regretful look on his face. Now that she realized it was him, she could clearly see the differences in their eyes. "I'm sorry, Trinity," he replied. "But I'm afraid you have no choice."

He lunged at her with lightning speed. But she was ready for him. Grabbing the backpack, she slammed the egg at his head with all her might, half praying it would just break, then and there, and end this once and for all.

But the egg remained intact. Caleb, on the other hand, collapsed onto the ground, out cold.

Trinity: one. Crazy evil twin from the future: zero.

Trinity tossed her head with satisfaction, kicking him a few times to make sure he was really out. Then she turned to the motorcycle, giving it a doubtful look. Even if she did figure out how to turn it on, she'd never be able to ride it. Instead, she yanked out what appeared to be an important wire, then took off down the road on foot. She turned back once, to make sure Caleb hadn't made a quick recovery. But he was still prostrate where she'd left him.

"Come on, dragon," she whispered to the egg in her pack. "Let's get out of here."

Chapter Seventeen

Trinity's skin glistened with sweat as she stepped into a sleepy little diner a few miles from where she'd left Caleb lying unconscious on the roadside. She'd chosen to skip the first town she'd come to—feeling it would be too obvious a hiding spot—and forced her feet to keep moving until she came across this tiny restaurant completely off the beaten path. There was no way he'd find her here. At least not anytime soon.

The bells hanging from the front door chimed merrily as she entered and the few locals sitting at the counter gave her curious looks before going back to their breakfasts. After catching sight of her reflection in the beer sign mirror hanging on the wall, she could see why. She was red-faced and wild haired from her run in the early morning air.

Breathing in the comforting smells of frying eggs and burnt coffee, she walked purposely through the diner, stopping at the ancient pay phone at the very back. Picking up the receiver, she shoved some change in the slot, then forced her trembling fingers to dial her grandpa's number. When there was no answer, she tried her best friend Caitlin's cell—the only other number she knew by heart.

After a few rings, her friend's cheery voice greeted her into voicemail. "Hi, you've reached Caitlin! I'm either on the other line or purposely ignoring you. Or maybe Mrs. Mitchell confiscated my phone for texting in class again. That bitch. Leave a message and if I deem you worthy, or at least hot, I'll call you back. Mwah!"

Trinity's heart sank. Of course. Caitlin's family had gone to Disney World for Christmas. They were probably hurtling down the Twilight Zone Tower of Terror that very second.

Leaving Trin stuck in this real-life version alone.

"Caitlin!" she cried into the phone, not willing to give up. "It's me, Trin." Feeling the eyes of the other patrons on her, she lowered her voice. "I'm...well, I'm at this diner. In some town in New Mexico." God, she didn't even know where she was. How could she expect her friend to help her? "I think I'm in trouble, Caitlin!" she confessed, her breath hitching. "And...well, I don't have my cell anymore. But I'll wait by the payphone, okay?" She read the number off the phone's base in case it didn't get picked up by her friend's caller ID. "Call me as soon as you can!" she pleaded before reluctantly hanging up.

"You just here to make calls or you want breakfast too?" asked the blond, ponytailed waitress behind the counter. Her voice was gruff, but there was something kind in her brown eyes, which crinkled at the corners. Trin slunk over to one of the red-vinyl stools and took a seat. Reaching her grubby hand into her pocket, she pulled out a few random coins—all the money she had in the world after making her calls.

"Can I get a cup of coffee for this?" she asked. She wasn't the biggest coffee lover in the world, but she was exhausted from her all-night ride.

The waitress—her nametag identified her as Mary—studied Trinity for a moment, then seemed to make up her mind. "Sure, honey," she said, reaching under the counter to pull out a cracked ceramic mug with remnants of pink lipstick still clinging to the rim. "In fact, we're running a Christmas special this morning. Buy one coffee, get eggs and toast free. And bacon too if you'd like it."

"Hey, Mary, how come you ain't told me about that special?" called the old trucker at the other end of the counter. The waitress shot him an amused look.

"Shut up and eat your oatmeal, Stu," she scolded. "Your wife would skin me alive if I let you eat bacon and you know it." She gave Trin a knowing look and Trin found she couldn't help but smile back. The down-home normalness of it all was starting to help her relax. All the horror of the last twelve hours was beginning to feel like a bad dream. "Now, did you want those eggs scrambled or sunny side up?"

Trinity ordered scrambled, her empty stomach growling in anticipation, and Mary turned to the griddle to start preparing her breakfast. Sipping her coffee, she looked over at the pay phone, praying Caitlin would call her back soon. Not that she had any idea how her friend would be able to help her. Especially from inside the Magic Kingdom. How would she even be able to explain what was going on—when she didn't even know for sure herself?

She closed her eyes, feeling defeated. What was she going to do?

"Are you sure you're okay, hon?" Mary asked, coming over to refill her mug. "No offense, but you don't look so good."

Trin's first instinct was to say she was fine. But something in Mary's face made her change her mind. "There's this guy," she confessed, squirming in her seat and sneaking a peek out the window into the nearly empty parking lot. "He's...well, I think he's after me." God, she sounded like a paranoid freak.

"A boyfriend of yours?"

Trin shook her head. "No. Just someone...I met." She looked up at Mary. "I'm in trouble," she confessed. "I'm far away from home. I don't have any money and I'm afraid he's going to find me."

Mary frowned. "That's it. I'm calling Sheriff Baker." She walked over to the phone behind the counter. Trin wondered if she should try to stop her. After all, she was a wanted felon at this point. If the police figured out who she was, they were going to take her away. Though at the moment a jail cell seemed like a better alternative than running into Caleb again. At least she could keep the egg out of his hands. Connor had told her the government was the least of their problems, that the Dracken were the biggest threat.

Connor. Where was he now? Did he have her grandpa with him? If only she could figure out a way to get back to Old Oak Grove. She looked around at the other diners. Maybe one of the truckers was going her way and could give her a lift. Of course it was dangerous to just get in a truck with a stranger. But considering the alternative...

A flash of movement outside caught her attention. She turned, her eyes widening in horror as they fell upon none other than Caleb himself, striding purposely toward the diner, his right eye swollen into an ugly purple bruise from where the egg had hit him. She dove off her stool and straight to the bathroom, her throat closing, cutting off air. How had he found her so quickly? It was as if he'd known she'd be there somehow!

She scanned the small room, desperate for an escape route, but realized there was no window and she was, for all intents and purposes, trapped. Outside, she heard the door bell's jangle; Caleb was now in the building. She slipped into the far stall and yanked the door shut behind her, sitting on the toilet with her feet up, trying to still her erratic pulse.

Maybe he was just here to order a cup of coffee to go.

Yeah, right.

A moment later, the bathroom door burst open. "Trinity!" he called. "Get out here now!" She heard a crash and realized he'd kicked open door number one. Followed quickly by door number two. How many stalls were there in this bathroom? Three? Four?

"I know you're in here!"

BANG! Door number three. She stifled a squeak of fear, not knowing why she bothered. He'd find her in a—

BANG! The door burst inward and she found herself face-to-face with her enemy. He gave her a disappointed look. "You're really going to have to learn at some point that I'm not the bad guy," he muttered as he grabbed her roughly by the arm and yanked her off the toilet seat. She struggled in protest until he pulled out a small pistol that looked just like Connor's laser one—and pressed it against her back. Her mind flashed to the man at the museum, his head exploding in a burst of green goo, and she reluctantly stopped fighting.

"That's better," he soothed. "Now let's go." He gestured toward the bathroom door. "Ladies first."

Somehow, some way, she managed to force her feet to

cooperate and shuffle forward toward the bathroom's exit. When she stepped back into the diner, the pay phone started ringing. She glanced at it longingly. *Caitlin…*

Caleb stiffened, turning to Trin, a horrified look of realization on his face.

"You didn't," he whispered accusingly.

"What if I did?" she demanded, somehow finding her voice. "Does that spoil your little kidnapping plan?" She forced herself not to look over at the phone, even though every fiber in her being wanted to dive across the room to answer it. She realized all the other diners had cleared out, probably after seeing Caleb's gun, and only Mary remained, a frightened but determined look on her face. The waitress started toward Caleb.

"Look here, you leave that girl alone!" she cried in a voice bordering on hysteria. Trin's eyes misted as the waitress came to her defense. At the same time she wished the woman would just turn and run out the front door—out of danger.

"You don't understand," Caleb cried, sounding exasperated. "I'm trying to save her life!"

Blue lights flashed through the diner's windows as two cop cars whipped into the parking lot. Caleb let out a frustrated breath. "You really are determined to make my job as difficult as possible, aren't you?" he groaned, shaking his head. He turned to Mary. "Is there a back door?"

"Like I'd tell you!" she shot back as the police officers entered through the front. The bells jingled merrily, the sound jarring with the current situation.

"Mary, what seems to be the—"

Before they could finish their question, Caleb had the

waitress by the ponytail, yanking her back. Mary screamed in protest as he dragged her in front of Trin, his laser gun pressed against her head. "Get back!" he screamed at the cops, who were now fumbling uselessly for their own weapons. "Drop your guns. On the floor. Or I'll kill her. I swear to God!"

The small-town cops, looking confused and frightened, obliged, dropping their firearms and crawling down to the diner's black and white tiled floor.

"Please don't kill me," Mary squeaked. "I have kids at home. Three little girls."

"Let her go!" Trin added, horrified by the fact she'd managed to drag a poor innocent mother into this whole mess. "I'll go with you. Whatever you want. Just let her go."

He ignored her. "Just be a good girl," Trin heard him whisper to Mary, "and lead us to the back door." Raising his voice, he added, "Stay still and count to a hundred. Or I'll kill her!"

As the cops began to count, the three of them backed through the kitchen and out the rear door. Trinity looked around, wondering if she should make a run for it. But Caleb still had the gun pinned on Mary, and she wasn't about to let the kindly waitress get hurt or killed on her account.

"Let her go!" she tried again instead, turning to Caleb with pleading eyes. "I'm the one you want, not her."

To her surprise, he nodded, releasing Mary. The waitress fell to the ground, crying out as her bare knees scraped against concrete.

"I'm sorry," Caleb said, looking surprisingly remorseful as he held out a hand to help the waitress to her feet. Mary refused his assistance, shooting him a death look as she scrambled up on her own. Her legs were cut and bleeding, her hair had come loose from its ponytail. Caleb sighed and dropped his hand. "Fine. Have it your way," he said with a shrug. Then he turned to Trinity, his face hard and cold.

"Now, if you're done messing around," he said, "we're late for our date with the Dracken."

Chapter Eighteen

"Y ou need to turn left at that stop sign up ahead," Caleb instructed from the passenger seat, after consulting his transcriber. "We'll be taking that road for the next hour or two."

Trinity put on her blinker, shifting in an attempt to get comfortable as the cracked vinyl seats pinched at her thighs. Caleb had stolen the old Ford pickup from the driveway of a darkened house near the diner and insisted she drive, making her wonder if cars were as extinct as airplanes in a post-dragon-apocalypse world. Though he *had* seemed pretty skilled on his motorcycle...

"And slow down!" he added, cradling the egg protectively in his arms as she stepped on the gas.

Damn. She'd been hoping he wouldn't register her sudden burst of speed—a desperate attempt to get a traffic cop to notice them and pull them over. She half wondered if she should just plow into the SUV ahead of her—or slam into a guardrail even—giving herself a chance to make a run for it. That sort of thing always worked great in the movies. But in real life, she feared, it might just land her with a broken leg... or worse.

"It probably would," Caleb agreed.

Startled, she snapped her head in his direction. "What?"

"Crashing the car like that. It'd probably kill you. Or at least hurt really bad. Definitely not a good idea."

She turned back to the road, gritting her teeth. "How did you know what I was thinking?" she asked finally, against her better judgment. She didn't want to engage him in another conversation, listen to his lies about "rescuing her" at gunpoint.

He looked surprised at the question. "I have the gift," he replied as if it were the most obvious explanation ever.

"*The gift*?" she repeated. "What gift?"

"*The* gift," he emphasized. "The one that gives us the spark."

"Yeah. Not really clearing things up."

Caleb sighed. "Didn't my brother tell you anything?" he muttered, shaking his head. Then he turned to her. "There are certain people in this world who are born with something special inside of them, a certain energy. We call it the spark. Those who are born with this spark can do amazing things. Some can sense emotion. Some can hear other people's thoughts. A few can go one step further and actually bend people's wills. They call that pushing. My brother can push. Which is one reason you have to be careful around him. You never know what he might try to get you to believe."

He paused, glancing over at her for her reaction, then continued, "Think about it. How else would I have been able to find you last night? Or at the diner this morning? I simply followed your fear and it led me straight to you."

Her hackles rose at the idea. The implication that it was some-how her fault—her weakness—that allowed her to be caught.

"Okay, fine," she snarled. "If you can read my mind, what am I thinking *right now*?"

Caleb chuckled. "That you want to kill me. Though, to be fair, I don't need to read your mind for that. It's written all over your face."

She groaned, forcing her focus back on the road. She wanted to tell him he was being ridiculous. That the only gift he had mastered was that of being a total dick. Yet, reluctantly, she had to admit he *had* known exactly what she'd been thinking. And he *had* found her—in the middle of nowhere. Both last night and just now.

And then there was Connor, his own twin. She thought about how he'd grabbed her back at the barn. She'd heard his thoughts, echoing through her head, though he'd never moved his lips. And when he'd finished, she'd wanted to do exactly what he'd told her to. Had that been this pushing thing Caleb was talking about?

She attempted to empty herself of thoughts, concentrating only on the road ahead, while Caleb continued to stare at her with piercing eyes from the passenger seat. His face was identical to his twin's, she realized, yet at the same time so different. How could she have not noticed it before? Whereas Connor's eyes were clear blue, the color of the sky on a cloudless day, Caleb's had flecks of gold and green, swirling about in a storm of color.

Connor. Where was he now? What was he doing? Did he have her grandpa with him? Was he trying to find her, wanting to make sure she was okay? Her heart panged as she remembered what must have been his shadow at her bedroom window, his desperate voice calling out her name just as Caleb stole her away. Did he know she'd been tricked? That his brother had assumed his identity? Or would he believe she'd left of her own free will, the evil dragon convincing her to join up with his worst enemy?

No, she decided. Connor would know. He'd know that she'd never take off on him willingly, leaving him and her grandpa behind. Not after what they'd been through—after what they'd shared. Her lips twitched involuntarily, still branded by his kiss. She barely knew the guy and yet there was something about him. Something...protective. Somehow she knew he wouldn't rest until he was sure she was safe.

"I have to say, you think pretty highly of a guy who wants to murder you," Caleb pointed out absently, turning to look out the passenger side window. His voice was calm, emotionless, but his eyes had darkened to angry thunderclouds.

"Excuse me?"

"Connor," he said slowly, as if speaking to a dimwitted child. "Your big knight in shining dragon scale. He would have killed you if I'd left you there."

"Oh, right," she retorted tartly. Seriously, why did she keep feeling the need to encourage his lies? "He wanted to kill me. Well, then why didn't he? He had plenty of chances and, at the moment, I still seem to be pretty much alive, don't you think?"

"That's only because your bond is not yet complete," Caleb replied evenly. "No offense, princess, but you're not worth killing until your death can bring down a dragon."

What? Her lips parted in surprise.

"Oh dear," he cried, catching her expression. His mouth twisted. "Could it be that my brother forgot to mention that pesky little detail when he was *rescuing* you?"

"What are you talking about?" Trinity demanded, getting annoyed. "Whatever it is, just come out and say it."

"Sure." He shrugged dismissively. "When you first touched Emmy back at the museum, a bond began to build between you."

She gritted her teeth. "I know that. Get to the part where Connor's trying to kill me."

"Patience, princess." Caleb's fingers danced lazily over the egg, still swaddled in his lap. "The great mysteries of the universe take time to untangle."

"I'll be happy to untangle you if you don't start explaining."

Caleb snorted. "It's simple, really. Once Emmy breaks free of her shell, the bond between you will be complete. Meaning you'll share a common life force. We call it Fire Kissed where I come from and it's a rare thing indeed." He looked down at the egg. "You should consider yourself lucky—it's a great honor to be chosen by a queen."

Trinity found herself glancing over at the egg, a shiver tripping down her spine. Emmy's words came whispering back at her.

We are destined…

"In any case, it's really tough to kill a queen dragon once she's hatched," Caleb continued in an easy tone, "especially with your current primitive technology. It would be *much* easier, let's say, for a Hunter to go after its partner instead—a weak little human with a fragile mortal coil. Not so difficult to kill." He gave her a winning smile. "Does that answer your question?"

Trinity found she couldn't reply, the implications of his words making her blood run cold. As much as she wanted to accuse him of lying, the story made a weird kind of sense. After all, why else would Connor have been so bound and determined to keep her around, even when she'd tried to push him away? Could she really have been his insurance policy all along—in case he failed in his mission to destroy the egg?

"Look, I don't mean to sound harsh," Caleb added, his tone softening. She could feel his pity but refused to give him the satisfaction of seeing her upset. "But why do you think my brother wanted you tagging along on his mission to save the world? So he could qualify for the two-for-one special at the local truck-stop cafe?"

She scowled, wishing he'd stop talking. She didn't want to hear anymore—not now that the doubts had already seeded themselves in her mind. Could Connor really be capable of such deception? Luring her in, making her feel protected and safe—all the while ready to cut her down if things didn't go to plan? The idea hurt more than she wanted to admit.

We have to do whatever it takes, he had said, *even if it means sacrificing ourselves.*

Had he been planning to sacrifice her as well?

Her troubled thoughts were interrupted as blue lights flashed in her rearview mirror. "Crap," she swore under her breath, making a move to pull over. "A cop." It was strange— just a few minutes ago, she'd been practically begging for a rescue. Now she wasn't so sure.

"No!" Caleb cried, grabbing the steering wheel and yanking her back on the road. "We can't stop!"

"But we have to," she argued. "There's no way we can outrun a cop in this hunk of junk." She'd been flooring it just to reach fifty-five. She started to pull over again.

"Fine," Caleb replied, reaching for his gun.

"Wait!" She jerked the truck back onto the road. "What are you going to do?"

"Whatever I have to to keep you and Emmy safe."

"But you can't just kill him!" she protested. "He's innocent."

"Trinity, no offense, but aren't you on the run from the law? What do you think Mr. Innocent will do when he discovers we're not exactly the poster children for innocence ourselves?"

Trinity's face fell, knowing he was right. There was no way the cop was going to just let them go once he checked the license and registration. There was sure to be an APB on them from the diner incident, and maybe a stolen car report to boot. And she didn't even want to think about the penalties that might be involved in basically assaulting two Homeland Security agents...

But she couldn't just let Caleb kill him.

Think! she berated herself as she slowed down and guided the truck to the shoulder of the road. The policeman pulled in behind her, stopping about twenty feet back. *There has to be another way.*

Caleb fingered his gun.

"Put it in the glove box!" she hissed, pointing to the dashboard compartment, a plan forming in her mind. A trick she'd seen her mother do, back when she still had command of her senses. "And follow my lead, okay?"

Caleb hesitated. "I don't know..."

The police car door opened.

"Just please, do it!" she begged.

"Fine." Caleb stuffed the gun in the glove box. "We'll do it your way. But if things start to go wrong, I'm going to shoot." He dropped the egg between his legs and shielded it with his jacket.

Relieved, Trinity placed her hands on the steering wheel, in the proper ten and two position, just as she'd been instructed in driver's ed, her heart beating a mile a minute and her palms damp with sweat. From her mirror, she watched the policeman get out of his car and amble toward them.

"He doesn't have his gun drawn," she said quietly. "That means he doesn't know the truck is stolen."

Yet.

Caleb reached into his pocket and slid a pair of dark sunglasses over his eyes, hiding the ugly bruise she'd given him. A moment later, the officer knocked on her window and she rolled it down, looking up at him with her best blinding smile.

"What seems to be the trouble, Officer?" she asked brightly, trying to conceal the tremble in her voice.

"Ma'am, do you know you're driving with a taillight out?" the officer asked. He was young—maybe a year out of the academy—tall, and well-built.

"Is it?" she cried, feigning surprise. Inside, she cursed Caleb for picking such a hunk of junk as their getaway vehicle. "I had no idea. This is my uncle's truck. He never fixes anything." She considered batting her eyelashes at the cop but decided it would be overkill.

Believe me! she begged. *Please believe me!*

Out of the corner of her eye, she could see Caleb shoot her a startled look, though she had no idea why. A shimmer of nausea fluttered in her stomach. She prayed he'd keep his promise to stay quiet.

The policeman's frown lifted. "I have an uncle just like that," he told her, shaking his head. "His guest toilet's been out of service for ten years if it was a day. He's always going on about fixin' it. But it never seems to happen."

"That must be really fun at Christmas," she joked, giving

him a forced laugh. She realized her hands were shaking and gripped the steering wheel a little tighter. "Speaking of, Merry Christmas!"

Walk away, walk away, she pleaded silently. *Please walk away.*

Her stomach lurched so forcefully she almost threw up right on the cop. With effort, she forced the smile back on her face. What was going on with her?

Keep it together, Trin. Just a little longer.

What are you doing? Caleb hissed in her head. It took her a moment to realize he wasn't speaking out loud. Like Connor back at the barn. Another part of the gift?

Shut up, she tried to send back, feeling a little ridiculous at her first attempt at mental telepathy. To the cop, she added, "I can't believe they make you work on a holiday!"

The cop glanced at his watch. "Actually I worked the nightshift," he told her. "I'm off in a few minutes."

"Going home to the family?"

Go home, go home, go home.

Pain stabbed at her forehead. Her vision swam. For a moment she thought she was going to pass out. What was wrong with her? This was so not going to help her case with the cop.

Thankfully, he seemed oblivious to her sudden distress. He reached into his pocket for his wallet. "My boy's one year old," he boasted, handing Trinity a picture of a chubby-faced cherub that looked a lot like his dad. "First Christmas!"

"Aww," she managed to choke out. "He's so cute."

She handed the photo back, the sick feeling intensifying. If she screwed this up, that adorable baby boy would have to grow up without a father—just as she had.

She had to make this work. Somehow. Some way.

She lowered her eyes demurely. It was time to go in for the kill. "I don't suppose we could just forget the taillight—in the name of Christmas and all? I'd promise to get it fixed the *second* we get home."

The officer's smile faded. "Now you know I'm supposed to at least run your plates, ma'am. It's protocol. I could get in trouble."

"Oh, I don't want you to get in trouble!" Trin protested. *Damn it.* "I just want you to be able to get home to your baby!" This time, she did bat her eyelashes, desperate for something to work.

The officer stiffened. She'd gone too far. "Why don't you just give me your license and registration? We'll get it done fast."

"Okay." She closed her eyes, realizing she'd failed. Epically failed. Slowly, she reached for the glove box, her heart filled with despair. In a moment it would all be over. The cop would see Caleb's gun. He'd reach for his own...

Caleb's fingers grabbed her hand. He turned to her slowly, his expression unreadable from behind the sunglasses. "Allow me," he said in a low voice, reaching for the glove box.

Trinity forced herself to nod. A trickle of sweat dripped down her back.

Please walk away, please walk away... she silently begged the officer one more time as sharp pain stabbed at her skull like knives. *For your son's sake, just please walk the hell away!*

The glove box started to creak open...

"You know what?" the officer interjected, his face breaking out into a big smile. "You're right. Who wants to give out a ticket on Christmas?"

Caleb pulled his hand away.

"Thank you!" Trinity cried, relief coming in a flood. "Thank you so much!"

"Merry Christmas," the officer said, giving her a small wave. "And get that taillight fixed."

And with that, he turned back to his car. A moment later, he was pulling off the shoulder and passing them on the road, leaving their lives forever. Trinity waited for him to disappear over the horizon, then stumbled out of the pickup truck, falling to her knees and vomiting on the side of the road, clutching her head in agony.

Caleb followed her out of the truck, clapping his hands slowly. "Wow, you really are Fire Kissed, aren't you?" he remarked, sounding impressed.

She looked over at him blearily, her stomach still roiling. "What are you talking about?" she asked, annoyed that he looked so pleased when she felt so terrible. "I just sweet talked him a little, something I learned from my mother."

"Trust me, no amount of sweet talk was going to make him drive away," Caleb insisted. "You pushed him—harder than I've ever seen anyone do. Which is probably why you feel like hell. Using the gift can kick the fleck out of you, especially without proper training."

"The gift?" Trinity looked up, confused. "You're saying I have the gift too?"

"Do you think a dragon would bond to a reg?" he replied, ripping off his sunglasses. His eyes shone. "Seriously Trin, I cannot wait to get you to the Dracken. They are going to be so excited to see you."

The Dracken. Trinity shivered. In her relief at escaping

the cop, she'd almost forgotten she was still trapped, still a prisoner—her life still in danger. Slowly, she rose to her feet, gripping the side of the truck, trying to regain her composure. The nausea was starting to fade, but she still felt overwhelmingly weak—not unlike how she felt after her trip to the Nether. As if she could sleep for a week.

"You know, I don't know what these Dracken people want from me, but I can tell you right now, they can just forget it," she managed to spit out, forcing herself to meet his eyes with her own. "It's not like I'm going to suddenly join them or whatever, just because you dragged me to their secret headquarters."

To her surprise, Caleb started to laugh. She shot him an annoyed look.

"What?" she demanded. "What's so funny?"

"It's just that…join us?" Caleb repeated, his eyes dancing in amusement. "But you're the one who started the Dracken in the first place!"

Chapter Nineteen

Trinity stared at Caleb, a clammy chill washing over her. "What?" she managed to scrape out in a hoarse voice. "What do you mean 'started the Dracken'?"

"Um, pretty much just like it sounds. You made it all happen. Brought everyone together, back in the day. Well, I guess more like ten years from now if we're being technical. You even came up with the silly name—the Order of the Dracken. Legend has it that it came from some video game you were into back then."

"What?" Trinity froze. Realization hitting her over the head with the force of a ten-ton truck. *Oh God.*

The Dracken. *That's* why the name sounded so familiar when Connor had said it back at the barn. Why had she not realized it before? The Order of the Dracken was a dragon-filled dungeon in the expansion pack of *Fields of Fantasy*. The very game that was probably still sitting under her grandpa's Christmas tree waiting for her to return.

The dizziness welled up inside her again, this time not as a side effect of the gift.

"But hey, don't take my word for it," Caleb continued, reaching into his bag and pulling out what looked like a high-tech tablet. He pressed a button and the screen illuminated into full-color video. She stared down at it; at first she thought she was watching some sort of movie—a fantasy epic straight out of *Lord of the Rings*. That was until the camera zoomed in for a close-up of a young woman, sitting on the back of an all-too-familiar-looking green dragon.

Trinity gaped. The woman had shorter hair than she did and was at least ten years older, but the resemblance was unmistakable.

"It's me," she whispered, unable to help stating the obvious. She watched in a mixture of fascination and horror as the woman and the dragon soared through the skies, looking elegant and elated and free. She wanted to protest that the footage had been doctored somehow, but what if it wasn't? What if Caleb was telling the truth? What if she really had started the organization? Connor had warned her about falling under the dragon's spell. Emmy had told her they were destined...

"It's a pretty great story, actually," Caleb said, turning off the device after the video faded to black. "A beautiful young girl, giving up everything she had to save the world's last dragons. Of course," he added, "it doesn't exactly end well."

She flinched. No, it didn't. She thought back to Connor's vision—of fiery skies and fallen friends, dragons destroying it all. What could have possibly prompted her future self to want to save these evil creatures who saw nothing wrong with burning the entire world to the ground? She couldn't imagine any spell that powerful.

"Don't feel bad," Caleb said, seeing her expression. "I mean, sure, things didn't turn out exactly how you planned, but you tried. Your heart was always in the right place."

"I don't understand," she protested. "Why would I form a dragon rights group? How would I even know about dragons to begin with? I mean, if the government took the egg immediately after it arrived at the museum the first time around, I would have never seen it again. I probably would have forgotten all about it."

"You didn't forget," Caleb corrected. "And a bond like yours and Emmy's is not easily broken. You heard her cries for years after they stole her, echoing through your head. At first you thought you were going crazy—like your mother had. It wasn't until Emmy lured you into the desert and you found a job at the facility they'd taken her to that you finally realized the truth."

"The truth?" Trinity repeated with encroaching dread. She turned to Caleb, trying desperately to swallow down her fear. "And what truth might that be?"

"That dragons have the power to save our world," Caleb replied matter-of-factly. "If only you could first save them."

Chapter Twenty

Caleb stared out the grease-smeared window of their small, dingy motel room, watching the wind outside swirl up debris. Trinity had suggested the place because it was the type that took cash and didn't ask for ID. Thanks to his little showdown at the diner, along with Trinity's performance with Homeland Security, the two of them were basically fugitives. The TV announcer had called them armed and dangerous.

Of course this was nothing new to Caleb. He'd spent most of his life considered armed and dangerous down in Strata-D. And while his brother, Connor, had racked up the accolades for his merciless dragon slaughter, Caleb picked up demerits. Hell, he'd probably been only an infraction or two away from a lifetime in the mines before meeting Darius, who recognized his gift and gave him a job.

Not an easy job, by any means. But an important one. A very important one.

His eyes left the window to check on Trinity, who'd thankfully fallen into an uneasy sleep. Poor girl. It'd been a rough journey for her so far. And pushing the cop had pushed her body to its limits.

If only his stupid brother hadn't gotten involved. Trin and her grandpa would already be reunited and the egg would be safe and sound at Dracken Headquarters, ready for hatching. But no. As always, the great and powerful Connor had to plow in and destroy everything in his path as part of his fanatical crusade.

And Caleb had almost lost Trinity—not to mention Emmy—because of it.

They still had a long way to go—both in physical distance and gaining trust. Sure, she'd been willing to listen to some of what he had to say, but he could see the disbelief reflected in her eyes. He didn't blame her, he supposed. It'd taken him a while to get on board with the Dracken as well. In fact, he hadn't truly believed anything Darius had said until the day he'd slipped the vial of dragon's blood into his mother's IV. The day she lived instead of died and the doctors called it a miracle.

The day, for the first time, Caleb was the hero, not Connor, even if no one knew it but him.

She was beautiful, he thought. The history texts did not do her justice. Sure, she had the same tangles of black curls falling down her back in waves, the same delicate features. But no photo could capture her long lashes, sweeping across freckled cheeks, or the way her lower lip plumped as she frowned in her sleep. And they certainly couldn't capture the fiery passion in her black eyes, illuminating the spark that was so strong within her.

Trinity moaned in her sleep, tossing and turning. He watched the stress lines wrinkling her brow and wondered if he should wake her from her nightmares. He hated to see her in such agony and prayed he hadn't been the cause of it. He'd never meant for everything to go so wrong, and the idea that she thought he was the bad guy tore at his heart.

"No one cares more about you than me," he whispered. He sighed, then turned back to the window.

"Shut up!" Trinity shot up in bed, boxing her hands over her ears and letting out a piercing scream. "Just shut up! Get out of my head!"

Caleb flew to her side. "Trinity! Wake up!" He grabbed her by the shoulders and shook her as hard as he could, forcing her awake. Her eyes flew open, wild and unseeing. Her face was blotchy and stained with tears.

"Are you okay?" he asked, his heart pounding in his chest.

"The voices..." she mumbled, still half in a daze. "So loud..."

He flinched. Of course. Why hadn't he thought of that before?

"Did my brother show you something?" he demanded. "Some kind of vision?" When Trinity reluctantly nodded, Caleb frowned. "I thought so. He probably opened up some doors by mistake. They're hard to shut if you haven't had the proper training." Stupid Connor. Always botching up people's heads.

"No," she protested. "I...I heard them earlier as well."

She said the words hesitantly, as if she was embarrassed to admit them aloud. "At the museum and then again at my grandpa's house." She moaned loudly, squeezing her eyes shut in agony. "God, I'm one shotgun blast away from becoming my mother, aren't I?"

"Oh, Trin." He gave her a sorrowful look, remembering

exactly how it felt, how horrible and confusing and maddening it had all been. It was all he could do not to reach out, pull her close, and wrap his arms around her in an attempt to draw out her pain. But he knew in his heart she'd only pull away, rejecting any comfort from his touch. To her, he was still the enemy. The one who had tricked her and stolen her away. He had a lot to prove to her before she would trust him. And there was no better time to start then now.

"Look, Trin," he tried, raking his aching hands through his hair in an effort to give them something else to do. "I can help you. But you have to trust me. Just close your eyes, okay?"

Her frown deepened. Her eyes remained open—stubborn as she was beautiful. "I know it hurts. But just do it, okay? I swear it'll help stop the voices."

"Fine," she said, snapping her eyes shut. "Happy now?"

"Ecstatic," he muttered. She was good at making things difficult, that was for sure. But he wasn't going to give up on her—as everyone had once given up on him. "Now listen. I need you to do a little visualization. Imagine each voice you hear attached to a person and each person standing at a doorway at the edge of your mind." He closed his own eyes, trying to remember how he'd been taught by Darius. "They're all trying to push past one another to enter." He paused. "Can you see it?"

She was quiet for a moment. He peeked an eye open and saw her squeezing her own eyes shut, a tormented look on her face. "Yes," she said at last.

"Good. Now slam those doors shut."

Her eyes flew open. "This is stupid."

"Do you want the voices gone or what?"

Reluctantly she shut her eyes again. "Okay, fine. I'm shutting the door…blocking out the big bad—"

She gasped. He opened his eyes. She was sitting on the bed, a shocked look on her face. "Oh my God," she murmured.

"Told you." He couldn't help a small smile.

"How did you do that?"

"*You* did it. I just showed you how. Don't worry. It gets easier with practice. Soon it'll be as natural as breathing."

She looked at him wonderingly, her eyes liquid pools of ebony. "How did you know? Are you cursed with voices too?"

"I told you: it's a gift," he corrected, though, in truth, that was not always the case.

She screwed up her face. "Some gift. My mother shot herself in the head over this so-called gift."

His heart squeezed at her words. At the naked pain blasting across her face.

"I'm sorry," he said simply. "It can be overwhelming for those who don't have proper training. The voices can get so loud they block out everything else." He thought back to one particular torment-filled night of his own, when he'd been sure he wouldn't live to see the break of dawn. "In any case, I won't let that happen to you. I can help you control them. To shut them out until you need to listen."

She started to nod, then winced.

"What's wrong?" he asked.

"There's still this one sound," she admitted, looking up at him, her face ghostly white. "This horrible, high-pitched sobbing. No matter how hard I try to block it out, it keeps slipping through the cracks."

Caleb's shoulders relaxed and he gave her a small smile.

"Oh right," he said. "I almost forgot about her. She's going to be a little tougher to tune out."

Trinity cocked her head in question. "She?" Her eyes widened as Caleb gestured to the egg, resting between two pillows on the adjacent bed. "You're trying to tell me the egg is crying?"

"Not the egg," Caleb corrected. "Emmy. She can sense you're upset and it's scaring her."

"She can sense my emotions?" Trinity asked, rising from the bed and walking curiously over to the egg. Caleb watched, breath caught in his throat, as she reached out hesitantly, then dared pull the egg into her arms. The bond was growing. He could see it in her face. Her touch. She was fighting it, but still….

"I feel like I should…I don't know…comfort her or something?" Trin dragged her gaze from the egg to Caleb. "But that's stupid, right?"

"Actually it's about the smartest thing you've said all day."

She gave him a withering look but turned back to the egg, stroking it softly with her hand. A moment later she looked up, her face mirroring her surprise. "She stopped crying!"

"She can feel your warmth. It's comforting to her."

Trinity stared back down at the egg, her face warring with mixed emotions. "I shouldn't be doing this," she murmured more to the egg than Caleb. "You're an evil dragon. I should be trying to destroy you. And yet…" She looked up at Caleb. "How did it all happen?" she asked slowly. "How did it go from this egg to a raging apocalypse?" She paused, then added, "And how do I fit in with the whole thing?"

Caleb paused, wondering what he should say. Then he

realized he didn't have to say anything. He could show her instead. It was the only possible way now to win her to his side. To get her to truly believe he meant what he said.

Reaching into his pocket, he pulled out a small amethyst, hoping it would do the trick. He walked over and pressed it into Trin's palm. "I'll show you," he told her. "I'll show you exactly what you did...and why you did it. All you have to do is take my hand."

Chapter Twenty-One

Trinity jerked up in bed, a sharp pain slamming through her with a force that almost knocked her back to her pillow. She looked around, rubbing her temples, trying to gain her bearings. She was no longer in the motel room with Caleb, but some kind of large dormitory, with rows of bunk beds lining the walls. A military base perhaps? But no, the others sleeping around her definitely didn't look like any soldiers she'd ever seen. The woman in the next bunk had to be eighty years old.

No! Please! Please stop!

She startled, recognizing the voice.

Emmy?

Suddenly it all came rushing back to her. This was another vision, like the one Connor had sent her of the Scorch. She let out a breath. At least this time she hadn't been dropped into the middle of an inferno.

Sliding her feet out of bed and onto the cement floor, she rose silently, careful not to wake anyone around her. She could feel herself being drawn toward the door at the end of the room and decided not to resist the urge. After all, Caleb had sent her here for a reason. He had something for her to see. And she needed to see it, whatever it might be.

"Show me what you will," she murmured, surrendering herself to the vision.

Her feet led her through the door, down a dark hallway, around a bend, and out of the dormitory altogether. Stepping into the warm summer night, she realized she was in some kind of military compound after all, with clusters of dark gray buildings surrounded by a barbed-wire fence. All the structures looked exactly the same, but at the same time, she somehow knew exactly which one she was looking for.

When she reached her destination, she found herself pulling out a set of silver keys she didn't know were in her pocket, slipping one into a metal lock, turning it, and pulling open the heavy door. Without pausing, she slipped into the building, wondering what she would find.

At first she thought she'd entered some kind of prison. But then she realized it was more like an animal testing site, with rows upon rows of multilevel cages, rising high to the ceiling and filled with apes and monkeys and gorillas and…

…a dragon.

She squinted down the rows. Sure enough, there was Emmy herself, standing in the very last cell. The dragon looked a lot different than she had in Trinity's previous vision. There, she'd boasted brilliant, almost blinding emerald scales, sparkling in the sunlight like precious jewels. Here, those shining scales had paled to a dull brown, so faded they appeared almost translucent.

Still, there was no mistaking it. It was Emmy. The dragon from the egg.

She started toward the dragon but stopped short, realizing Emmy wasn't alone. A scruffy, older man dressed in filthy coveralls was lugging a large hose in the dragon's direction. Trin watched from a distance, unseen, as Emmy shrank back in her cage, her eyes bulging with fear. The man gave a cruel laugh.

"Sorry, dragon," he chortled. "It's bath time." He turned on the hose, full force, shooting Emmy square in the chest. Emmy fell backward from the force of the water, her fear and panic engulfing Trinity as if it were her own. As the high-pressure blast slapped against an open sore on the dragon's left flank, Emmy bellowed in pain. Desperate, she lifted her mighty head, her massive jaws creaking open, preparing to unleash her fury on her captor. Trinity watched, almost rooting for the dragon as she waited for the fire to come.

But to her surprise, no flames shot from the dragon's mouth—only a sputter of spark and the most pitiful puff of smoke. Emmy closed her mouth, looking confused. The man laughed again.

"Good try," he snorted. "But your fire-breathing days are long over."

Emmy's face fell and she resignedly put up with the rest of the bath. Finally, the man turned off the hose and grabbed a mop, attached to a long pole. He stuck the mop into the cage, in a rough attempt to rub the dragon down. In response, Emmy turned her head, grabbing the mop in her teeth and playfully tossing it to the back of her cage. The dragon looked so proud of herself that Trinity wanted to laugh. The poor beast might have been robbed of her fire and dignity, but she wasn't entirely helpless.

Sadly, the man didn't find the scenario so amusing. "That's it!" he declared, stalking over to a nearby wall and grabbing the hugest electric cattle prod Trinity had ever seen off a hook before heading back to the dragon. "You will behave," he declared, jabbing Emmy in the neck with the prod. "If it's the last thing you do!"

Emmy let out a bloodcurdling scream and Trinity was sent reeling as echoes of the dragon's pain rocked her to her core. But the man refused to stop, jabbing the poor beast over and over again, electricity crackling from the stick and through the dragon's trembling frame until Emmy finally collapsed, her body convulsing and her mouth foaming.

"Emmy!" Trinity cried in horror, involuntarily giving herself away. The man whirled around, his eyes locking upon her. Uh-oh.

"What the hell do you think you're doing here?" he demanded, stalking over to her, still gripping his electric prod. Trinity took a hesitant step back, then forced herself to stand her ground.

"Leave her alone!" she found herself saying. "You're hurting her!"

"So what?" the man shot back. "In two weeks she's going to be monkey meat." He glared back at the dragon, who was still writhing in her cage in agony. "And good riddance too. She's been nothing but trouble since she hatched from that stupid egg."

Please. Trinity. Help me.

Fury overcame Trinity—fury at the coldhearted man for abusing this poor, helpless beast; at this compound—whatever it was—for caging her in the first place. On impulse, she charged the man, shoving him with all her might. He stumbled and fell onto the concrete floor, screaming in anger. Trinity lunged again, this time grabbing his cattle prod.

"Get the hell out of here," she growled. "Or I'll stick this thing so far up your ass…"

The man's face went white and he lost his confident swagger as he scrambled to his feet, not taking his eyes off the prod. "Give that back," he tried in a trembling voice.

"Not likely."

"You don't know what that thing can do. There's enough electricity in there to kill a man."

"Then I suggest you get moving if you want to live till morning."

The man rolled his eyes, disgusted. "You just wait until your supervisor hears about this. You'll be fired for sure." He turned and fled, the exit door clanking loudly behind him. The primates in the other cages whooped and cheered for their newfound hero. The sound was nearly overwhelming.

But Trinity only had eyes for Emmy. Setting down the prod, she approached the dragon's cage slowly, peering inside. At first she worried the dragon might already be dead, but then she caught Emmy's ribcage heaving up and down with effort. Trin let out a sigh of relief.

She scanned the creature; from this close proximity, she could see that the dragon was missing a whole section of scales, as if they'd been ripped from her body one by one. Her right wing was misshapen—broken and not set properly, maybe in an effort to keep her from flying. Under the wing, several ugly welts and burn marks marred the dragon's flanks, some festering and crusted with oozing, yellow pus. And the spot under her neck where the man had poked her was still smoking.

Trinity's heart wrenched and it was all she could do not to

throw up then and there. This beautiful creature…so abused. But she forced herself to stay strong.

"Are you okay?" she asked Emmy, daring to reach through the cage's bars to stroke the dragon's long nose. She knew it was probably a good way to get one's hand bitten off, but somehow she knew Emmy wouldn't harm her.

Sure enough, the dragon nuzzled her giant head against Trinity's hand, her whiskers tickling Trin's sensitive skin. The dragon opened her large, liquid eyes, staring up at her savior with such gratitude it made her want to cry. She observed, sadly, how Emmy's once brilliant blue eyes had faded to a dismal gray.

My thanks, Fire Kissed, Emmy whispered in her mind, her voice weary and broken.

"Who was that?" Trinity demanded, glancing back at the door, praying the man wouldn't reemerge. She couldn't stay long. He might return with backup. Still, she had to make sure Emmy was okay first.

Just a man assigned to care for me. He's worse than some, but not as bad as others.

Trinity shuddered at the idea that there could be worse. "But why?" she asked. "I mean, how could anyone do this to you?"

She tried to remember the other vision—the city engulfed by flames—but instead all she could see was this one gentle giant before her and her great suffering at the hands of mankind. Was this why the dragons rose up and destroyed the world? Was it merely an act of survival?

I do not know, Emmy whispered in her mind. With great effort, the dragon managed to right herself, letting out a long, surrendering sigh. Then she met Trinity's eyes with her own. *But I need your help.*

Trinity found herself nodding. Of course. At that moment, lost in the dragon's beseeching eyes, she would have done anything she'd asked. "What can I do?"

My time grows short, but my children...they still have a chance to live.

"Children?" Trinity cocked her head in question. "You have children?"

A shadow of confusion passed over the dragon's face. *I have not laid any eggs,* she admitted. *And I've never seen their faces. But I can hear them call to me all the same. My children are here. Somewhere nearby and still unscarred. They still have a chance to fly free.*

Trinity remembered what Connor had told her. The government had cloned Emmy. They'd taken her DNA and created a whole race of dragons. That's why they didn't care about Emmy's condition. She was nothing more than a tissue sample, to be used and discarded. The keeper's words came rushing back to her.

In two weeks, she'll be monkey meat.

Trinity gritted her teeth, squaring her shoulders. She wouldn't let that happen—couldn't let that happen. Not to this poor beast who had suffered so greatly, who was willing to sacrifice her own life to save her children.

"I'm going to get you out of here," she declared, giving Emmy her most confident look. "You *and* your children. You won't die in here, Emmy. If it's the last thing I do, I will set you free."

Chapter Twenty-Two

The scene faded and, once again, Trinity found herself in the motel room with Caleb, the egg still cradled in her lap as tears streamed down her cheeks. Caleb reached out and stroked her hand gently. She didn't pull away.

"That night, you went online," he told her, "you emailed everyone you could. The most passionate, the most militant, the most dedicated animal rights' activists out there—you told them of Emmy's plight and asked for their help. Of course they were more than willing to join up. After that, it was just a matter of breaking into the facility and freeing Emmy and her offspring."

Trinity drew in a breath. Before now, she couldn't have fathomed why anyone would want to unleash a pride of dragons on the world. But after seeing Emmy's suffering…

"What did we plan to do with them?" she asked. "I mean, they're not exactly stray pets, ready to find forever homes once they're out and about."

"The history texts are vague on that account," Caleb admitted. "But I'm sure you had something in mind. Or maybe you didn't—maybe you were only focused on setting Emmy free. All I know is, as I said earlier, your heart was in the right place."

Trinity frowned at that. "Yeah, I'm sure that made people feel a hell of a lot better once the dragons started chowing down on their children," she retorted bitterly. "I mean, sure, we miss little Lucy, not to mention the entire planet's infrastructure, but hey, at least that chick's heart was in the right place."

Caleb gave her a wry look. "Seriously, don't beat yourself up. At the time, you had no way of knowing the fifteen baby dragons you rescued alongside Emmy had been genetically altered."

"Altered?" She cocked her head in question.

"Their technology wasn't as good back then as it is in my time," Caleb explained. "They had to combine Emmy's DNA with some other lizards—nasty, violent things. And then, to keep them alive once they were born, they pumped them full of steroids." He shrugged. "Some historians will tell you their goal was to turn them into weapons. And, well, weapons they became, breaking free of their Dracken rescuers and flying wild." He gave her a rueful look. "You can probably guess the rest."

"The Scorch," she said in a dead voice. "The end of the world. All thanks to me. Wow. That's going to look awesome on my college application."

"Actually it won't," Caleb contradicted. "Because it's not going to happen this time around. Don't you get it? That's why we've come back. We're going to change things. We're going to get that happily ever after—for both the human race and the dragons themselves." He beamed widely.

She stared at him. "Are you stupid or just utterly insane?"

His smile faded. "What do you mean?"

"Um, gee, I don't know. Maybe the fact that you seem to think bringing dragons back into the world is a good thing? I mean, hello? Fire and brimstone? Worldwide apocalypse? Didn't you guys learn *anything* the first time around?"

"Yes! We did. We learned tons," Caleb replied eagerly. "Don't you see? That's why we decided to come back and do it all over again. This time *we* have control of the dragon, not the government. Those mutated dragons will never be born. Instead, we'll just breed more Emmys. Sweet, gentle creatures, with gifts to help mankind."

Trinity gave him a skeptical look. "Gifts? What, like helping Boy Scouts cheat on their campfire merit badges?"

"Try curing cancer," Caleb shot back, "eradicating diabetes, wiping out AIDS. Dragon blood has almost magical healing properties," he informed her. "Not to mention the creatures are pretty much unsurpassed at sniffing out natural resources buried deep in the ground. Oil, precious metals, water, new food sources—the types of materials we need for continued survival on this planet—dragons can help us excavate them all."

He sounded like he was quoting from a press release. "Okay, fine. Say that's true. What do the dragons get out of the deal?" she asked. "I mean, seeing as they're basically being volunteered to dedicate their lives to save the human race and all?"

"Everything," Caleb declared staunchly. "They'll be treated like royalty—given food to eat, space to fly. They'll be protected, honored, worshipped around the world." He paused, then added, "And most importantly, they won't be dead. Which, you know, is kind of the biggest thing, if you think about it."

He met her gaze, as if daring her to argue with his logic. When she didn't immediately reply, he continued, "We've done our calculations, Trin. We need dragons as much as they need us. Without them, very soon *we're* going to be the ones on the endangered species list." He squeezed his hands into fists. "I, for one, am not willing to let that happen."

Trin didn't know what to say. "You really believe this?" she found herself asking. "You really, truly believe that this dragon egg here has the power to save us all?"

Caleb gave a fierce nod. "*Everything* depends on her survival."

PART 3:

SPARK

Chapter Twenty-Three

The Surface Lands—Year 183 Post-Scorch

*D*ad's about to slay the dragon, Connor. Come on, come on!
Ten-year-old Connor looked up from his reader just
in time to see Caleb come bursting into the crumbling church
sanctuary. His brother was bouncing with excitement, his blue
eyes shining and his mouth twisting into a gleeful grin. *Could
this really be it?* Connor rose from the pew slowly, setting down
his reader, his heart thudding in his chest.

Are you sure? he sent back, using their silent twin language.
The one they used when they didn't want anyone else to hear.
He tossed a cautious glance to their mother, who was hum-
ming quietly to herself as she stirred soup over a makeshift
fire pit at the other end of the church. She didn't look up.

Of course I'm sure. Come on! Before it's too late! Caleb turned
back to the door.

Scrambling over the pew, Connor dove after his brother,
out of the sanctuary, and down the burnt-out hallway. They'd
been camped out in the ruins for weeks now, waiting for Dad
to draw the dragon near, and they'd been practicing the quick-
est route to the roof for nearly as long. As they leapt over

charred cinderblocks and ducked fallen archways, Connor could barely believe that this time was for real. The last song must have done the trick.

They weren't supposed to leave the sanctuary, of course. Their father would have had their hides if he'd known they'd traded the safety of four walls and a barricaded door for the fully exposed rooftop of the Pre-Scorch church. But the chance to watch the legendary Dragon Hunter finally down the fiery serpent they'd been chasing for weeks was more than worth risking his wrath.

Connor followed his brother through a caved-in wall, taking the rotted-out wooden steps two at a time. At the top of the steeple, Caleb didn't pause, dodging the cracked church bell and squirming through the broken window, making his way out onto the steeply sloped roof. He turned back to his brother.

Come on! Hurry!

A cry cut through the night air. Screeching, inhuman. Connor paused, fear sliding down his back. His eyes fell upon the jagged shards of glass jutting out from the window. The roof outside, slick from recent rain.

*I don't know…*he hedged. It was different now from when they'd practiced. More real. More dangerous. Outside, the dragon let out another cry, chilling him to the bone.

Caleb gave him a disgusted look through the window. *You really want to miss this?*

He sighed. Of course he didn't. Pushing down his rising dread, he forced himself to step through the window slowly, carefully, so as not to cut himself on the glass. Up here on the Surface Lands, even the smallest cut could turn deadly.

Once outside, he cautiously slid down the roof to join Caleb below. It was even slipperier than he'd imagined; the sudden drop in temperature had made it almost icy. When he finally reached his brother, he let out a sigh of relief. Caleb gave him an approving grin, then pointed to the ground below. There, their father readied himself for battle, unaware of his sons watching from above. *This was it!*

The sky darkened, causing Connor's heart to stutter all over again. Looking up, he caught a large, dark shadow eclipsing the setting sun. He gasped, fear thrumming through his veins. There she was, in the flesh.

She was huge. The hugest he'd ever seen, with shiny, blue scales sparkling in the fading light. Connor drew in a breath. She must have been old—maybe one of the original fifteen even—and he knew the Council would pay top silver for her head. Enough to keep their mother in medicine, pay their rent down below, and maybe even have a little left over for Caleb's tuition to the academy. So the first-born twin could carry on the family tradition and become a Hunter himself.

"She's so beautiful," Caleb marveled. "It's almost a shame Dad has to kill her."

Connor shook his head. He had no idea how his twin could see beauty in the empty-eyed, overgrown lizards with razor-sharp teeth and bulletproof scales, especially considering what these creatures had done to the world. In his opinion, they all deserved to die—as painfully as possible.

Pride flowed through him as he watched his father line up his target with deadly precision. He could almost hear his Hunter's song as he enticed the beast closer and closer, until she was finally within range.

BANG!

The recoil from the gun-blade echoed through the Surface Lands, shaking the roof of the church. The dragon squawked as the bullet bounced harmlessly off her sapphire scales. Their father swore under his breath. He'd missed the sweet spot. The one soft scale under the left wing that could take down even the mightiest of beasts. His father liked to brag about one-shot kills. But today evidently wasn't his day.

The creature retaliated immediately, opening her mouth and releasing her flames. Searing the ground mere inches from where their father stood. Connor watched, drenched in sweat from the sudden heat, feeling as if the pounding of his heart would crack his ribs. *Come on, Dad!* he urged. *Kill her already!*

The dragon stopped short. She turned slowly, abandoning his father, her beady black eyes scanning the sky until they fell upon Connor. He gasped, shrinking against the roof as the creature met his gaze. Had she heard his thoughts somehow? Had they broken his dad's spell?

They had to get inside. Now. Before it was too late.

Come on! he cried to Caleb, who sat unaware, still mesmerized by the creature. *We've got to go!*

He grabbed his brother's hand, trying to drag him to the window. But Caleb wouldn't budge—he just kept staring into the dragon's eyes. Connor yanked him again—there was no way he was leaving his twin behind—but the jerky movement only served to throw him off balance. A moment later, Connor found himself sliding down the roof at top speed. He screamed.

"Caleb! Help!"

But Caleb didn't seem to hear him. And as Connor

tumbled from the rooftop onto the ground below, the dragon's screech reverberated in his ears. He slammed onto the desert floor, a sharp pain shooting up his leg as his ankle crumpled beneath him.

"Connor!" he vaguely heard his father cry. But the dragon was already on him, black smoke billowing from her nostrils, sparks crackling at the back of her throat. Connor tried to scramble away, but his foot dragged uselessly behind him, trapping him where he stood. Unprotected. Exposed.

The deadly beast pulled back her gigantean head, opening her mouth, ready to release her inferno upon him. One more moment and the fire would come. If he was lucky, it'd be over quickly. If not…

Suddenly he was tossed to the side like a sack of potatoes. He hit the ground hard, a few yards away, the pain shooting up his leg all over again. Grasping his ankle, he looked up just in time to see the dragon let loose a stream of fire—hitting his father square in the chest.

"No!" he cried as his father collapsed, engulfed in a sea of flames.

The dragon turned back to Connor, her mouth curling into a sadistic smile.

On instinct, Connor dove for the discarded gun-blade, ignoring the brutal pain in his ankle. Gripping the weapon in both hands, adrenaline pounding through him, he charged the creature full force, putting everything he had into the weapon's thrust, just as his father had taught him. The blade sung true, sliding into the dragon's one soft scale like a hot knife through butter.

The beast bellowed in agony, collapsing to the ground and

writhing in pain as the steel pierced her unprotected heart. Black blood oozed from the wound and Connor met the creature's eyes with his own, staring her down with defiant rage. He yanked the blood-soaked blade free, then stabbed the fiend again. And again. And again. And—

"Connor, stop! She's dead. The dragon's dead!" He felt his mother's arms grab him from behind and drag him away. He fell to the ground, still half lost in an adrenaline-induced haze. His mother dropped to her knees, searching his face with her own tear-stained one.

"Dad?" he managed to blurt out, even though he knew in his heart what her answer would be. No one survived a full-on dragon blast—not even the best Hunter in the land.

Mom shook her head. "I'm sorry, Connor," she said, tears streaming down her cheeks. He buried his face in her shoulder, allowing the grief to consume him. His mother held him close, rocking him gently, soothing him in soft whispers. "But he died a hero. A true Hunter."

Her words were meant to comfort but only served to wrack Connor with guilt. He'd acted foolishly, disobeyed orders, and now, because of it, a great man was dead. His father was dead. And more would likely follow too—with the people of the strata now left without a trained Hunter to protect them. Who knew how long it would take for the Council to send reinforcements to this forgotten corner of the world? They barely had enough Academy graduates to protect the big cities.

It was up to him now. He had no choice but to shoulder his father's birthright. It was the only possible way to make himself worthy of his father's sacrifice. He rose and limped over to the dragon's corpse. The beast looked smaller now.

Shrunken. A shadow of the deadly creature she'd once been. As he stared down at the monster who had stolen his beloved father away, disgust and fury threatened to consume him.

He squeezed his hands into fists, his nails cutting into his palms. "I will hunt your kind until you've been wiped off the face of the Earth. No matter what I have to do."

✦ ✦ ✦

"Dad!"

Connor shot up in bed, a sharp pain drilling through his skull. He was in a small room—two matching beds, simple furniture—smelling slightly of mildew. A radiator in one corner rattled and spit while the TV on the dresser blared an advertisement for soap. Outside the window, a neon sign buzzed and flickered, matching the beats of his throbbing head.

He sank down onto his pillow, sucking in a breath, forcing the nightmare to retreat to the back of his mind. It had been seven long years since his father's death and yet hardly a night went by when his brain didn't manage to conjure up a full-color torturous play-by-play of that day.

The day he'd killed his father.

He'd told Trinity he was here to save the world. But that wasn't the whole truth. He wanted to save his father.

"I'll do whatever it takes, Dad," he whispered.

"Whatever *what* takes?"

Connor looked up. The bathroom door at the far end of the room squeaked opened and Trinity's grandfather stepped out, buckling his belt as he limped back over to the motel television, palming the remote and increasing the already near-deafening volume. He'd been glued to the set since they'd arrived in New Mexico a few hours before—the last location Connor had felt Trinity's spark before it had sputtered out.

"Nothing," he said quickly, sitting up in bed. The last thing he wanted to do was talk about his father's death—or hear the comforting rationalizations that were bound to follow. That it wasn't his fault, that there was nothing he could have done. It wasn't true. And it didn't make him feel any better either.

He sighed. What a mess this all was. If only he'd woken Trinity up when he and her grandfather had first returned to her mother's house the night of the Reckoning. Everything would be different now. They'd have the egg. They'd be on their way to the volcano to destroy it. Mission practically accomplished.

But he hadn't. Mainly because she'd looked so exhausted. So dead to the world. And once again, the soft spot he had for her had botched his common sense. And so, instead of waking her and bringing her downstairs where he could keep an eye on her all night, he'd let her sleep alone. It wasn't until he heard the banging on the rooftop a few hours later that he realized something was wrong. Unfortunately, by the time he'd reached her room, she was already on the back of his brother's motorcycle, zooming into the night.

God, he'd been such a fool. He'd had the egg. He'd had the girl. His whole mission practically wrapped up in a Christmas bow. And yet he'd screwed it all up, underestimated his brother, and let it all slip through his fingers.

His father would be so disappointed.

I'm sorry, Dad, he thought. *I won't let you down again.*

His thoughts were interrupted by the television, blaring

some kind of news broadcast at top volume. Trinity's grandpa, Connor realized, must be going a bit deaf.

"Could you please turn that—" he started to beg, but his mouth snapped closed as his eyes caught the video on the screen: black-and-white surveillance tape of a small convenience store. Two very familiar people walking up to the cash register.

Connor dove off the bed, joining Grandpa in front of the TV. He stared, mouth gaping. Could it really be?

"Suspected terrorist Trinity Foxx was last seen at a Santa Rosa Circle K," the announcer informed them. "She and her unidentified partner purchased food and drinks, and then took off in a green Ford pickup, according to witnesses. Anyone with information on the pair's whereabouts should call the Crime Stoppers' hotline. Police warn not to approach them; they are considered armed and dangerous."

Connor watched as the tape looped, his stomach swimming with nausea. On the screen, Trinity turned to his brother, poking him playfully in the ribs before setting her snacks down on the counter. The two of them started to laugh.

"What are they doing?" her grandpa cried, furrowing his bushy gray eyebrows. "I thought you said he'd kidnapped her." He turned to Connor, his eyes filled with accusation.

Connor shrugged helplessly, still staring at the TV in horror. All this time he'd been so sure Trinity must have been tricked, taken against her will. But looking at the video made him wonder. His brother had always been charming—could he have convinced her somehow that he was out for her own best interests? That Connor was the bad guy, not him? Or was it the dragon bond itself? Poisoning her mind against him more and more each day. He shuddered at the thought.

At least that explained why he'd lost her signal. He'd been following her spark, reaching out to her through the back door he'd created in her mind when he'd shown her the vision of the Scorch. But as of yesterday, he'd found himself at an impasse, her mind blocked against him. Caleb must have shown her how to shield herself, which would make it nearly impossible to find her.

"Santa Rosa, New Mexico." Connor glanced over to see Trinity's grandpa consulting an old-fashioned paper map. The man looked up. "It's not even fifty miles from here. Let's head out." He rose to his feet, his eyes shining with eager desperation.

Connor sighed, feeling old and defeated. He wanted to tell the man it would do no good. That they could follow them to the ends of the earth, but they'd always remain one step behind as long she kept herself blocked to him. If she didn't want to be found...

"Are you coming?" her grandfather asked, hovering at the open door.

He reluctantly rose to his feet, resigning himself to the fool's mission. At least it would make her grandfather feel better. To feel like he was doing something instead of just sitting around uselessly, waiting for news.

They're quite a pair, he thought as he followed Trin's guardian to his parked car. *So devoted to one another. Ready to risk everything to keep one another safe.* He tried to imagine what it must be like to have someone like that in his life. Someone who cared more about him than even the end of the world.

Of course, his father had once. And he'd died because of it.

He firmed his resolve. In the end, nothing had changed. His mission was still on, still vitally important to the survival of the world. And if Trinity didn't believe him? If she refused to go along with the plan they'd made? Well, that made her his enemy. Just like his brother.

Don't give up on her, Connor.

He started at the sudden thought slamming into his brain. No, not just a thought—a push. A powerful push. So strong that even he, with all his training, had to fight to keep it from lodging into his consciousness. He looked around, wondering where on Earth it could have come from. After all there were no—

He stopped short, catching Trinity's grandpa squeezing his eyes shut, as if he were in sudden pain.

"Did you…um…say something?" Connor stammered, searching his deeply lined face.

The old man's eyes snapped back to the road, but not before Connor caught a flash of guilt cross his face.

"I don't know what you're talking about," he muttered. "Now, are you ready to go or what?"

But you do, Connor thought excitedly. *You know exactly what I'm talking about.*

Aloud he said, "Yes, I'm ready. Let's go."

Her grandfather grunted and pulled out of the parking lot, the car's tires screeching as he turned onto the street. As they drove down the road, toward Trin's last known whereabouts, the sharp push came again.

She's worth fighting for. She's worth everything.

Chapter Twenty-Four

If you'd asked Trinity what she thought Dracken Headquarters would look like, she probably would have guessed like something out of a sci-fi movie—deep in the desert with watchtowers and electric fences, maybe a few landmines littered along the way. Not to mention the requisite men with machine guns, high-tech security gates—all the stuff that was supposed to go along with any self-respecting top-secret military operation. So she was quite surprised when Caleb directed her to pull off the highway and into the parking lot of a seemingly abandoned shopping mall instead.

"We're here," he announced, gesturing for her to stop the truck and put it into park. "Home sweet home at long last."

"Um." She looked around doubtfully. "This is it? *This* is Dracken Headquarters?"

The Nevada mall sprawled out before them had presumably seen better days. The store signs were crumbling, and colorful graffiti had been splashed over almost every available surface. Tall weeds poked defiantly from cracks in the pavement, and the sidewalks were lined with rusty shopping carts from days gone by.

Caleb looked at her with piercing eyes. "Is something wrong?"

Trinity shook her head. "Sorry, I guess I just didn't expect the secret headquarters of a dragon-worshipping sect from the future to have a JCPenney."

He snorted. "The actual mall went bankrupt five years ago, princess, after a developer built an open-air shopping center a few miles down the road. The Dracken were able to scoop it up cheap. It's actually the perfect home base if you think about it. Lots of space. Lots of bathrooms. They've spent the last two years converting it. The outside's just to scare off the tourists. Wait till you see what's beyond the front doors."

He shot her an excited grin; he'd been in a good mood all morning, becoming more and more animated the closer they got to their destination. As if he couldn't wait to introduce her to his world and his friends. She, on the other hand, felt more than a little apprehensive about the impending meet-and-greet with the Dracken. Unfortunately she had little choice in the matter. While Caleb didn't treat her as a prisoner, he also wasn't about to let her go.

They parked the car and headed into the mall's main entrance, Caleb triggering some kind of special sensor at the door that pricked his finger and matched his DNA before unlocking and swinging open. As he gallantly suggested "ladies first," Trin gathered her nerve and stepped into the belly of the beast.

The two-story mall was dimly lit and more than a little dusty, the entryway caked with cobwebs and littered with debris. Just more props to scare away potential intruders, Trin wondered, or were the Dracken simply lousy housekeepers?

At first glance, the place seemed deserted. At the same time, she got the uneasy feeling of being watched as their footsteps echoed down the hall—by a hundred pairs of unseen eyes. The whole thing was unnerving to say the least. Even more so when the doors behind them clanked shut with a booming crash, effectively sealing them in.

"What, no welcoming party?" she managed to joke, shoving the fear down her throat. "You'd think for the Fire Kissed they'd at least spring for a few balloons. Maybe some chips and dip?"

Caleb smirked. "Just wait, princess," he replied. "You'll get all the welcome you want. And then some."

Sure enough, not a moment later, Trin caught a mop of blond curls poking over the mall's second floor railing. "He's back!" the girl shouted, her voice echoing through the empty corridors. "Hey, guys! Caleb's back!"

The mall sprang to life, dozens of people spilling out in every direction, rushing toward them with wild abandon. Soon Trinity found herself completely engulfed in a sea of excited faces, all babbling over one another, trying to get her attention.

"You're here!"

"You're finally here!"

"We've been waiting so long!"

"We've been dying to meet you!"

"Where's the egg? Has she hatched yet? Did you bring the dragon?"

Overwhelmed, Trin took a hesitant step back, shooting Caleb a "help me" glance. He laughed, then clapped his hands together loudly.

"Hey, hey! Back up!" he commanded the crowd. "Let the poor girl breathe." As the multitude sheepishly complied, he turned to Trin. "Guess I should have warned you," he said with a sly grin. "You're a bit of a legend here."

Trinity's eyes darted around the crowd, trying to take it all in. The group standing before her appeared to be all kids around her own age, dressed identically in navy blue sweats, white T-shirts, and matching tennis shoes. But the similarities ended there. Some were tall; some were short. Some were athletic, while others were fat or thin. Male and female, fair-skinned and dark—seemingly from every country under the sun. As if someone had managed to gather up an entire teen-age United Nations under one roof.

"Are these the Dracken?" she asked hesitantly. "Are they all from the future?" The idea that all these kids had traveled back in time together was hard to believe.

Caleb shook his head. "These are the Potentials," he explained. "All from your time."

"Potentials?"

"Potential Dragon Guardians," he clarified. "For the last two years the Dracken have been busy combing the world, looking for kids born with the gift. The ones they find are brought here to be tested. If they pass their initial trials, they're initiated into the organization. Eventually each one will be assigned a dragon to bring back to his or her country. It's the best way to make sure everyone gets to enjoy the dragons' gifts in a peaceful, ordered way."

"Right." Once again, Trinity couldn't help but wonder what the dragons themselves would think of such an arrangement. Would they get to choose their country or just be randomly assigned? Like, what was the poor dragon stuck shivering in Siberia going to think of his friend happily firing things up in Fiji? There were still a lot of unanswered questions to the Dracken's master plan.

Before she could ask, a tall girl with smooth, olive skin and large, golden eyes stepped out from the pack of Potentials. She offered Trin a wide smile, then, without pause, threw her arms around her in a big bear hug. Trinity stiffened at the sudden spontaneous display of affection, but somehow managed to stand her ground.

"I'm Rashida," the girl said as she pulled away from the hug. "May I be the first to welcome you home."

Welcome home. Trinity couldn't help but flinch at the all-too-familiar greeting. The same one she'd always hear when walking through the front door of yet another foster family. As if it could be that simple. As if the strangers standing before her could somehow become an insta-family—just add water!—by simply uttering those magic words. And while sure, some of the foster families had been nice enough and she'd eventually settled into their rules and routines, never once had any of those houses ever felt like home.

But this girl looked so happy. In fact, they all did. Every face in the crowd glowing with enthusiasm, as if completely thrilled to have Trin join them at last. She found she didn't have the heart to disappoint them.

"Well, there's no place like home," she declared, flashing the Lollipop Guild a smile she didn't feel. Now if only she could score some ruby slippers…

As Rashida retreated back into the crowd, a sudden rumbling echoed through the mall. Trin's eyes lighted on an elevator at the center courtyard, its doors yawning open with a loud groan. The crowd immediately parted like the Red Sea as a man and a woman stepped out and made their way toward Trin and Caleb.

They were dressed simply—not unlike the rest of the Potentials. But something in their manner—something fluid and graceful—made them stand out from the pack. They were also older. The man was probably in his late fifties, black hair speckled with gray. The woman's age was harder to judge; she had a seamless face but dark, serious eyes and long blond hair cascading down her back like flowing water. They glided through the crowd, and the Potentials bowed their heads one by one as they passed.

These had to be the Dracken, Trin determined. The real ones who had come back from the future with Caleb.

"Welcome," the man said, his voice warm and rich, a blinding smile spreading across his clean-shaven face. He reached out, pumping Caleb's hand vigorously while the woman opened her arms, enveloping Trin into another hug. These Dracken people certainly were touchy-feely. She shot a furtive glance at Caleb and realized he was smiling broadly.

"Trinity, I'd like you to meet Darius and Mara," he said. "Darius is Master of the Dracken and Mara is our Chief Birthing Maiden."

"Um, hi," she managed to spit out, not sure the proper Miss Manners etiquette for greeting visitors from the future. "Nice to meet you." She realized her hands were shaking and shoved them behind her back.

Thankfully the Dracken didn't seem to notice. Darius turned to Caleb. "You have done well," he told him. "Even with the extenuating circumstances. I am very pleased." He gave him an approving smile and Caleb beamed back happily.

From the way he was acting, Trin got the feeling the Dracken leader must be some kind of father figure to him.

"And you, my sweet girl," Mara said to Trinity, her voice light and musical. "Welcome to our humble headquarters. I know this must all seem very strange to you, but we hope you will find a way to make yourself at home here. You are our honored guest. Our Fire Kissed. And we are here to meet your every desire. Anything you need, you must only ask."

"Can I go home?" Trinity blurted, not missing a beat. She could hear the other Potentials snicker until Darius shot them a look. "Sorry," she muttered. "But you did say *anything*."

Mara gave her an apologetic smile. "You're right. I did. And if only we could honor your request. It would be my greatest pleasure to allow you to return home. But I fear it's not safe for you there, and your safety is of utmost importance to us."

Trin frowned. Of course they'd play the safety card. And, she had to admit, it was a tough one to argue with. "I'm sure I'd be okay," she tried. "If I could only—"

"I don't think you understand," Mara interrupted in a kind but firm voice. "Your government has labeled you a terrorist, dealing in what they consider biological weapons of mass destruction. If they capture you, they will hold you without trial for as long as they wish. Torture you even. Are you prepared to face something like that?"

Trin stared at her, heart pounding in her chest. Terrorist? Sure she'd broken some laws. But terrorists were Osama Bin Laden, the Taliban, not teenage girls from West Texas who only advocated violence when it came to zombie-blasting video games.

"Not to mention the Hunter is still at large," Darius added.

"If he tracks you down—and I have no doubt he would if we allowed you to leave—he will kill you in order to slay the dragon. And we cannot, under any circumstances, allow that to happen. After all, this little dragon holds the future of the world in her hands. And so, through her, do you."

Trin swallowed hard, looking around the room. And here she thought Caleb was intense. What had she gotten herself into? She tried to force her pulse to steady, to order her thoughts. Okay, fine. They wouldn't let her go. *It wasn't a big surprise, really*, she tried to tell herself. But there was one thing she could ask for. Something they might still agree to.

"If I can't go home to my grandpa," she said, after gathering her nerve, "then can you bring him back here to me? He's the only family I have and I won't be able to settle in until I know he's okay."

Darius looked at Mara. She nodded. "Now that's something we can arrange," she said.

Trin's shoulders slumped in relief. "Thank you. That would be great. Really."

"We'll put our best men on it," Darius assured her, laying a hand on her arm. "They'll find him and bring him back here and he can live as our honored guest just like you. If we're quick, perhaps he'll even be able to arrive in time to witness the dragon's birth."

Trinity nodded enthusiastically, loving the idea of her grandpa getting to see Emmy hatch. After all, he was the one who had brought the egg into their lives in the first place. Without him, none of this would be happening.

"Thank you," she said sincerely. "I can't tell you how much that means to me."

"Not half as much as you mean to us," the Dracken returned grandly. He turned to Rashida, who was still hovering at the front of the crowd. "Now, would you mind, Sister, taking our guest to her chambers? She must be exhausted from her trip." He turned back to Trin. "We have prepared everything for your arrival—rooms, clothing. Even now your handmaiden is drawing you a hot bath."

Trinity raised her eyebrows. She had to admit, a bathtub sounded good in and of itself after their days on the dusty road. But a freaking handmaiden to boot?

Emmy, we're not in West Texas anymore.

But where am I? she wondered as she followed Rashida down the darkened hall, the creepy feeling returning with a vengeance the further they went. *And what do they want from me, now that I'm here?*

Chapter Twenty-Five

"Hey! Fire Kissed! Over here!"

Rashida waved wildly across the food court, attempting to get Trinity's attention. Trin waved back awkwardly, then headed over. She could feel the stares of the other Potentials as she wove through the tables and tried to acknowledge each of them as she passed, not wanting people to think she was a snob. At school, Trin always tried to avoid being the center of attention, but she realized there was no helping that here.

"This place is like a maze," she remarked as she slid into her seat. "I got lost three times trying to get here from my room."

"That's because you were given a crap tour guide," the tall, blond boy across from her quipped, playfully poking Rashida, the tour guide in question. She poked him back twice as hard.

"As if you don't still get lost going to the bathroom," she retorted, "and you've been here half a year."

"This was the biggest mall in Nevada before they shut it down." The petite Asian girl on Rashida's left looked up from the journal she'd been scribbling in. Some kind of poetry, Trin noticed. Or maybe song lyrics? "But I found the original blueprints if you ever want to learn your way around."

"If you ever want to be a complete nerd," the boy shot back, but he was smiling at her.

"This is Aiko," Rashida introduced, ignoring him. "Our very own rock star, straight from Japan. She may look like a tiny little thing out of an anime film, but don't let her fool you. The girl's got mad pipes." Aiko blushed prettily, closing her notebook and reaching out to shake Trin's hand. Her fingers were dainty but calloused on the tips, assumedly well acquainted with guitar strings.

"And this is Malia," Rashida continued, gesturing to a broad-shouldered, dark-skinned girl across from Trinity. "She's from Kenya and serves as our resident gamer girl. Many of the boys have tried to take her down," she added with dramatic flair. "But the girl somehow manages to frag them all."

Trinity raised an eyebrow. "You have video games here?" she asked, her heart beating a little faster.

"Of course," Malia replied shyly. "The Dracken turned the old Apple store into a game room. We have every system and all the best games. A few of us meet up on Friday nights to play. You should join us sometime. We could use more girls on the team."

"Do you have *Fields of Fantasy*?" Trin dared to ask, her breath caught in her throat. "The new expansion pack?" Maybe it wouldn't be so bad to be stuck here after all.

Sadly, Malia shook her head. "Sorry, nothing that requires a Wi-Fi connection," she told her. "We can play on a closed LAN line with one another, but Darius has strict rules about going online."

"Which means no satellite TV to watch the matches," the

blond boy added gloomily. "I don't suppose you know who won the Rugby World Cup this time around? It's been bloody killing me."

Trinity shook her head. "Sorry," she said. The boy sighed loudly, dropping his head onto the table with over-exaggerated despair.

Rashida rolled her eyes. "And last but not least, this is Trevor," she introduced with an impish smile. "As you can probably tell, he's from Australia and like most Aussies will never let you forget it."

"It's a bloody great country," he declared, breaking out into what Trin assumed to be some kind of national anthem in a loud, booming, and terribly out-of-tune voice. The girls groaned and threw their napkins at him, which only made him sing louder.

Trin shook her head, watching their antics, surprised at how normal the whole scene felt, as if they weren't in the middle of an abandoned shopping mall, but rather some kind of European boarding school or something. It was hard to believe, just by looking at them, that these kids weren't study-ing for their SATs. They were training to take care of dragons.

"So where do we get the food?" she asked, gesturing to her tablemates' heaping trays.

Rashida waved an arm around the food court. "Each of the stations has food from a different continent," she told her, "to make sure all of us get to eat what we're used to. Well, not all of us," she added, glancing teasingly at Trevor. "The Dracken come from a long line of animal rights activists, which means no shrimp on the barbie for poor Trevor here."

"I could skip the shrimp," the blond boy protested, "if

only I could score a nice, juicy T-bone once in a while." He stabbed a piece of tofu with his fork and stuffed it into his mouth with a miserable look. The girls giggled.

"So how long have you guys been living in this place?" Trin asked curiously. They all seemed so at home here, so comfortable with one another. And their English was impeccable. She could barely detect any accents.

"Malia was one of the first to come here. You've been here almost two years, right?" Aiko asked the girl across from Trin, who nodded in agreement. "I've been here just over a year myself."

"I've been here a year and a half," Rashida offered. "Trevor's the baby of the group. He only arrived six months ago."

"And yet I'm already beating you in your lessons," Trevor shot back. Rashida patted him on the back patronizingly.

"Sure you are," she said.

"Wow," Trin marveled, looking them over. "That's a long time to be gone. Do you get, like, spring break or summer vacation to go visit your families?"

The four Potentials exchanged looks. "We don't have families," Malia replied quietly.

"What?" Trinity asked, completely thrown by the answer.

"We're all orphans," Aiko explained.

"All of you?" Trinity glanced around the bustling food court. There had to be a hundred Potentials eating lunch here alone. Did none of them have parents? Family? People back home?

"My parents died in the tsunami," Aiko said matter-of-factly. "My entire village was wiped out. I had no family left, no place to go."

"I was living on the streets of a Mumbai slum," Rashida added. "I'd spend my entire day just trying to find a place to sleep where I wouldn't be attacked or robbed."

"My mother died of AIDS when I was young," Malia said quietly. "My aunt took me in until the drought hit. Then she had to make a choice—her own children or me."

"What about you, Trin? What happened to your parents?" Trevor asked pointedly. "If you're here, you must be an orphan too." They all turned to look at her. She felt her face heat and she stared down at her hands.

"She doesn't have to say if she doesn't want to," Rashida scolded him. "It's not any of our business." She gave her a kind look. But Trin knew they were expecting her to say something. After all, they'd all shared their stories with her—stories that must hurt to talk about just as much.

"I…I never knew my father," she said at last. "He died before I was born. My mother…well, I guess she was one of us. She had the gift too. But the voices got too loud…" Her own voice cracked on the words and she found she couldn't continue. In any case, what could she say? That her mom preferred to blow her own head off than spend Christmas Eve with her only child?

The girls looked at one another. Then, without saying a word, they reached out, grabbing Trin's hands in their own and squeezing them tight. She watched, puzzled, as they closed their eyes in unison and bowed their heads. For a moment she was convinced they were about to break out into prayer. Or at least a rousing round of "Kumbaya." But no words came from their lips. Instead, suddenly Trin felt an overwhelming sense of comfort pass through her. As if she were being wrapped up in a warm, billowy blanket and hugged tightly.

They're using their gifts, she realized, fascinated. Trying to send her comfort. And it was working too. She could actually feel the anger and pain slipping away. *Which was cool*, she tried to tell herself. But also massively weird—not to mention invasive. Like, what if she wanted to keep that pain? Hold on to that anger? What if it was a part of her she wasn't ready to let go of yet? They hadn't even asked permission. Just dove inside her mind and—

She yanked her hands away.

The girls opened their eyes, gazing at her with pity. She averted her own eyes, staring down at the table in front of her, trying to still her erratic pulse. *They're only trying to be nice*, she tried to tell herself. *They aren't trying to hurt me.*

"In any case, that's when the Dracken came," Aiko continued, breaking the awkward silence. "They found us and rescued us and brought us back here, where we no longer have to worry about anything. Food, shelter, school—it's all provided by the Dracken." She stared off into the distance, a dreamy look on her face. "We owe them our lives."

"We're a family," Rashida declared. "And now you're our family too."

They fell silent, as if waiting for her response. She bit her lower lip. She knew what they wanted her to say. The foster families had always wanted the same thing—for her to be thrilled to be a part of it all, for her to consider herself one of them. But try as she might, the words stuck in her throat, just like they had a dozen times before.

I'm not like you, she wanted to scream. *I don't belong here.*

And this time it was especially true. After all, these kids had come here willingly, following the pied piper of dragons and his promises of a better life. They'd given up their freedom, their free will—and evidently the chance to wear something other than navy blue sweat pants. And yet they all seemed so happy, perfectly content to live out their lives in this creepy mall without Internet access or TV.

Content? something inside of her nagged, *or brainwashed?*

Either way, now she was stuck here right alongside them, she realized, as the panic rose inside of her once again. Whether she liked it or not.

Chapter Twenty-Six

Two hours later—or was it three?—Trinity paced the soft-carpeted floor of the most luxurious chamber she'd ever seen, located in a space that had once held a Baby Gap. Draped in lush crimsons and accented in gold, the room had all the luxuries Trinity could have ever imagined and then some, all done up in her favorite colors and styles.

It was almost as if someone had gone into her head and plucked all her secret fantasies from her brain and made them real. From the king-sized canopy bed wrapped in sheer silk curtains to the stylish sitting room with plush upholstery and a glittering chandelier. There was even a gigantic marble bathroom, complete with steam shower and whirlpool tub—and one of those fancy Japanese toilets with all the extra buttons that Trin had always been curious to try.

The other recruits—the Potentials—all lived in dorms, she'd been told, located in the former Sears at the other end of the mall. The boys on the second floor, the girls on the first. But the girl who had founded their organization—the Fire Kissed herself!—was too special to be subjected to those humble accommodations. She deserved only the best.

And only the best it was. The best prison cell ever.

It was the silence that was the worst. When she'd gotten back to her room after lunch, she'd tried to reach Emmy, to restore the connection between them. She'd gotten so used to the dragon babbling and chirping in her head over the last few days, the sudden absence felt deafening. Where had they taken her? Was she okay? She wondered if she'd made a mistake allowing them to make off with the egg in the first place. But Caleb had assured her they would take good care of the dragon. That was the whole reason they'd come back in time to begin with, after all. But still, Trinity couldn't help but wonder.

A knock sounded on the door. She turned to it reluctantly. "Who's there?" she asked.

"Caleb."

Her heart started. Where had he been? She hadn't seen him since they'd first arrived and she realized, annoyingly, that she'd kind of missed him. Which was stupid, she knew, to miss someone who'd basically kidnapped you and held you against your will. What did they call it? Stockholm syndrome? Ugh. What a total cliché. Just because he'd been kind to her, helped her shut out the voices in her head, held her hand as she cried for Emmy. Big freaking deal. At the end of the day, he was still sardonic and cynical and kind of a douche. Nothing like his brave, heroic brother, Connor, who had honor and dignity and…

…*wants you dead*, a voice inside jabbed.

She sighed, stalking to the door and ripping it open. "Where have you been?" she demanded, her voice sounding angrier than she'd meant it to.

183

"Nice to see you too, princess," he replied coolly as he stepped into the room. He had changed from his dusty road clothes and was now wearing a plain white T-shirt and slouchy jeans. His hair was still damp, slicked back from his face, and he smelled of Irish Spring soap. She cleared her throat, pretending not to be affected, as she stole a glance at herself in the mirror, wishing she'd taken the time to comb out her curls after her bath, then scolded herself for caring.

She realized he'd come bearing gifts—namely a cart of covered silver platters, linen napkins, fine tableware, and a carafe of what appeared to be coffee and another of soda. Prison room service? She would have laughed if she weren't so pissed.

"I'm not hungry," she declared, forcing her eyes away from the cart.

Caleb didn't reply. Instead, he busied himself with the covers, removing them one by one. Heaping bowls of pasta, steaming platters of rice, pizzas dripping with cheese—it went on and on, the rich, savory smells torturing Trinity until her stomach betrayed her with a feral growl. After her uneasy conversation with the Potentials, she'd been too freaked out to eat and now she was absolutely ravenous. But still. She scowled and turned away, plopping down on her bed, arms crossed over her chest. She would not be bought by something as simple as a mall-cooked meal.

"I don't want it," she repeated. "Take it away."

But Caleb only continued his reveal—mountains of mashed potatoes, buttery rolls fresh from the oven, glistening vegetables, and sugary desserts. Every single dish one of her favorites.

"Are you sure about that?" he asked, giving her a skeptical look. "After all, everything's been prepared exactly the way you like it according to our records."

She frowned. According to their records. In other words, the time travelers had studied her life like it was some kind of history project—just like with the bedroom—thinking they could win her over by plying her with her favorite things. It should have felt good, for them to have given so much thought, taken so much care. But instead it felt invasive, an unfair advantage.

"Come on, Trin," Caleb cajoled. "It's just food. It's not like I looked up your bra size." He gave her a winning smile. She scowled back.

"What, do you want a medal for that?"

"Hey, I think I exhibited tremendous restraint!" He joined her over on the bed, dropping his impish grin and giving her a serious look. "Okay, what's wrong?" he asked. "I thought you'd be pleased. The Dracken went through a lot of trouble to design all of this for you. We did extensive research into what makes you happy. So why aren't you happy?"

He made it sound so simple, like a math problem or something. They gave her what she wanted; she'd do what they wanted. But it didn't work like that.

"How can I be happy?" she demanded, turning to him and meeting his eyes with her own. She realized her hands were shaking and shoved them under her thighs. "I've lost everything I ever had. My only family is MIA and I'm trapped in a freaking shopping mall with the children of the corn. Trust me, no amount of pineapple and feta cheese pizza is going to make this any better."

"Even if it came from Deluca's?"

She involuntarily glanced over at the pizza sitting on the tray. "*Did* it come from Deluca's?"

"Sadly, no." Caleb shrugged. "I was just curious if it would have made a difference."

She groaned, grabbing a pillow and shoving it into his face. "You're so not helping."

"Oh really?" He tapped the side of his head, his eyebrows quirking. "Mind reader, remember? I know for a fact that I'm helping. Helping a lot, actually. You don't want to admit it, I know. But that doesn't make it untrue."

Her face flushed. Rising to her feet, she stalked over to the other side of the room. "That's so unfair," she growled.

He laughed. "I know, I know. I'm sorry." He pranced over and grabbed her hands in his. "But you've got to try to relax, princess. You're going to drive yourself to an early grave. Which, I might selfishly mention, would be catastrophic for the rest of us sorry humans. After all, you're—"

"The Fire Kissed," she finished for him in her best over-the-top fantasy-film voice. "The one who will save our world." She yanked her hands away. "Seriously, if you start telling me there's one ring to rule them all or that the force will be with me always, I'm going to smack you upside the head."

"Please," he scoffed. "You don't need the force or some silly ring—not when you have a dragon by your side."

She groaned loudly, pressing a hand to the wall and leaning against it. "I'm going insane. That's the only explanation for any of this. I'm going insane and the men in white coats will be showing up at any moment to tell me this has all been a psychotic delusion. They'll take me away and lock me up, and

I'll be free to drool in the corner of my padded cell for the rest of my life without a care in the world."

"But then you'd never see me again," Caleb reminded her with a wink.

"Really? Can I get that in writing?"

He gave her a mock offended look, then grabbed her arm, dragging her back over to the bed. He sat her down, taking her hands in his own. She tried not to notice the way her skin warmed under his touch—or the shivers that tripped up her spine as his eyes turned serious.

"Look, I get it, okay?" he said. "I understand how hard it must be for you to be here. And the Dracken can come off as pretty radical—"

"Radical?" Trinity repeated. "Come on, Caleb. If you looked up 'evil cult out to destroy the world' in the dictionary, you'd find these guys' pictures."

He shook his head vehemently. "You're getting the wrong idea. I'm telling you. Darius and Mara and the rest of them aren't like that at all. They're good people. They believe in what they're fighting for. They're trying to save the world. And you're so important to that mission. *Everything* they've worked for their whole lives rests on you—and their ability to keep you safe. Imagine yourself in their shoes. You'd want to keep you under lock and key too, wouldn't you?"

Trinity bit her lower lip, hating the fact he was making so much sense. She turned to face the wall, feeling his stare burning at her back but refusing to meet his eyes. For a moment he was silent. Then he spoke.

"I was homeless," he stated flatly, "living on the streets of Strata-D, probably only a few demerits away from a lifetime in the mines. Everyone had dismissed me, the no-good shadow of my hero brother." He sighed, remembering. "But then Darius came. He plucked me from the streets and offered me hope. Recognized my gift and gave me a job. He told me I could be great if only someone would give me a chance." His voice cracked. "And then he gave me that chance. So here I am, working every day to prove he wasn't wrong about me."

His words were so earnest, so proud. But Trinity could hear the doubt threaded just below the surface. As if he himself wondered if he was worthy of the chance he'd been given.

"He can save you too, Trin," Caleb said softly. "If only you'll let him."

A silence fell over the room as she struggled for a clever reply. But her mind had gone completely blank. The silence stretched, awkward and long. Finally, Caleb let out a long, deep sigh.

"Look," he said, "do you want to get out of here for a bit?"

She turned, her eyes widening. "Can we?"

"Well, not like you're probably thinking," he admitted. "I mean, your physical body has to stay here in the mall. Darius would kill me if I put you at risk. But we could go to the Nether."

"The Nether?" she repeated doubtfully. "You mean the place with the dragons?"

Caleb nodded. "It's a place beyond time and space," he replied, "ruled by the collective unconsciousness of dragons. Before they're born and after they die, they exist here, in this Nether space. Those with the gift have the ability to travel there, channeling our energies through special gems." He reached into his pocket, pulling out two glittering rubies, and grinned. "It's like this big, amazing playground—and it can become anything you make of it."

"Will Emmy be there?" she asked, intrigued despite herself.

"Absolutely. And my dragon too."

"You have your own dragon?" The thought had never occurred to her. But she supposed it made sense. "Is it an evil mutant one out to destroy the world?"

Caleb laughed and shook his head. "Sorry to disappoint, but we don't clone mutants anymore. Our technology is a bit more advanced than yours. My dragon was made from a pure strand of DNA from one of Emmy's true children. Darius gifted her to me after I passed my Guardian trials. Wait until you see her, Trin. She's so beautiful—sparkling teal scales, huge golden eyes, a wingspan that could block out the sun." He smiled dreamily. "First time I laid eyes on her, I fell in love."

"Cool. What's her name?"

His smile faltered. "Um…what?"

"Her name?" Trinity repeated. "Your dragon, I mean. Does she have a name?" She glanced over at Caleb curiously, surprised to see he'd gone bright red.

"Oh. Um, yeah. Sure she does. Her name is…Fred."

Trinity burst out laughing. "Fred?" she repeated incredulously. "Your beautiful, majestic, not to mention female dragon is named Fred?"

"Hey! You're the one who called your dragon Emmy," Caleb protested, his face now a peculiar shade of purple. "That's not exactly High Goth'Or the Great and Terrible either!"

"Okay, okay!" She held up her hands in innocence. "Fred it is. Fred the dragon." A snort escaped her, despite her best efforts.

"Are you going to laugh at my poor dragon all day or would you actually like to meet her?"

She forced herself to sober. "Explain how this works again?"

"The how is irrelevant," he assured her. "I mean, you don't need to know how one of your cars works in order to drive it, right?" He reached out, taking her hands in his, pressing the ruby gems between their palms. "All you have to do is enjoy the ride."

Chapter Twenty-Seven

The thunder came first. Then a sharp wind, scraping her face and stealing her breath. Her eyes flew open, a screech of surprise tumbling from her lips, as the world shot back into focus.

She was flying—or riding at least—on the back of a mighty dragon.

"Oh my God!" she cried, throwing herself against the creature's back, terror surging through her. Her arms flailed, seeking handholds around the dragon's thick neck as her thighs squeezed its midsection, desperate to hang on.

Please don't let me fall. Please don't let me fall.

She dared, for a split second, to look down, and her stomach rolled as the earth seemed to weave dizzyingly in and out of focus miles below her.

Please don't let me fall. Please don't—

You okay?

She opened her eyes in surprise at the voice. In her initial panic of waking up on the back of a dragon, she'd all but forgotten she'd come to this nightmare of her own free will. With Caleb holding her hand. He pulled up alongside her, astride his own dragon, flashing a cocky grin. He was wearing black leather pants that molded to his thighs and a black T-shirt that couldn't disguise his strong, flat abs. He looked confident and happy and, well, pretty damn hot, she had to admit, despite herself. Something about a guy on a dragon… And the dragon herself, Fred, was as beautiful and majestic as he'd promised, despite her silly name. Her massive wings steadily beat the air currents into submission—leather cracking, membranes stretching—as an elegant tail flapped lazily behind her, serving as rudder.

Caleb lifted a hand, offering a casual salute, a teasing smile playing at his lips. Trin gritted her teeth, refusing to give him the satisfaction of seeing her frightened. Instead, she forced herself to straighten and her shoulders to drop, as if she were on some casual bike ride—no big deal.

We couldn't have started this out on the ground? she sent, realizing it was the only way to communicate over the thunderous flapping of dragons' wings.

He shrugged playfully. *Why waste time walking when we can fly?*

Gee, I don't know. So I could learn to steer?

She couldn't hear his laugh but she could see the amusement dance across his face and it made her hackles rise. So this was a big joke to him? He thought it was funny? What if she fell? What if she careened to her death? If you died here, in this Nether place, did you die in real life? She remembered her real-life burn from the last time she'd visited and shuddered.

Just tell Emmy where you want to go. She'll get you there.

Emmy? Trinity's gaze shot down to the dragon beneath her, eyes widening in realization. This was Emmy? But she was so big! And besides her green scales, she looked so different than the dragon she'd met dying in her cage. This dragon wasn't sad and defeated and wounded—she was gorgeous, alive—with emerald scales that snared the very sun and reflected the rays back tenfold.

In the Nether I can be anything I want to be, look any way I want to look, Emmy broke in, her voice unmistakable. The beast turned her giant head, acknowledging Trin with a quick nod. It was then that she recognized the dragon's eyes. Such pretty eyes—all blues and golds swimming together in the depths of the deepest sea. *And so can you.*

Can I be someone who isn't afraid of heights? Trin winced as she accidentally looked down again. Maybe if she just stared straight ahead, the nausea would go away.

Emmy's laugh was rich and affectionate.

You can trust me, Fire Kissed. I'd never let you fall.

Trust. It had never been one of Trinity's strong points. Not when so many people in her life had let her down. Her own mother even—with all her promises that they'd be a family again. Promises as empty as the shotgun barrel she'd left behind. And then there was Connor, who'd promised to keep her safe while secretly planning to kill her. No, it was better in the long run not to trust anyone in this world.

But I'm not just anyone. I'm your dragon.

Emmy's words sent a shiver down her spine, as if she could feel them as well as hear them. And strangely, suddenly, she found herself wanting to trust those feelings, to let herself go. To feel what it would be like to soar through the skies. To understand what it really meant to be Fire Kissed. To become one with a dragon.

She shook her head. *Okay, where had that thought come from? Let yourself go, Trinity. Trust me.*

On impulse, she reached down to stroke the dragon, surprised to find the creature's scales soft and satiny to the touch. As her fingers tripped down the beast's neck, Emmy wiggled appreciatively and made throaty noises that reminded Trin of her cat purring. She drew in a shaky breath.

"Okay, fine," she declared, squaring her shoulders. "What the hell. Let's do this."

You won't be sorry!

And with that, Emmy took off, soaring through the heavens at top speed. Trinity squealed and grabbed on tight, her pulse skyrocketing and her heart lodging in her throat. It was as if she was on some living, breathing rollercoaster, rolling and dipping across the sky, and it was hard to believe a creature so big and gangly looking could be so graceful. Soon as they whirled and swirled in their dragon dance along the horizon, she found herself laughing out loud—an unguarded, joyous laugh. This was actually fun!

Faster! she cried to Emmy. *Go faster!*

Emmy tossed her head excitedly, then turned her snout to the sky. Higher and higher she pushed, chasing the currents of wind, gaining more altitude every second, until Trinity half wondered if they'd collide with the sun. Finally, the dragon stopped, hovering in midair, turning to face her, a challenging look on her face.

Are you ready? she asked teasingly.

Trin gulped but somehow managed to nod. No sooner had she finished than Emmy turned her nose down, dive-bombing the ground, fast and furious. Trinity screamed in a mixture of delight and fear, white-knuckling the dragon's neck as the earth rushed to meet them at frightening speed.

Trust her. Trust Emmy. You can trust her.

Emmy stopped on a dime, practically throwing Trin from her back with the sudden halt of momentum. She gasped as she realized they were hovering only a few yards off the ground. Had they really been so close to colliding? Emmy snorted excitedly, then shot back up into the air again, the wind pounding at Trin's face, drawing tears from her eyes. She laughed and shook her head.

Show off, she admonished her dragon.

Oh, you liked it, Emmy shot back. And Trinity had to agree.

And so they kept going, dipping and diving, soaring and seeking, skimming trees and ponds, then shooting high into the atmosphere, teasing the sun. Emmy even attempted a few clumsy barrel rolls that made Trinity's stomach lurch. But through it all, she couldn't help the big grin spreading across her face. For the first time in her life, she felt free. Absolutely, one hundred percent free.

What do you think? Caleb asked, leading his own dragon up beside her. *Is Emmy taking good care of you?*

Oh my God! she cried. *This is, like, the best thing ever!*

I told you, he teased. *Now come on. Race me to that ledge!*

Before she could respond, he urged his dragon forward, diving down toward the craggy cliffside before them at top speed. Trinity stared after him with amused outrage.

"Cheater!" she cried out after him. *Go, Emmy! Don't let them get away!*

The dragon shifted position, diving after Caleb and his mount. Trinity cheered her on as the wind thundered in her ears. It wasn't long before the two beasts were neck and neck again, beads of dew sparkling on Emmy's shining scales as her muscles rippled beneath her thighs. The boy and his dragon may have stolen a head start, but it was obvious to Trin who really ruled the skies.

Yeah, baby! she taunted Caleb. *Wingspan definitely matters.*

Oh, you think so? he replied without missing a beat. He gave her a cocky grin. *Watch and learn, princess.*

Trinity glanced over just in time to see Caleb waving his hand in the air. To her surprise, a piece of raw meat, dripping with blood, seemed to appear out of thin air. He grabbed it in his hands, then tossed it in the direction of her dragon.

The meat flew temptingly through the sky, causing Emmy to stop short, her eyes locking onto the bloody snack. Before Trinity could protest, the dragon was suddenly dive-bombing for her dinner, the race all but forgotten.

No, Emmy! Trinity tried. *Go back!*

But the dragon either couldn't hear her or chose not to answer. A moment later she caught up to the meat, snapping it into her massive jaws. Trinity sighed as she watched Caleb and Fred come in for a triumphant landing on the ledge above. First by more than a snout.

"Cheater!" she yelled up at them, shaking her fist. But Caleb only laughed, sliding down his dragon's wing in a graceful dismount.

"The first rule of the Nether," he yelled back. "There are no rules in the Nether."

"Now you tell me," she muttered as Emmy finished her meal and headed up to join Caleb and Fred on the ledge. Once she'd landed, Trinity attempted a graceful dismount, but only managed to land painfully on her butt.

"Better luck next time," Caleb teased, holding out his hand.

She refused it and stuck out her tongue at him—childish but pretty satisfying all the same.

She looked around, taking in their surroundings; they'd landed on the edge of a rocky cliff face, with an overhang that created a small cave. As she watched, Caleb started gathering a few chunks of wood and branches that the wind had blown their way, creating a makeshift fire pit. When Trin looked at him questioningly, he shrugged. "I don't know about you, but I'm freezing."

She nodded, letting out an involuntary shiver as the icy wind pricked at her skin. It was strange—she hadn't felt the least bit cold when she was riding Emmy. Maybe it was the adrenaline. Or maybe dragons were just hot-blooded. Whatever the case, she hastened to help Caleb with the wood.

When they had finished, she stepped back, regarding the fire pit with critical eyes. "Do you have a match?" she asked.

Caleb laughed. "Are you kidding? Watch and learn!" He turned to Fred. "Light my fire, baby!" he crowed to the mighty beast. Fred cheerfully obliged, puffing out a small fireball in the direction of their woodpile.

Trinity smiled. "I should have known."

As the fire crackled to life, she settled down on a nearby log, holding out her hands to warm them by the flames. A moment later, Emmy curled up by her side, contentedly snorting a few puffs of smoke from her snout before closing her large blue eyes. Trin reached over and stroked the dragon's nose, thanking her for the amazing ride.

But next time, no lunch breaks! she scolded her gently. *And no letting them win. They're already too cocky as it is.*

She heard a loud snort and glanced up to find Fred looking

at Caleb expectantly, her golden eyes shining with eagerness and a large splotch of drool dripping from the corner of her mouth. Caleb rolled his eyes and waved his hands in the air. Once again, a piece of meat appeared, even more bloody than the one Emmy had devoured if that were possible.

"Okay, okay, I guess you deserve this," he said grudgingly. "I'm still in shock you let the other one go." The meat dropped to the ground with a bloody plop and Fred dug in with gusto. When she had finished, she looked up, her mouth smeared with blood like some crazy clown lipstick, batting her eyelashes at Caleb, obviously hungry for more. Trinity giggled. She was worse than a Labrador Retriever.

"No more!" Caleb cried, playfully shoving her huge snout away. He turned to Trin. "Lesson one when raising dragons: they're all complete gluttons. They'd eat until they exploded if you let them." He gave Fred a scolding look. "Now settle down and go to sleep. You're not getting anything else from me today."

Fred hmphed her disapproval but eventually gave up, settling down beside Emmy. A moment later, her eyes drifted closed and she started snoring like a buzz saw. Caleb groaned. "Gotta love dragons," he said derisively, poking the beast with his boot to get her to quiet down. Then he settled in front of the fire himself, closing his eyes and holding out his hands, as if he were meditating. Trin was about to ask what he was doing, but before she could speak, a bag of marshmallows dropped from the sky, out of thin air, just like the meat. Two large toasting sticks soon followed.

"Wow," she breathed. "How are you doing that?"

"Ask and the Nether shall provide," Caleb replied

nonchalantly, though Trin caught him wiping a sheen of sweat from his brow. Whatever he'd done, it'd taken a lot out of him. "That's what makes this place so cool. We can do anything we want to do. Be anyone we want to be. It's limitless! Well, until you get back to real life that is," he amended. "Then you have to face the fire."

"What do you mean?"

"Remember how you felt after using your gift on that cop?" Caleb reminded her. When she nodded, he added, "Imagine that but ten times worse. Like a hangover, I guess. And your spark is totally depleted." He gave her a rueful look. "Sorry, I probably should have warned you in advance."

She shrugged, taking a marshmallow and stuffing it onto her stick. "Whatever," she said, waving a hand in dismissal. "This is well worth a little hangover." She looked out over the valley below, at the sky, flaming red from the setting sun. "To be here. To see this." She shook her head. "It's unbelievable really." She gave him a shy look. "Thank you. It's just what I needed—a chance to get my mind off everything."

"So you enjoyed your ride?"

"It was incredible," she admitted, watching the marshmallow turn a golden brown as she held it over the flames. "I can't even put it into words. And it wasn't just the flying either. But the chance to let go like that—to just be able to enjoy the ride." A warm glow flowed through her. "Let's just say that's not something I've been able to do much in my life."

"I know exactly what you mean," he said with a slow smile. "I'll never forget my first time. I thought I was going to die. Instead, it's when I finally started living."

A silence fell over them, each lost in their own thoughts

as the fire crackled between them. She looked over, watching him gazing tenderly at his dragon and she felt a warmth settle in her stomach. He was so different here than he acted in the outside world. As if just being here allowed him to shed his prickly skin and reveal his true self underneath. Here he seemed relaxed, gentle, kind. Almost sweet. So unlike the sullen, sarcastic boy he pretended to be.

He looked up, catching her gaze. His eyebrows raised. She felt her face heat and she turned quickly away. As she stared purposely into the fire, she could feel his eyes rake over her with curious intensity, as if asking a question she wasn't sure how to answer.

"Wow, this fire is pretty hot," she stammered, pushing back on her log.

"Yeah," he answered slowly. "Some might say scorching."

Scorching. Yes, she felt scorched all right. But not by the fire. She cleared her throat, trying to still her pounding heart as her stomach flip-flopped madly. She tried to tell herself it was because she still hadn't eaten. But deep down, she knew that wasn't it at all.

"So do you only do this in the Nether?" she asked quickly, desperate for a subject change. "Or do you ride Fred in real life too, back home in the future?"

Caleb's face sobered. "I used to," he replied, a bitterness creeping into his voice. "Before."

"What do you mean? Did something happen?" Trinity glanced worriedly over at Fred, who was smacking her lips in her sleep and moaning loudly—likely dreaming of jerky treats. Had someone hurt her? Or worse?

"Remember what I told you—only dragons yet to be born

or those who have already died can exist here in the Nether," Caleb said slowly. "In other words, Fred is no longer a part of the real world. I can only see her when I come here."

"What happened to her?"

He gave her a hard look. "How do you say it in your world? Oh yeah: I'll give you three guesses, but the first two don't count."

She stared at him, dread rising within her. It couldn't be true. Could it? "Oh God. Not..."

"Oh yes. The great and glorious dragon hunter," he spat. "My own brother."

"How could he do that?" she blurted out, horrified. But even as she asked the question, she realized she already knew the answer. Connor believed dragons were evil. They'd killed his father. They'd destroyed his world. None of them were pardoned from his bloody crusade—not even sweet, silly Fred.

And especially not Emmy.

Caleb scowled. "He actually had the nerve to tell me he was doing me a favor," he ground out, "that I had been brainwashed by an evil fiend and he was only doing his brotherly duty, breaking me free." His hands curled into fists, his fingernails cutting into his palms. "But Fred didn't do anything wrong, Trin. She wasn't a monster. Her only crime was belonging to me."

His voice broke. Trinity's heart wrenched at the naked pain she caught in his eyes. She couldn't imagine what it must have been like for him—to lose someone he loved at the hands of his own twin. No wonder he was so bitter. So angry. So sarcastic. He was hiding a mountain of pain behind those sullen eyes.

"But I don't understand," she tried. "If you were bonded to a dragon and she died…"

"Our bond hadn't yet been completed at the time he did the deed," Caleb explained. "That was one of the excuses he gave, actually—he had to kill her to save me." His expression darkened. "I told him not to do me any favors."

Trinity nodded slowly, knowing all too well what he meant. That helpless feeling of being left behind. Of having someone you love ripped away and the sudden realization that you're all alone—and will be forever. After all, hadn't she herself once stared down the barrel of a certain shotgun, hopelessly broken inside, wondering if Mom had seen fit to leave her dear old daughter a spare bullet? If her grandpa hadn't walked in at that very moment, things could have turned out very differently.

"Fred was the only one I could trust," Caleb continued. "The only one who gave a fleck about me in this stupid world. And Connor murdered her in cold blood. Left me all alone." He looked up. "And now he's after your dragon too."

Trinity flinched. She glanced over at Emmy, sleeping peacefully by her side, her emotions spilling over. She knew, in her head, why Connor would want Emmy dead. But at the same time, her heart told her it wasn't fair. To punish Emmy for something she didn't do.

She turned back to Caleb. "You must miss her," she said softly, not sure what else to say. Words seemed so inadequate in the face of such exquisite loss.

"I do," he admitted. "It's one reason I travel to the Nether so often. It's tearing my body apart in the real world and I know I should stop before I suffer some kind of permanent damage. But," he whispered, looking sorrowfully at his dragon, "how can I leave her here, all alone?"

Trinity's heart tore at the wretchedness in his voice, the pain she saw in his eyes. Even if he won this fight, she realized, he'd already lost—lost the one thing he cared about more than anything in the world. All of a sudden, she understood why it was so important for him to help the Dracken succeed. While nothing could bring Fred back, with Emmy, he still had the chance to usher new Freds into the world. Giving other lonely, orphan Potentials a chance to feel valued and whole.

On impulse, she rose to her feet, walking over to his side of the fire and sitting down beside him. Without a word, she reached out, pulling him into her arms. At first he didn't move, as if startled by her offer of comfort. Then, slowly, he wrapped his hands around her waist, burying his face in the hollow of her throat. She could feel his erratic heartbeat against her chest as he struggled silently with his demons.

For a moment, they just sat there, completely still, locked in their embrace. Then, without warning, Caleb pulled away, pinning her with a dark, hungry gaze. She shivered as she recognized the naked need on his face—the worship in his storm-tossed eyes. As she drew in a shaky breath, he reached out, tracing her cheek with a trembling finger, his touch speaking words she wasn't sure she was ready to hear.

And then he kissed her. Not the whispering kiss Connor had given her back at her mother's house. Not tentative, not shy, not the wisp of a butterfly's wing brushing against her skin, but hard, angry, almost brutal in its intensity—as if trying to punish her for what they'd done to him. Hot blood pounded in her ears as his mouth moved over hers, his hands clamping the sides of her face.

She knew she should break away, to get as far away as possible as her emotions whirled and skittered. But her traitorous body seemed to have other ideas, pressing closer against him, wrapping her legs around his, digging her hands into his hair. As if she could simply melt into his embrace and be done with it all. In that moment, there truly seemed to be nothing else in the world. No dragons, no apocalypse, no loved ones in danger. Just a boy and a girl tangled in one another's arms.

"You have to admit," Caleb murmured against her mouth. "You're suddenly feeling a lot, lot better."

Oh God. She froze, his words breaking the spell. What the hell was she doing?

Ripping herself from his grasp, she somehow managed to scramble to her feet, staring down at Caleb with wild, unfocused eyes. How could she have let this happen? It was wrong. So wrong. On so many levels.

Caleb looked up to her, his lips swollen and his face torn with confusion. "What's wrong?" he asked, his voice hoarse and horrified, and sounding so very scared. He started to rise to his feet. She held up a hand, stopping him in his tracks.

"I'm sorry," she cried. "But this isn't right. There's too much going on. Too much at stake. I can't afford to be distracted. I can't lose…" She trailed off helplessly, unable to finish. But from the look on Caleb's face, she knew she'd said enough. Maybe too much.

"I'm sorry," she said again. But he was no longer listening.

✦ ✦ ✦

Trinity's stomach roiled. She leaned over, spewing her guts out onto the hand-scraped hardwood floor, sickly yellow bile pooling at her feet. She groaned, her head aching, as she looked around the room, trying to gain her bearings. No longer was she sitting by the fire on the side of a cliff, two dragons curled up nearby. She was back in the real world—and with the promised Nether hangover to boot, ten times worse than she'd imagined it would be.

She looked down, her breath catching in her throat as she found Caleb's hands still wrapped in her own. The ones that just minutes before had been touching her so desperately. It was all she could do not to grab him all over again. Surrender to the hot blood still coursing through her veins.

But it was wrong. She had to stay strong. She had to focus on the task at hand and not let anything else distract her. This kiss was nothing more than another trap—like the fancy rooms or the delicious food—seeking to wrest her under Dracken control. To make her forget her real life outside these prison walls.

But she would not surrender. She would not lay down and die. She would not kiss him again.

Caleb opened his eyes. For a moment he sat still, looking dazed and confused. Then a shadow crossed his face and he ripped his hands from hers, ruby red dust flying as he stood up and stalked to the other side of the room. She looked down at her empty hands, a sudden aching emptiness throbbing in her fingers. She frowned and shoved them under her thighs.

"Look, Caleb," she tried. "I'm—"

Her words were interrupted as the bedroom door flew open. Rashida burst into the room, her eyes wide and frightened.

"Mara sent me," she told her in a voice that betrayed her fear. "She said you have to come now."

"What is it?" Trinity asked, rising to her feet, sudden fear pounding in her chest. She knew somehow, before the Potential even opened her mouth, that it must have something to do with her dragon. "Is Emmy okay?"

"She's hatching," Rashida told her in a tight voice. "They tried to stop it—it's far too early—but they couldn't." Her mouth quivered. "The dragon's coming, Trinity. And the Dracken need your help."

Chapter Twenty-Eight

Trinity raced after Rashida, through the mall corridors, past curious Potentials, trying not to puke again as the aftereffects of her Nether trip still thrashed at her insides. Her head pounded, her legs felt like lead, but still she pressed on, only one thing on her mind. One name on her tongue.

Trust me. I'll never let you fall.

Yet now it was Emmy who was falling, who was failing. Fighting for her life. And Trin was the only one who could help her.

Hang on, Emmy, she sent. *I'm on my way.*

The birthing chamber had been constructed out of a two-floor Neiman Marcus, repainted entirely in white save for intricate, silver runes etched into the cathedral ceiling. Men and women—presumably other Dracken she hadn't met yet—bustled about the room, occupied with equipment Trinity couldn't identify. In the center of the room sat the egg itself, swaddled in a bathtub-sized pool of crystal. From high above, water cascaded down onto the egg, splashing over its shell.

Trinity drew in a breath. She remembered how blown away she'd felt the first time she'd laid eyes on the egg under the glass case in the Millennium Chamber. But that was nothing compared to how she felt now, as she watched the egg trap the chamber's light and toss it around in a kaleidoscope of color. Emmy was more beautiful than ever—luminous and glowing and ethereal. But it was not her shell's outer brilliance that brought tears to Trin's eyes—rather the slight movement, the desperate struggling, just beneath the now translucent surface.

Is that you, Emmy? she whispered, mesmerized by the dark, dragon-shaped shadows. *Is that really you?*

"Thank God you're here." Trin turned to see Mara on approach. The Birth Maiden's eyes were vivid but frightened.

"What's wrong with her?" Trinity asked worriedly. Her eyes searched the egg, catching the hairline fracture at the top. She stepped forward, reaching out to trace the crack with a soft finger, warm water sluicing over her hand. But the warmth was short-lived as she felt Emmy's chill of terror wash over her. Her stomach clenched.

"We don't know," Mara confessed, giving her a helpless look. "I've assisted in countless dragon births over the years. But the equipment we have to work with here is practically prehistoric—it can't tell me what I need to know. All that I can tell is that she's trying to break free of the egg, but she's not having any luck. Maybe the shell hardened somehow, by being in the ice so long. Maybe its composition changed after so many years. All I know is the baby dragon's struggling. And her vital signs are weakening. If we don't get her out now, she'll likely die before she can ever be born."

Trinity cringed and pressed her palm flat against the egg, closing her eyes. Somehow she knew it was up to her. That she was the only one who could save the dragon now.

Or you could end it all, a quiet voice tugged at the back of her brain. *This is the perfect opportunity—they'd never know it was you.*

Her pulse raced as she stole a glance around the room—at the men and women all around her. The dragon sympathizers who had inadvertently sparked an apocalypse once upon a time in another future. Caleb promised that they had the best intentions, that they knew what they were doing this time around—that by saving dragons they would save the world.

Save the world? the voice whispered. *Or leave it vulnerable to attack?*

Her mind flashed back to Connor and his talk of the Scorch. Of his father, burned alive by dragon's breath. Of the vision he'd shown her: the screams of agony, the smell of burning flesh, the shadows falling, never to rise again. The entire world all but destroyed because of one single egg.

This one, single egg.

What if the Dracken couldn't stop history from repeating itself no matter what their intentions? Would keeping Emmy alive be putting the entire human race at risk?

Once she's born, it'll be too late, the voice whispered. *You'll be as hunted as she is. Your life forces intertwined. And if anything happens to the world—like it did the first time around—it'll be your fault.*

She pulled her hand away and felt the eyes of the Dracken shift in her direction, watching, waiting to see what she would do. Pressure started to expand inside her chest, building and pushing against her ribs until she felt as if she were going to explode.

She could end this all now and hope for the best. And maybe the Dracken predictions were wrong. Maybe mankind would find a way to survive without the dragons' gifts. At least they wouldn't be burned alive. At least the earth would remain intact.

But what about Emmy?

She closed her eyes, remembering her flight through the Nether. The majestic dragon, soaring through the skies, brave and beautiful, her eyes bright and her head held high. She'd carried Trin on her back. She hadn't let her fall. Didn't Emmy deserve the same chance now? The chance to live her life? The chance to fly free?

Emmy didn't start an apocalypse. She didn't burn the world to the ground. It was man who caged her, tortured her, stole the spark from her eyes. Man who robbed her of her dragon's dance and created monsters from her DNA. Emmy didn't bring about the end of the world—man did, with his lust for war and power. And who was to say he needed dragons to do it the next time around?

Trin shook her head. In the end, she realized, this wasn't a question of whether dragons would save the world or tear it apart. It didn't matter what destruction they might bring or what gifts they might offer. This was about a life—one single, precious life, struggling to enter the world. Emmy was pure; she'd committed no folly. She had caused no harm. Her life should not be held forfeit to pay for mankind's sin.

There was no more decision to make. Trin pressed her hand against the egg once again. *Are you there, Emmy?*

Nothing. She pulled the egg from the basin, out of the water. A few of the Dracken jumped in alarm, but Mara held out a hand. "Let her try," she told them. They reluctantly stepped back. Trin took Emmy and brought her to the floor, cradling her in her lap.

Emmy? Can you hear me?

Still nothing. Then…

Trinity?

Her heart leapt. She was alive!

Yes, Emmy! I'm here. Are you okay?

So…weak. So…tired.

As Trin rolled her hand over the egg, stroking it gently, she felt an overwhelming exhaustion come over her. Emmy's exhaustion, she realized, threatening to crush her with its intensity. But she forced herself to swallow it back, gritting her teeth with the effort.

Listen to me, Emmy. You can rest later. Right now, I need you to fight. You must break through your shell.

I can't do it. I'm not strong enough.

Then take my strength instead. Take whatever you need. The Potentials had been able to push comfort to Trin's mind back in the food court. Surely she'd be able to do the same, giving her dragon the strength she required.

Are you sure? I don't want to hurt you.

I'm sure. In fact, Trinity had never been so sure of anything in her life.

She emptied her mind, sweeping all the doubts and insecurities away, preparing to give everything she had inside to the dragon and then some if need be. At that moment, she told herself, she was no longer Trinity Foxx, broken orphan of West Texas. She was the Fire Kissed. The one Emmy had chosen out of all the others. And Trinity wasn't about to let the dragon down.

Emmy hadn't let her fall. Now it was Trin's turn to return the favor.

Do it, Emmy! she cried. *Break free!* She pushed with all her might.

And then the pain came. Excruciating, all-encompassing agony, lashing at her insides and stealing her breath away. Her muscles clenched and her eyes lost focus, sharp screws drilling into her brain while a thousand spiders crawled up and down her skin. She was sure, at one point, she would pass out from it all.

But instead she fought it, refusing to give up on her dragon. Clinging to consciousness as hard as she clung to the egg. Bright lights popped in and out of the room and a strange wailing sound echoed in her ears. It took her a moment to recognize it as screaming. Another to realize it was coming from her own lips.

"Her vital signs are weakening!" she heard somewhere in the distance.

"She's not going to make it," another voice cried. Trinity didn't know if they were talking about the dragon or her. Or maybe both.

She turned her attention back to the egg. Why wasn't it working? She was giving all she had and it still wasn't enough. Emmy still wasn't breaking free. She reached out to the dragon, combing her mind, desperately trying to figure out what was wrong. Why she still was too weak to—

And suddenly she realized the problem. It wasn't that Emmy was weak or powerless at all.

She was scared.

In fact, she was petrified. But of what?

Trin squeezed the egg between her hands, gritting her teeth and forcing away the pain. *What's wrong, Emmy?* she begged the dragon, praying there was still time to make things right. *What are you so afraid of? Whatever it is, you can tell me.*

And so...the dragon did.

Chapter Twenty-Nine

Emmy watched from inside her egg as her mother, Lyria, paced the low-ceiling cave, her muscular legs making short work of the distance between the walls. It was nice to finally be able to see her mother—really see her at last— through the haze of her growing-translucent shell. Before today, Emmy had only been able to hear her mother's low growls and comforting snorts and had to imagine what she must look like on the outside. Now she realized she could have never envisioned how beautiful her mother really was, how noble and regal she could be. With emerald-green scales and massive, golden wings, she looked like an angel sent from the Nether. Emmy stole a glance down at her own pitiful flaps and wondered if she'd ever have anything so grand.

The temperature had dropped and snow swirled madly outside the shallow cave, which had been cut into the side of a steep cliff. Lyria had landed here the week before, the encroaching storm preventing her from reaching safer ground further south, where the other mothers had gone to lay their eggs. Now they were stuck here until the eggs hatched and the baby dragons could spread their wings and fly. A fact Emmy knew made her mother increasingly nervous.

She also knew her brother wasn't far from hatching; he'd been pecking at his shell all night long. She'd tried to work on hers as well, but her shell seemed so thick, so unyielding to her soft snout, and she was getting a little worried. She'd tried calling out to her mother, to beg for some help, but the elder dragon seemed not to hear her. Emmy narrowed her eyes and tried again. She couldn't give up—no matter what.

A loud cracking broke through the silence and Emmy turned just in time to see her brother poking his snout from his golden shell. Their mother approached, snorting in excitement, nudging the shell with her nose, widening the crack. A moment later, a tiny, red head poked out from the egg, followed by a gangly body, tripping out of his shell and onto the cave floor. A ruby dragon! The rarest of all. Emmy's mother tossed her head in pride. The other mothers would be filled with envy at such a living treasure.

Emmy watched as her baby brother took a few awkward steps, then worked to spread his fledgling wings. They looked so fragile but at the same time so strong. A moment later, he tripped over the left wing, falling flat on his face. He scowled, shaking his tiny head, puffing smoke from his snout. But Emmy's mother only laughed, giving him a long, wet slurp from her massive tongue.

What about me? Emmy pleaded as she tried once again to poke through her unyielding shell. The storm outside was getting worse. They had to leave soon or be trapped here forever, buried in a ton of ice. But try as she might, she couldn't break free.

Help me, Mama! I need your help!

But her mother was too busy with her brother—the

precious ruby—to hear her call. And Emmy was beginning to despair. She knew what happened to dragons who couldn't break out of their shells. They returned to the Nether. Forever. Emmy liked the Nether. It was fun to play there. But it was also lonely. Her family was here.

Outside, the lightning danced across the sky, followed by a crack of thunder. The cave shook, stalactites crumbling from the ceiling. Emmy's brother squawked in fear as a rocky spike came crashing down only inches from where he'd stood. Lyria quickly scooped him up with her paw, pulling him protectively against her massive chest. She seemed to hesitate for a moment, then stepped toward the edge of the cave.

Emmy's heart stuttered. *What was she doing?* She watched in terror as her mother inched closer to the edge, still holding her brother under her arm. Once she'd reached the precipice, she paused, then turned back to the unhatched egg, indecision warring on her face.

No! Emmy cried, realizing what her mother was contemplating. *Don't leave me, Mama! Please don't leave me here alone!*

But her mother didn't answer. Instead, she turned away, unfurling her massive wings and gliding off the edge of the cliff, her precious ruby son cradled protectively in her arms. Emmy watched as they soared off into the distance until they had disappeared from view. A lone tear slipped down her snout. She knew in her heart they were not coming back.

And she would be alone forever.

✦ ✦ ✦

"Emmy!"

Trinity opened her eyes, heart wrenching and tears coursing down her cheeks. She was back in the birthing chamber, back with the Dracken, still clutching the egg with both hands. Her body was shaking uncontrollably and she was drenched in sweat, but she paid it no mind, looking down at her dragon, reliving her pain, feeling her fear. Finally she understood. In fact, she understood perfectly.

Oh, Emmy…I'm so sorry.

No wonder the dragon was so hesitant to enter the world. The world had left her behind. Everyone she knew was dead. Had been dead for millions of years. They'd abandoned her, sacrificed her to save themselves—left her all alone.

My mother left me too, she told Emmy. *I trusted her and she let me down. Left me behind without even saying good-bye.* She stroked the shell with gentle fingers. *I promised myself I'd never trust anyone again after that day—until I met you.*

The dragon stirred from inside the shell, swimming around in a hazy black shadow. Trin dug her fingers into the crack, trying to widen it as she'd seen Emmy's mother do.

You flew me through the skies. You took away my fears. You told me you'd never let me fall. She drew in a breath. *Well, Emmy, I'll never let you fall either. You can trust in that. You can trust in me. As you told me, we are destined…*

She closed her eyes, the exhaustion overwhelming her at last. There was nothing else she could do. Nothing else she could say. She only hoped Emmy could hear her. That she believed what she'd said and—

"The egg! It's cracking!"

Trinity looked down at the egg. Sure enough, it had cracked

wide open, all the way down each side. She watched, not daring to move, as a tiny, birdlike head popped out from the now broken shell, bobbing up and down on a wobbly neck. The dragon regarded her with large, serious blue eyes rimmed in gold—eyes she would recognize anywhere.

"Emmy!"

The dragon let out a triumphant squawk, tiny wisps of smoke puffing from her snout. The room exploded in applause, everyone rushing to witness the miracle for themselves. But Trin held up a hand, forcing them back. To give her baby dragon space to breathe. To protect Emmy as she'd promised she would.

She was the Fire Kissed, after all.

She ached all over, as if she'd been hit by a truck. And she was so exhausted she could probably sleep for a month. But it was all worth it to watch Emmy spread her tiny, webbed wings and give them a tentative flap. The dragon looked up at Trinity shyly, inquisitively. Trin found herself laughing, tears still splashing down her cheeks.

"They're beautiful," she assured the tiny dragon. "Just like your mother's."

The dragon squawked happily, making her way up Trinity's arm and settling contentedly on her shoulder. Her claws tickled and tugged, but Trinity didn't mind at all. She reached up and scratched her dragon on the ridge of her nose. Emmy purred in delight. Trin felt a little like purring herself.

For the first time in her life, she felt whole. Complete. And she would do anything to keep this baby dragon from harm.

Chapter Thirty

Two nights later, there was a massive celebration—all the Potentials, all the members of the Dracken gathering together to celebrate Emmy's birth. The tables and chairs at the food court were cleared away and a few of the Potentials who were musically inclined set up a makeshift stage and blasted out the tunes. Aiko turned out to be quite the talented singer, belting out hit after hit to the cheering crowd. Even Trevor got into the spirit, asking Rashida to dance. And she didn't even tease him before saying okay.

Through it all, Trinity sat in a special seat of honor at the head of the room, gaudily decorated with green ribbons and bows. She was too drained to dance or join in with the festivities, but she was having a blast watching everyone else. And little Emmy, sitting proudly on her shoulder and wearing a red ribbon, wasn't bad company either.

"She's so cute!" Malia cried, coming over with Rashida and Aiko during the band's break. They'd been allowed to change out of their training uniforms for the night and each wore sparkling emerald cocktail dresses in honor of Emmy.

"It's hard to believe she's really here!" added Aiko. "I feel like we've been waiting forever."

"Some of us never believed it was going to happen at all," added Rashida, giving Trevor a knowing nudge. He rolled his eyes and blushed.

"Yeah, yeah," he muttered. Then he turned to Trinity. "She's brilliant, Trin. Truly brilliant. Good work."

Trinity grinned with pride, reaching over to stroke Emmy on the nose. The little dragon danced and purred happily, causing the Potentials to crack up. Malia reached over, daring to touch her tiny nose and Emmy rewarded her with a big slurp of her tongue. Malia screeched in surprise, yanking her hand away, then laughed sheepishly and reached out to pet her again.

"I can't wait to get one of my own!" she cried. "It's going to be so amazing."

Trinity nodded happily, a strange sense of contentment washing over her. It was strange. In some ways, nothing had changed—she was still technically trapped here, still unable to walk out the front doors. And yet now, with Emmy here, she wasn't all that sure she'd want to even if she could.

It wasn't easy taking care of a newborn dragon, and it didn't take long for her to realize she had no idea what she was doing. Thankfully, the Dracken had been endlessly patient, showing her how to feed Emmy, to bathe her, to keep her warm. Not to mention babysit her at times when Trin just needed a few precious hours of sleep. And most importantly, they showed her how to use her gift to communicate with the dragon, to ensure Emmy not only felt safe but loved. That was the fun part, actually—to spend hours just cuddling her dragon while whispering in her mind all the things they would do together. Trinity found she never felt happier than when Emmy was in her arms.

She tried to imagine what it would have been like if she and Emmy had been out in the world when the dragon was born. The creature probably wouldn't have made it through her first night—or have been able to hatch at all. The Dracken had made it all happen, continued to make it all happen, and Trin found herself left with a grudging sense of gratitude and respect for the ragtag team of time travelers and orphans. And she felt bad for being so suspicious at first.

It still wasn't home, but at times it felt pretty darn close. And it would feel even more so, she knew, when her grandpa joined her at last.

Wait until you meet him, Em, she sent. *You're going to love him as much as I do.* The little dragon bobbed her head excitedly, and Trin tried to imagine her grandpa's face when she presented Emmy to him for the first time. The moment he would realize, without a doubt, that he'd been right all along—that all his lifelong dreams had finally come true.

She looked up just in time to catch sight of a dark figure skulking across the back of the room. Her heart snagged. *Caleb.* She hadn't seen him since their little trip to the Nether. He hadn't even shown up with the others after Emmy's birth. After all the work he'd done to bring the little dragon here, he should have been first in line to greet her. But instead he stayed away, lurking in the shadows. And she was pretty sure she knew why.

She sighed. Time for an apology.

"I'll be back," she told her new friends. The girls gave her knowing looks and smiles as they followed her gaze.

"Take your time," Aiko teased.

"Yeah, no rush at all," added Rashida with a wink.

She shot them a weak smile—at times, they really did seem like sisters—then pushed across the dance floor. It took a while to cross—everyone wanted to talk to her and meet Emmy—but finally she managed to reach the edge of the food court. Spotting Caleb trudging down the darkened hall some distance ahead, she picked up the pace.

"Wait!" she cried.

He stopped, stiffened, then turned around slowly, his face unreadable. "What?" he asked.

She faltered, words failing her as her eyes caught his, flashing and cruel. "About what happened," she started.

Caleb waved her off. "Please. Don't embarrass yourself on my account. It's really no big deal."

"But—"

"I was in the mood. You were ready and willing. It happened. Now it's over and done. Let's move on with our lives, shall we?"

His words stung. Badly. Even though she was the one who had pulled away. But that wasn't because it hadn't meant anything. It was just—

"What, do you think you're the first girl I took into the Nether?" he scoffed, catching her anguished expression. "Please. I've had half the Potentials in there. Nothing like a good dragon race to get a girl all hot and bothered." He snorted. "You should have seen when I took Aiko in there three months ago. She was practically ripping off her shirt before I could even manifest a single marshmallow."

Trinity's throat seemed to close up. "Oh," she stammered. "Wow." She no longer had anything to say—at least nothing she could force past the huge lump that had formed in her throat. Her mind flashed back to the cliff side, to Caleb's tormented face. The story that had broken her heart. Had it all been an act? A signature move honed and perfected over the years to lure Potentials in? Make them feel sorry for him so they'd agree to hook up?

"Now why don't you go back to your little birthday party and your little friends?" he added with a sneer. "I've got things to do."

"Yeah. I'm sure being a full-time douche keeps you pretty busy," she retorted, feeling the tears well up in her eyes. She turned and walked away before he could see them fall. Thank God she'd had the sense to break things off first. How far would he have taken it if she'd lost herself in his arms?

She stalked down the corridors, no longer in the mood to party. The happy, carefree faces of the Potentials would only serve to torment her. Had Caleb really taken Aiko into the Nether? Had he broken her heart too?

Not that her heart was broken, she reminded herself. Like Caleb said, it was no big deal. Just a kiss. Nothing more. And not even a good idea. She had enough going on with her newfound mission to save the world to be wasting time on some doomed romance. She was the Fire Kissed, after all. She didn't have time to be some guy's girlfriend too.

A tear slipped down her cheek.

Don't cry, Trin.

She gave the dragon a rueful look. Emmy gazed back at her with concern deep in her blue and golden eyes. She reached out a hesitant paw and brushed Trinity's cheek, swiping away a tear. Trinity gave the dragon a sad smile. At least she had someone who cared.

"You know, that was the first thing you ever said to me," she reminded Emmy. "Back at the museum. When I thought you were fake." She twisted the ring on her finger. "It seems a million years ago at this point."

She sighed. She was so tired. So, so tired. But she squared her shoulders and shook it off best she could. Emmy needed her to be strong after all, to keep the promise she'd made. And so when the dragon gave her a doubtful look, she reached out to pat her wing reassuringly.

"I'll be fine," she said. "I just need a good night's sleep."

"You do indeed," boomed a deep voice. Trinity whirled around, startled. The Dracken Master himself, Darius, stood not two feet away, dressed in a smart black tuxedo, his hair slicked back with a bit too much grease. She hadn't heard him approach. "Your training begins tomorrow. And I must warn you, it will be nothing if not intense."

She forced herself to smile back at him. "Intense is my middle name," she declared, mustering up her bravado. "I can hardly wait." She turned on her heel, ready to head back to her bedroom.

"Stop," he commanded suddenly in a voice that caused her heart to leap to her throat. Turning back slowly, she leveled her eyes upon his face. His smile had disappeared.

"Yeah?" she asked, biting her lower lip.

For a moment the Dracken leader said nothing, just regarded her with solemn eyes. Then he sighed deeply. "Before you go, I have some news. About your grandfather."

Her heart fluttered. "News?" she repeated warily.

"Maybe you should sit down. We could go to my office and—"

"No." She shook her head vehemently, scarcely able to breathe. "Just tell me."

Looking regretful, he reached into his jacket's interior pocket and pulled out a folded newspaper, holding it out to her. "What is this?" she asked, heart pounding madly now as she took the paper and unfolded it with shaky fingers. Her eyes widened as she realized she was holding a copy of the *Old Oak Grove Gazette*. Today's *Old Oak Grove Gazette*. She looked up at Darius, confused. "I don't understand."

Without a word, he took the paper from her and flipped it over. She looked back down. "The obituaries?" she asked. "What...?" She trailed off, her eyes falling on the single entry for that day. She nearly dropped the paper.

"No," she stammered, her world falling out from under her. "There must be some mistake."

Darius shook his head slowly, then opened his arms. She fell into them, sobbing hard against his chest. He wrapped his hands around her, rubbing her back with long, even strokes. She didn't have the strength to pull away.

"I'm so sorry, Trinity. I wanted to wait to tell you, so you could have your celebration. After all you've been through, I didn't want you to have to deal with this too. At least not before you regained your strength."

"What happened?" she asked, pulling away, searching his face. Out of the corner of her eye she could see Emmy, dancing nervously around her, clearly upset at her mistress's distress. But she needed answers first—before she could reassure her dragon.

He gave her a sorry look. "From what my men could gather, your grandfather was found a few days ago, down by exit 13 off the old, abandoned interstate. He had been beaten within an inch of his life." He cringed. "They tried to operate but his heart couldn't take it. He was in a coma for a few days before he finally let go."

He kept talking but Trinity could no longer focus on his words. Exit 13. That was where she'd told him to meet her. But then she'd sent Connor instead. The Dragon Hunter who she hadn't realized at the time was trying to kill her.

She broke out into a fresh set of tears. Had Caleb been right about his brother all along?

"I'm so, so sorry," the Dracken leader murmured, taking her face in his hands and peering down at her with intense brown eyes. "I know how much he meant to you."

"He was my family," she sobbed. "My only family."

"No!" Darius's eyes flashed fire. His hands tightened against her face until she almost cried out in pain. "We're your family now. And we'll always be there for you no matter what. We'll never let anything happen to you. I promise."

His words were fierce and passionate, and probably meant to comfort, but instead chilled her to the bone, realization hitting her hard and fast. As nice as they were and as helpful as they'd been...

They were never going to let her go.

Forcing the fear back, she looked down at the paper again, as if she could somehow change what it said by sheer force of will. But, of course, the words were written in indelible ink.

She looked up. "The funeral is on Friday," she managed to say past the lump in her throat. "I'd like to go."

Darius regarded her for a moment, then shook his head slowly. "I'm sorry," he said. "That's not possible."

"Please," she begged, her voice trembling. "I'll leave Emmy here. You can send guards with me. We'll leave immediately after the service." She gave him a pleading look. "I just want to have the chance to say good-bye."

Darius gave her a pitying look. "I know. But I can't allow it. It's too dangerous." He shook his head. "We'll hold our own memorial here," he told her. "We'll all come together as a family to honor his memory. He was important to us too, Trinity. Without him, Emberlyn might still be trapped in a glacier. It was his dedication to his work that set her free." He smiled sadly. "Why, we owe him our very existence."

Trin frowned, unease itching at the corners of her mind. His words were exactly right and yet something still felt wrong—something hazy just around the edges. On impulse, she attempted to push into his brain, as Caleb had done to read her thoughts, but found herself blocked by a solid, black wall. And suddenly doubt seeded in her mind.

Maybe it was just desperation—of not wanting to believe a truth too horrible to swallow. Or maybe she was just going crazy—with all that had happened, it didn't seem too far-fetched. But what if there was something else going on here? What if he was lying? Doctored the paper to say what he wanted it to? What if her grandpa wasn't dead after all? What if this was just another way of trying to keep her here?

"Look," she tried. "I just want to—"

"I'm sorry, Trinity," he interrupted, his tone final. "But it's too dangerous. You will not be allowed to leave these walls."

"For how long?" she demanded, the anger and frustration inside of her threatening to boil over. "How long are you going to keep me locked up in this damned place?"

The Dracken didn't reply, simply bowed his head respect-fully, then turned to walk away. Trinity watched him go, furious beyond belief, then found herself reaching out again, trying desperately to break through his wall.

And then, just before the Dracken leader slipped into the shadows, she heard it. Escaping his mind like a tendril of smoke, twining its way back to her and her dragon.

What do you care? it taunted. *It's not like you have anywhere left to go.*

PART 4:

SMOLDER

Chapter Thirty-One

"Have you seen this girl?"

Connor watched wearily as Trinity's grandfather approached two teenage girls walking out of the convenience store, flashing the five-by-seven school photo in their faces. "Her name is Trinity. She might have been traveling with a brown-haired boy who looked something like him." He pointed over at Connor. The girls studied him with interest, giggled, then shook their heads before walking away. Connor sighed. This was beyond useless.

Trinity's grandfather dropped the photo to his side and rejoined Connor by the car. "I think we've hit a dead end," he admitted mournfully. "I can feel traces of her spark, as if she were here at one point, but no one remembers seeing her."

Connor clamped a comforting hand on the old man's arm. He looked beyond exhausted and for good reason. Maybe it had been a mistake to teach him how to glean energy signals from the atmosphere. It was a useful Hunter trick when tracking down dragons and it could work on others with the gift as well. But while Connor had discovered Trinity's grandpa to be a natural-born Hunter, he was also very old and very weak. Energy gleaning took a lot out of even the hardiest of

Hunters and was a technique to be used sparingly. But once Grandpa had learned what he could do, he refused to stop doing it. Every second she was gone, she was in danger, he'd reminded Connor. They'd come this far; they couldn't give up now.

"It's as if she's vanished off the face of the earth," Grandpa muttered, raking a hand through his thinning gray hair. His whole body was trembling, Connor noticed, and he looked as if he could barely stand.

"Look, why don't we find a hotel and get some rest," he suggested kindly. "Once you've regained some spark we can try again." He was pretty drained himself and could use a small break before pressing on.

"No." Grandpa frowned. "There's no time for rest."

Connor gave him a stern look. He was beginning to realize where Trin had gotten her stubbornness from. "You're dead on your feet. You'll be no good to her if you collapse and I have to bring you to the hospital."

Trinity's grandfather groaned in response but thankfully didn't try to argue. "Okay, fine," he said. "But just for a short time. Then we'll try again."

"Right. Now wait here and I'll grab us some supplies." Connor gestured to the convenience store. "You want anything special?"

Trinity's grandfather shook his head and Connor headed inside the store to make his purchases. In addition to water, he grabbed a few oranges and energy bars. It was important for a Hunter to properly fuel his body in order to achieve maximum spark. And at this point, they could both use as much spark as they could get.

Once he had paid for his purchases, he headed back outside. "Are you ready to…?" He started to say, but then realized Trin's grandfather was no longer leaning against his car. In fact, he was nowhere to be seen at all. Connor's gaze darted from one end of the street to the other, anxiety prickling at his skin. He tried to tell himself that the old man had probably gone to find a bathroom or something—his bladder was beyond useless at his age. But as the minutes ticked away, that idea started to seem more and more unlikely.

Charlie? He reached out, grimacing at the effort. His spark was so low at this point it wasn't even funny. *Where'd you go? Are you okay?*

I'm fine! Grandpa's excited voice shot through Connor's head a moment later. *I met some guys—they know where she is! They're going to take me to her!*

Connor tensed, warning bells clanging in his head. *No!* he cried. *Wait for me. Don't go anywhere until I get there.*

It's fine, Connor. They're real nice fellas. They're going to—

His send stopped abruptly, as if the connection were severed by a knife. Fear throttled Connor as he tried to find the old man with his mind. But it was as if a brick wall had slammed down between them.

Flecking hell. What had he been thinking—leaving him alone like that? Trinity had told him her grandpa was gullible, but he didn't think even *he* would be so stupid as to go off with a bunch of strangers alone. Evidently he underestimated the man's determination to find his granddaughter at any cost.

Suddenly Connor heard a cry—an old man's cry of pain—echo through his head. He sprang into action, racing down the street in the direction of the sound. Stomach churning, he pushed past curious bystanders, not bothering to apologize, as his pulse drummed out his fear.

This couldn't be happening. Not after he'd promised Trinity he'd keep her grandpa safe. If he couldn't come through with that, how could he expect her to trust him with anything else? And it wasn't just that, either, he admitted to himself. He'd grown fond of the crotchety old geezer in the last few days. He couldn't let anything happen to him.

He swung into an alley and stopped short, dropping down behind a trash compactor at the sound of men's voices. Peering around, he froze as he saw Trinity's grandpa surrounded by a group of thugs who were glaring at him menacingly. The old man's face was awash with confusion and fear as he looked back at the men.

"I don't understand," he babbled. "I thought you were going to take me to my granddaughter."

"Oh, we'll take you to Trinity all right," one of the men said with a nasty sneer. A scar slashed across his cheek and, from the way the others looked to him, Connor figured him the leader. "You'll make a good dinner for her dragon."

Connor stifled a groan. He'd been praying this was just some kind of robbery—a group of street rats taking advantage of an old man. But no, these men knew about Trinity and they knew about her dragon. Which could mean only one thing.

They were sent by the Dracken.

Oh, Trinity, he thought. *Be careful who you trust.*

Grandpa's face paled. He made a move to escape, but the men grabbed him, yanking him back. One slammed a foot into the back of his knees, sending him flying forward. The other clubbed him across the face, hot blood splattering as his nose burst open. A third drew his gun, shoving the barrel up against the back of his head, execution style. Connor cringed.

"No!" The leader wrestled the gun away from his buddy, giving him a scolding look. "Darius says we have to make it look like a heart attack." He peered down into Grandpa's terrified eyes with a mocking grin. "You'll be a good old fart and come along quietly, now won't you?"

"Why are you doing this?" Trinity's grandpa cried, tears streaming down his wrinkled cheeks, mixing with the blood.

The Dracken mercenary didn't answer. But Connor didn't need him too. In fact, it all made perfect sense. Grandpa was Trinity's only family—the only tie she had left to the outside world. Cut that tie and she'd have nothing left except them and the dragon and their empty promises to save the world. She'd be completely under their control.

It was the perfect plan except for one thing. He wasn't about to let them get away with it.

His mind raced for a plan. This is what he'd trained for, why they'd sent him here in the first place. But he hadn't bargained on being so weak—practically out of spark. Group pushes were tricky at best, even at full energy levels, and he was running on empty. But he had to try. He couldn't take on five armed men by himself. Closing his eyes, he pulled deep within, drawing up all his reserves, not holding anything back.

You've got the wrong guy.

He opened his eyes, scanning the group, praying they'd heard him and would obey. But they were busy dragging Grandpa to his feet and shuttling him to a nearby van with blacked-out windows. His push hadn't affected them at all.

Connor tried again.

The cops are on their way. You need to leave. Now!

Icy pain stabbed his skull and he nearly passed out from the effort. But when he opened his eyes, he realized it was all for nothing. The men kept at their tasks, as if nothing had happened.

He gripped his head in his hands, trying to think past the pain. This was not going well. A few more minutes and they'd be gone—Trinity's grandpa never heard from again. He watched, helpless, as the old man struggled uselessly against his captors. From this close proximity, he could feel Grandpa's terror and confusion as if it were his own. He certainly was a strong sender. Maybe one of the strongest Connor had ever met, save for Trinity herself.

That's it! The idea struck him like a lightning bolt. If he could get Grandpa to help him, maybe their combined spark could complete the push. He didn't know if the old man could focus past his injuries, but he had no other options and they were running out of time.

To me! he sent out. *I need as much spark as you can spare!*

He watched, praying for some reaction, some clue to tell him Grandpa had heard him and would obey. For a split second, he thought he saw something in the man's eyes, but he couldn't be sure. Still, he had no time to send again. He had to hope for the best.

Pushing past the pain in his skull, he closed his eyes one more time. Drawing his energy into a tiny, bright white ball and thrusting it as hard as he could.

You've got the wrong guy. Walk away now. The cops are almost here.

He fell back, seeing stars, unable, for a moment, to even

move. His legs and arms were Jell-O and his stomach swam with nausea. Still he watched, waiting. Praying. They'd almost reached the van. If this hadn't worked, it was all over. It was too late to try again.

For a moment, he saw no sign. Then one of them looked up. "I don't think we have the right guy," he said.

"What?" the leader lashed at him. "What are you talking about? Of course it's the right guy."

"No," his buddy agreed, looking at Grandpa, his face awash with confusion. "I don't think it is."

"Do you hear sirens?" added the third man. "I think the cops are on their way."

The leader's face twisted in rage. "You morons. What's wrong with you? There're no sirens. And no cops either. Now get him the hell in the van and let's get out of here."

But the men had already released Grandpa, the old man collapsing unceremoniously down onto the pavement. They looked at one another, fear clear in their faces, then rushed to the van, jumping in and closing the doors behind them. A moment later the engine roared to life.

"What are you doing?" screamed the leader. "Get back out here! Get him in the van!"

But his cries were for nothing. And the vehicle soon sped away. Connor let out a silent cheer. Now it was one on one. Even in his weakened condition, he liked those odds. Too bad his gun was back in the car—that would have made it almost easy.

"Aw hell," the leader was growling, watching the van disappear around a corner. Then he turned back to Grandpa. "If you want something done right, you have to do it yourself."

He reached into his pocket and pulled out the pistol. "Guess I have no choice now."

This was it! Connor dove in, throwing himself on top of the man. The gun went off with a loud bang and for a split second Connor thought the guy had missed, that the bullet had rang out into thin air. But then he felt a warmness soak his arm, followed by a stabbing pain. No such luck.

But he had no time to consider the extent of his wound. Instead, using his good arm, he managed to wrestle the gun from the mercenary's grip, tossing it away. Then he clamped his fingers around the man's neck, squeezing as hard as he could. The man struggled, kicking and gasping, but Connor had him well pinned.

"This is for Trinity!" he growled, digging his thumbs into the man's sunken flesh. "This is for my dad!" He dug in harder, finding himself oddly enjoying the terrified bulge in the man's eyes.

"Connor, stop! You're going to kill him!"

He felt a hand grab his injured arm and he screamed in agony as the pain exploded all over again. But the jolt was enough to break the spell. He loosened his grip, looking up to see Trinity's grandfather looming above him, a scared but determined look on his wrinkled face.

"Come on," he hissed. "We have to get out of here."

"Wait," Connor said, his soldier training conquering his raging emotions. "I need to get information from him first." Ignoring his throbbing head, he plunged into the unconscious man's mind, gasping at what he found inside.

It was ugly—black and decrepit and rank. Smelling of death and decay. The Dracken had evidently chosen their mercenaries well. There was no pity in this man, no sense of humanity. If he had ever lived and loved and hoped and dreamed, all of that had died out a long time ago.

The ugliness made Connor's stomach turn, but still he pressed on, crawling through the darkness until he finally reached the small nugget of information he needed. He yanked hard, grabbing it and securing it into his own consciousness. Only then did he allow himself to pull back. Once he was out, his stomach wrenched and he vomited, the ugliness spewing out in black pools onto the pavement.

He looked up, staring blankly at Grandpa, all his energy expended. The old man grabbed his good arm. "Come on," he pleaded. "I can hear sirens. You'll be no good to her if they lock you up."

Connor forced himself to his feet. He glanced at his arm, horrified at the blood soaking through his shirt. Cradling it against his chest, he ran after Grandpa, back toward their car and away from the scene of the crime.

When they reached the outskirts of town, Connor finally allowed himself a much-needed breath. His arm throbbed, his head felt thick and dizzy. He was losing too much blood, he realized vaguely.

"We need to get you to a hospital," Trinity's grandfather said, glancing over at him with concerned eyes. He didn't look in much better shape than Connor felt. His nose had swollen to twice its size and blood had crusted on his unshaven chin. They made quite a pair, he thought grimly.

"I'll be all right," he assured the older man, reaching into his bag and pulling out his precious burn salve. In addition to soothing burns, it did a good job of closing wounds and preventing infection. He winced as he forced himself to smear the salve over the spot where the bullet had hit him. Thankfully, it appeared to have gone right through. He wouldn't have to dig it from his skin.

"I'm sorry, Connor," Grandpa said, watching him with dismay clear on his face. "I should have never taken off on you like that. I was just so hopeful that they really knew where she was."

"They knew," Connor replied grimly, relaxing against the back of the seat. The burn salve was doing its job and the pain was thankfully subsiding a bit. "Believe me, they knew. And now, thanks to you, so do we."

Chapter Thirty-Two

A re you there, girl?"
Caleb had to duck as he entered the low-ceilinged cave, narrowly missing a hanging stalactite. Blinking, he peered into the darkness, searching for something Fred shaped.

"Come out, come out, wherever you are."

He took another few cautious steps, careful not to step in a hole. Even here in the Nether, where dragons no longer had to worry about predators, the beasts gravitated toward hard-to-reach places—preferring dark, dank crannies to flower-strewn fields where they could more easily stretch out and worship the sun. Lingering instinct from the old days, perhaps, when they would hoard huge troves of treasure, deep in their lairs, safe from even the cleverest of thieves. Some dragons—the really old ones—still kept the tradition, manifesting shiny gems and glittering gold anytime they had the spark. Fred, on the other hand, preferred treasures of a more edible sort.

A bellowing roar echoed through the cave and a moment later Caleb found himself almost knocked over by a rampaging beast. *His* rampaging beast. He laughed as a solid snout rammed into his chest, tickling him as it sniffed at his various pockets.

"Hey, hey! Put that thing away!" he protested, playfully shoving the dragon's nose. "You could hurt someone with that, you know."

Fred snorted and twin puffs of smoke twined from her nostrils as she gave Caleb an offended look. He rolled his eyes. *Dragons.* "Don't you even think about getting huffy with me," he scolded, wagging his finger at her, "or you won't get what I brought you."

Fred's eyes widened and she stumbled backward so fast it made Caleb laugh out loud. "Thought so," he said with a nod. As Fred watched him, he closed his eyes, envisioning a large chunk of horsemeat—one of his dragon's favorite foods. (Not that Fred was all that picky.) At first nothing appeared and he could hear his dragon's impatient panting beside him.

"Hang on, girl," he promised, sucking in a breath and pushing again. "Just one more…"

The horsemeat fell from the cave's ceiling—smaller than he'd aimed for and a bit rotten from the smell, but Fred didn't seem to mind. She attacked the flesh with gusto, smacking her lips in appreciation between bites. Once it had been completely consumed, she gave Caleb a baleful look, batting her eyes and lolling her giant tongue.

"Are you kidding me?" he scolded, forcing his laughter at bay. "That last manifest nearly killed me. Have some mercy on your poor Guardian. Besides, you keep eating like that and you're going to get fat."

It wasn't strictly true—in the Nether, Fred could look svelte or swollen, depending on her mood—but Caleb had been harassing her about her caloric intake since they'd first met in the real world and old habits died hard.

"Are you ready to fly?" he asked. Flying was the one thing Fred liked better than eating. Or at least she pursued both with equal gusto.

Sure enough, the teal dragon bobbed her head excitedly. Then she glanced behind Caleb, her golden eyes searching.

He looked over his shoulder. "What?"

Did you bring my namesake?

Caleb groaned loudly. *Not again.* "Are you going to ask me that every time I come visit you?" he admonished. "I'm beginning to get a complex. And she's not your namesake anymore either. We talked about this. You're called Fred now, remember?"

Fred is a silly name for a dragon.

"Well, you're a pretty silly dragon, so it works out just fine," Caleb retorted, feeling his face heat. He hadn't been prepared when Trinity had asked him his dragon's name back at Dracken Headquarters and had blurted out the first thing that came to mind. Because the alternative—to admit whom he'd really named his dragon after—well, that would be beyond embarrassing. "In any case, no, I didn't bring her. Sorry I'm not enough for you."

He meant it as a joke, but the words came out more bitterly than he'd intended. Fred seemed to hesitate. *You like her. You're happy when she's here.*

Ugh. Maybe going off the food conversation had been a mistake. He closed his eyes, tried to manifest something else for his dragon to eat, but it was no use. His spark had gone out. And it would be hours, maybe days, before it regenerated. Opening his eyes again, he caught Fred giving him a disapproving look, but brushed her off.

"Look, Trin has more important things going on right now," he told his dragon. "She and Emmy have a lot of training to get through. You remember how brutal training can be. Trin doesn't have time to come to the Nether. She's got things to do in the real world."

And you do not?

Caleb flinched at Fred's pointed question. Seriously, for a ridiculous, food-obsessed reptile, his dragon could also be startlingly perceptive at times. But what could he say? That he was hiding out in the Nether to avoid the mess he'd created in real life?

He should have never kissed her. That was his first mistake and probably the stupidest thing he could have done. She was a legend. A leader. The Fire Kissed, for God's sake! She deserved a match of the highest order. A real man with character and integrity and power.

And what was he? Nothing. Nobody. Just a petty criminal from Strata-D—not even his own family wanted him around. He wasn't good enough for someone like her. He wasn't even worthy of licking her boots to clean them.

And yet…

His mind flashed back to her hands, gripping him tightly and pulling him close. Her heart matching the erratic beats of his own. The look in her eyes, the catch of breath at her throat, her soft, silky skin melting against him—he'd lost himself in the fantasy of it all. And as her lips clung to his as if her life depended on it, he'd allowed himself—for one precious moment—to believe she could see beyond what everybody else saw. Just once, he wanted someone to look up to him.

Instead her dark eyes gazed upon him with apology. With…pity.

Anger rose as he remembered that look. Shards of glass, tearing into his soul as she yanked herself away. She'd had excuses, many, many excuses. But the truth remained the same. She only felt sorry for him. The boy with the dead dragon.

He scowled, digging his nails into his palms. Well, she could keep her pity. He was doing just fine on his own. And as for Fred? Well, who cared that she was technically deceased? He could see her anytime he wanted to here in the Nether.

Not anytime. Not if you value your health.

Caleb grunted, waving off his dragon's warning. But deep down he had to admit she was probably right. The extended trips to the Nether were taking a massive toll on him. In fact, he'd hardly recognized his face in the mirror that morning. Sallow skin, sunken eyes, cracked lips. And that was just on the surface. He didn't want to think about his hands shaking uncontrollably. His heart palpitating far too fast. His mind unable to focus on something as simple as tying his shoes.

He'd told himself he'd take the day off. Spend some time in the real world, regain his strength. But then he ran into Trinity in the corridor. Saw the haunted look in her eyes. Remembered all the things he'd said the night of the party— his desperate attempt to save some sort of face. And before he knew it, he was palming the sapphire.

He knew he had to be careful. While a single trip to the Nether would leave you with a headache, extended trips could cause your brain to go into permanent stasis. You'd still be alive—your heart would still beat and blood would still flow through your veins—but your mind would be gone, on a one-way trip to Dragon Land, never to return.

And while sometimes the idea didn't sound half bad, Caleb knew he could never allow himself to succumb. Darius was counting on him. He'd seen something worthy in the rat he'd plucked from the gutter. How could he let his mentor down?

His ruminations were interrupted as he felt Fred twitch. "What's wrong, girl?" he asked, snapping back to the present. But before the dragon could answer, he saw for himself.

His brother was dressed in formal Academy attire—black pants, white shirt, crimson jacket, adorned with scattered medals and pins, each representing one of the Dragon Hunter's kills. Caleb couldn't help but wonder which shiny medal Connor had been awarded for slaying poor Fred, and in a moment of rage considered ripping each and every one of them off of his brother's chest.

You think they make you a hero, he thought bitterly, *but you're nothing more than a killer.*

Forcing his anger aside, he stepped between his dragon and his brother, squaring his shoulders and lifting his chin. He knew Connor couldn't hurt Fred in the Nether—he'd already done all he could to his poor dragon in real life—but he felt a bristle of protectiveness all the same.

"How did you find me?" he asked, not bothering with pleasantries. But even as he voiced the question, he knew. Too much time in the Nether had obviously weakened him, made him easier to locate by those with the gift. Another reason it was good that Trin was spending all her time in the real world. The last thing she needed was for his brother to track her down. "And what do you want?"

"I wanted to congratulate you," Connor said simply, ducking under the cave's low entrance and strolling toward him with deceptively casual steps. As he drew closer in the dim light, Caleb got a better look at the Dragon Hunter, raising his eyebrows in surprise. Connor looked in worse shape than he did—evidently he'd been power-using his gift as well these past few days. Though, of course, his reason was very different than Caleb's—seeking to find Trinity, not escape her.

"Congratulations from you?" he drawled, keeping his face neutral. No need to let his brother see his upset. "Have pigs finally learned to fly?"

"No, but I understand dragons have. Or one particular dragon in this case."

Connor spoke lightly, easily, but Caleb could detect the flicker of annoyance cross his brother's otherwise smooth face. And suddenly he realized why. He must have found out somehow that the egg had hatched. That he had lost. The great Dragon Hunter had been defeated at last. And not only defeated, but defeated by his own no-good, Strata-D criminal twin! A smile tugged at the corners of Caleb's lips.

"Don't thank me," he replied smoothly, running a hand along Fred's long neck. "It was your girl who did it all."

Connor's eyes narrowed. "That's the worst part, you know. You couldn't have just gone and done this stupid thing on your own. You had to drag poor Trinity down with you."

"Oh, I'm sorry, should I have left her behind to make it easier for you to kill her?"

"I wouldn't have had to kill her if you'd just left the flecking egg. It could have gone down the volcano and everything would have been fine. No one would have had to die."

247

"Um, yeah, except for the entire world," Caleb reminded him. "The human race needs dragons to survive. Otherwise we'll be the ones going extinct."

Connor groaned loudly. "Is that how the Dracken are playing it now? That they're on some mission to save the world?" He shook his head. "Seriously, Caleb, how could you believe that? You saw what dragons are capable of. You saw what that one did to our own father."

"What, defend herself against a man who was trying to slaughter her for no reason?" Caleb asked. "Face it, Connor. Our father wasn't a hero. He was just a money-grubbing mercenary, killing for coin."

"And what's Darius willing to kill for?" Connor shot back. "What does he hope to gain from striking down a poor, helpless old man?" He screwed up his face. "Trinity's grandfather barely escaped with his life, you know."

"What are you talking about?" Caleb blurted, against his better judgment. "Trinity's grandfather is dead." His brother was starting to piss him off. "And it's pretty obvious who killed him."

To his annoyance, Connor started to laugh. "Oh, so they're trying to pin it on me, are they? I should have known." He rolled his eyes. "Well, you can call off the lynch mob, seeing as he's very much alive."

Caleb stared at him, a strange flurry of emotions hitting him hard and fast. Joy at the idea of Trinity's beloved grandpa being alive; fury at Connor for trying to blame his friends for his attempted murder.

"You're lying," he stammered, trying to catch his breath.
He's not.

Caleb whirled around. Fred was still standing behind him. The dragon gave him a hard look.

Listen. You know he's not.

"But why would Darius do something like that?" Caleb demanded, turning away from the dragon. "He wants Trinity on his side."

"Exactly. He needs her," Connor agreed. "If she leaves, his whole operation is botched for good. So why not take out the one thing she cares about more than anything in the world? Leave her completely dependent on the Dracken with no place left to go."

Caleb frowned. He wanted to tell his brother that he was crazy. That Darius was good and kind and had rescued him when he had nowhere else to turn. But that would just prove Connor's point, wouldn't it? Everyone here—every Potential they had—was orphaned or otherwise alone in the world, with no ties to their previous lives. That way Darius never had to worry about divided loyalties; no one had anything left to lose.

But Trin was different. She hadn't come here of her own free will. She hadn't needed a rescue. She had a life outside these walls. And as long as she did, she could never fully become part of the Dracken. Not in the way Darius wanted her to anyway.

He looked up at his brother. "Why are you telling me this?"

Connor leveled his eyes on him. "Because Trinity deserves to know the truth. And since she's shut me out, you're the only one who can tell her." He shrugged. "But don't take my word for it. Meet me in Tucson. See her grandpa yourself and hear what he has to say." He paused, then added, "You say you care about her. Well, now's your chance to prove it."

Chapter Thirty-Three

"Argh! That was so close! Try again, Em! I know you can do it!"

Trinity reached down, palming the tennis ball, then stretching to full height again, preparing for another throw. Emmy hovered a few feet away, her wings beating madly at the air, her eager eyes glued to the ball. Trin could barely believe how big the dragon had gotten, going from the size of a baby bird to a plump, full-grown Chihuahua in just a few days. She supposed it wasn't too surprising, though, given the dragon's never-ending appetite. Caleb had told her dragons would eat until they exploded; Trinity was now beginning to believe it.

The little dragon did a showy flip, then tossed Trin an impatient look, once again eyeing the ball in her hand. Trinity let the ball fly, watching it spiral high into the open-air court-yard of the west wing. "Have at it, Emmy!" she crowed. "Go, go, go!"

Before Emmy's birth, if you'd asked Trinity what being a Dragon Guardian meant, she probably would have guessed it was just hop on a dragon and hope for the best—as she had with Caleb in the Nether. But in real life, it turned out, there was a lot more to it than that. The Dracken had created a highly regulated training regimen—one, they insisted, all Guardians go through. From offensive maneuvers to healing arts, defensive tactics to stealth operations—the program covered it all. It was like training to be all the character classes in a Dungeons and Dragons handbook at once—all with the aid of an actual dragon.

The green dragon's face was awash with concentration, her eyes drilling into the falling ball. She pulled back her head, waited for just the right moment, then opened her mouth.

Whoosh! The flames shot from deep in her throat, hurtling through the air and smacking the tennis ball square on. The ball burst into flames before falling harmlessly to the ground in a puff of black smoke. Trinity let out a loud whoop of triumph, pride gushing through her.

"Yeah, baby! That's how it's done!" She held out her hand as the dragon flew by, slapping her palm against an outstretched wing. Emmy squeaked in excitement, dropping to the ground and doing a little victory lap around the still-smoking tennis ball. Trinity couldn't help but giggle.

"You're pretty proud of yourself, aren't you?" she teased.

Out of the corner of her eye, she caught the guard making his move, crossing the courtyard, then disappearing through the door at the far end of the room. She glanced at her watch, her smile fading. *Right on time.* She turned to Emmy.

Okay, we've got five minutes. Let's do this.

She ran to the edge of the courtyard to the west wall, where a colorful tapestry, depicting a dragon fighting a medieval knight, hung from floor to ceiling. To a casual onlooker, the wall would seem solid and seamless behind its flashy decor. But Trin had studied Aiko's blueprints and knew there had once been a door, covered up by drywall when the Dracken remodeled. A door that led to a series of twisty passageways which employees had once used to transport trash or receive deliveries. From what Trin could determine from the blueprints, these back hallways culminated at a large underground garage, where a single elevator offered an unguarded exit—a chance to escape.

Trin pulled back the tapestry, scanning the blank wall, running her fingers over its smooth surface. She'd been timing the patrols all day and had calculated five minutes between shift changes. Which meant they didn't have time to get this wrong.

It should be right about here, she told the dragon. *Give it a try.*

Emmy pulled back her little head, letting loose a long, steady stream of fire. The drywall cracked and hissed under the heat but soon melted away, revealing, to Trinity's excitement, the outline of a door underneath. She beat out the flames with the emergency fire blanket they'd given her for training purposes, then turned to her dragon.

Good work! Now let's get out of here.

As she grabbed chunks of charred drywall, ripping them away to unblock the door, she wondered what the Potentials would think when they realized she'd gone. She felt a little guilty, to be honest, just taking off without even saying good-bye. They'd been so nice to her, so welcoming. But she couldn't trust them to stay quiet if they learned of her plans and she really couldn't blame them either. Their entire lives had been constructed around the idea that Emmy would stay and grow and hatch baby dragons that they would be assigned to take care of. Without Emmy, there would be no dragon program. No reason for them to remain. She didn't want to think about where they'd end up if the Dracken turned them out on the streets.

But she had no choice. She had to know for sure whether Darius was telling the truth. If her grandpa was really dead. And if he was, well, at least this way she'd get a chance to attend his funeral. To give him a proper good-bye. Maybe after all was said and done she'd consider coming back here to resume her training. But under her rules this time. She refused to be made a prisoner. Even if it was for her "own good."

Trinity studied the door. It appeared as if its handle had been removed when it had been covered up, meaning it wouldn't be easy to pull it open. She bit her lower lip, glancing at her watch. They only had about two minutes left.

Try to pry open the door, she told Emmy. *Use your claws.*

She still wasn't exactly sure what she was going to do with her dragon once they were out in the wild. It wasn't as if Emmy could exactly blend in. And at the rate she was growing, she couldn't be a house pet for long. But when Trin had floated the idea of the dragon remaining here, where it was safe, Emmy refused to even consider it.

I go where you go. We are destined…

Deep inside, Trinity was relieved to hear it. The little dragon was a part of her now. She needed Emmy as much as Emmy needed her.

Come on, she urged her dragon. *We almost have it.*

The sound of a door slamming behind her interrupted their progress. She whirled around, startled, to see a lone figure entering the far end of the courtyard. Horrified, she yanked the curtain down over the gaping hole, obscuring it from view. *What is he doing?* she thought furiously. This place was supposed to be off limits while she was training except for the regular patrols. *Who would dare to interrupt the Fire Kissed at work?*

Then she realized exactly who.

Caleb.

Her heart fluttered involuntarily in her chest. She hadn't spoken to him since the night she'd learned of her grandpa's death—the night he'd been so cruel. Now, as he approached, she couldn't help but notice his gaunt face, his hollow, shadowed eyes. He looked terrible, she realized, as if he hadn't slept in weeks. And was his arm wrapped in some kind of sling?

"What happened to you?" she asked, forcing her voice to stay casual as she gestured to his arm. "Some girl get a little too feisty in the Nether?" She said it as a joke but caught a tinge of bitterness thread through her voice all the same.

Caleb didn't reply. Instead, he walked straight up to her, coming too close, invading her space. She found herself trembling, her heart pounding in confusion, as he took her hands in his and squeezed them tight. What was he doing? Desperately, she attempted to clear her mind, force it into blankness so he couldn't discover what she was hiding just beyond the curtain.

"What you do want?" she demanded angrily. "I don't have time to—"

She stopped short as her eyes met his own—eyes as clear blue as the sky on a cloudless day. Eyes she'd recognize anywhere.

Her face clouded with confusion. "You're not Caleb," she gasped. "You're—"

Connor clamped his mouth over hers, silencing her with a

hard, long kiss just as the guard stepped back into the room. She struggled to free herself, but his hands closed around her forearms. As his lips moved against hers, she felt a voice sweep through her consciousness.

Look under your bed. I left you something.

Then he released her, pushing her away. Out of the corner of her eye she caught the guard giving them an amused look before continuing his rounds. She stared at the Dragon Hunter, unable to speak, unable to move. What was he doing here? Had he come to rescue her?

Or finish her once and for all?

Chapter Thirty-Four

Trinity ran to her room, Emmy flying high above her. When she got there, she dismissed her maid and shut the door, locking it behind her. Dropping to her knees, she peered under the bed, pulse beating erratically as she wondered what Connor could have left for her there. Her eyes widened in disbelief as she pulled out a small laptop accompanied by a pair of headphones.

"What the...?" she trailed off, walking the computer over to her desk and setting it down. With shaking hands, she lifted the cover, bringing it to life. She gasped as her eyes fell upon the sole program sitting on the desktop.

Fields of Fantasy. With the expansion pack already installed.

"Oh my God," she whispered, glancing up at Emmy. Of all the possible things she could have imagined, this was definitely not it. The dragon looked down at the game with mild curiosity, her eyes narrowing at the splash screen depicting a knight slaying a dragon. She gave a disapproving snort.

"Sorry, this game does have its share of dragoncide," Trin admitted with a rueful grin. "But it's pretty awesome all the same." She stared at the screen, elated yet confused as hell. Why had Connor left this for her? Surely it was more than a late Christmas present.

"Guess there's only one way to find out." She looked up at Emmy. "Wait for me outside," she said. "Sound the alarm if someone comes." She wasn't sure what the Dracken would do if they found her with an unauthorized laptop, but she didn't want to find out.

The dragon tossed her head in agreement and Trinity opened the door to allow her to exit. Then she returned to the laptop. It had been rigged, she noticed, to some kind of wireless hot-spot device, giving her Internet access even in this dead zone of a mall. Very clever. With trembling fingers, she somehow managed to log in with her character and waited for the game to load. The expansion pack had a spanking new intro scene that she was desperate to watch, but she forced herself to click through it, not wanting to waste any time.

A moment later, her Elven mage StarrLight appeared on the screen, exactly where she'd left her: dancing on the table in the middle of the town tavern, scantily dressed and double-fisting two large mugs of beer. Trin couldn't help but laugh. The last time she'd played was with Caitlin, who passionately believed the game's only redeeming quality was its hook-up potential. Trin had never had the heart to tell her that the majority of the strapping elves she flirted shamelessly with were probably actually forty-year-old men living in their mothers' basements.

Quickly, she did a search for her friend.

>>HotElfChick69 is not online.

She sighed. That would have been too easy.

She turned her attention back to the situation at hand,

directing her character to jump off the table and walk out of the tavern. *Now what?* she wondered. What did Connor want her to do?

>> *Stegosaurus65 has come online.*

Wait, what? Trinity scrolled back up the dialog box at the bottom of the screen to make sure she'd read that right. At the same moment, a big, burly, and very familiar-looking level one barbarian walked out of the tavern. Stegosaurus65— she'd recognize him anywhere.

"But that's impossible," she whispered. Stegosaurus65 was the character she'd helped her grandpa create last year when he'd been curious to see for himself the game that took up so much of his granddaughter's time. He'd lasted all of ten minutes before declaring that all the colors and sounds were making him dizzy and he'd never logged on again.

>>*Stegosaurus65 invites you to join his party.*

She swallowed hard, then hit accept, grabbing the headphones off the desk and shoving them over her ears.

"Um, hello?" she said through the microphone. "Who is this?"

She waited, breath lodged in her throat, for his reply. As the moment stretched on, she tried to prepare herself for inevitable disappointment and—

"Is this thing on?" There was a rapping on the microphone. "Goddamn futuristic technology…"

"Grandpa!" she screeched, then clamped a hand over her

mouth, glancing worriedly at her closed door. The last thing she needed was to get caught now. "Is that you?"

"Trinity?" His voice was so loud she had to turn down the volume. "Speak up, girl! I can't hear you over this blasted thing."

She laughed even as the tears streamed down her cheeks. "It's me, Grandpa," she told him as loud as she dared, while she watched the barbarian on the screen stumble into a tree and get stuck in its branches. *What a noob*, she thought, her heart soaring with affection. *What a total noob.*

"Where are you?" she asked. "They told me you were dead." Her hands fell to the keyboard and she instructed StarrLight to give Stegosaurus a hug. It wasn't the same as a real-life one, but at the moment she'd take what she could get. The whole thing was just so surreal—she could barely believe it was happening.

"Please. You think I'd go off and croak, and let you have all the fun raising the world's last dragon?" he retorted gruffly, his voice cracking at the edges. On the screen, his barbarian broke out into a jig. She laughed and joined him, feeling totally silly yet totally happy too. Seriously—best game ever.

"I'm so sorry," she whispered, then repeated herself louder so he could hear her. "I should have believed you from the beginning."

Her grandpa's voice was firm. "You believe now. That's all that matters."

He was right, she thought, as she looked around the colorful town square, drinking in all the familiar sights and sounds. It was funny—though the Dracken had created real-life accommodations made of her wildest fantasies, this simple video game felt a thousand times more luxurious.

>>*ConnorTheDragonHunter has joined the party.*

"Pretty clever, huh?" Connor's voice broke in through her headphones, just as a dashing blond warrior wielding a two-handed sword walked onto the screen. Trinity's heart melted a little at the sight of him. Talk about a knight in shining armor…

"It was your grandpa's idea," the dragon hunter continued. "I needed to talk to you and you'd blocked me from your mind. But your grandfather knew you wouldn't be able to resist logging into your precious game." He walked over and joined Stegosaurus in his dance.

"He knows me too well," she said with a groan. She wondered where he was now—was he still inside Dracken Headquarters? She glanced at the door, both longingly and fearfully. A part of her wanted to see him so badly, but the other was afraid of what he'd do. He'd obviously seen Emmy in the courtyard. He knew she'd hatched. And if Caleb and the Dracken were to be believed, that meant he was here for one thing and one thing only.

"Why are you here, Connor?" she asked, deciding there was no time to be coy. "What do you want from me?"

Connor's knight stopped dancing. "What do you mean?"

"Don't play dumb," she snapped. "I know all about your little mission to save the world. Specifically the part where you were planning to kill me if things didn't go your way."

"Wait, what?" her grandpa broke in. "What are you talking about? Connor's there to rescue you, not kill you."

"He probably told you that, Grandpa, but that was never his true mission," she said in a flat voice. "Was it, Connor?"

She waited for him to deny it. To tell her that Caleb had been lying. That he'd made it all up just to get her on his side. But Connor only sighed deeply. "Yes," he said at last. "That was my mission."

She glared at the screen—at his avatar—wanting to be furious, but instead feeling only hurt and betrayal clawing at her insides. "You kissed me," she seethed. "You made me think we were on the same team. I trusted you. I saved your life from those government agents. And the whole time you were just leading me on! To get me to trust you so you could cut me down when the time was right."

"It wasn't like that!"

"Then what was it like?" she demanded. "I think I deserve to know the truth."

"You'd better start talking," her grandpa added, the level one barbarian stepping in front of the knight, his massive arms crossing over his beefy chest. "Now."

The knight nodded, sinking down onto a nearby bench. "You have to understand," he began in a low voice. "When I first got my orders, I didn't know anything about you except what I'd learned at the academy. They taught us you were evil, that you'd set dragons on the world. They told us you were the one responsible for all the destruction. For millions of deaths." She could hear his hard swallow in her ears. "For my father's death."

Trinity cringed. In all her self-righteous anger, she'd conveniently forgotten about her future self's role in this whole mess. She, with the help of her Dracken friends, had inadvertently released monsters upon the world, destroying everything Connor loved. She supposed she could understand why he might be a little reluctant to confide in her.

But still…

"It's a bit harsh to judge me for something I haven't even done yet," she pointed out, "something that I might not even do."

"You're right," he said simply. "You're absolutely right. And when I finally did meet you—when I started to get to know who you were—I realized the history texts had to be wrong. You weren't some cold, world-destroying monster. You were just an innocent girl who had no idea of the situation she was about to be put into." He sighed. "Do you have any idea how hard it was to know I might have to kill you to save the world, all while you're trying to help me figure out a way to do it?" He paused, then added, "Let's just say suddenly things didn't seem so black and white anymore."

Trinity twisted her mother's ring. "I guess I know what you mean," she admitted. "It was kind of the same—once I met Emmy." She remembered how much she wanted to destroy the egg when she'd first learned of what it was capable of. To snuff out Emmy's life force before she even had the chance to be born. It was inconceivable to think of now. And maybe Connor felt the same way about her.

"It doesn't help that I've had to spend the last week sharing hotel rooms with this old guy," Connor added, his character tossing his head toward the barbarian. "Having to hear how amazing you are. How smart and dedicated and loyal you are. How hard you work every day to keep him and his museum afloat. Blah, blah, blah."

"Well, it's true!" Grandpa blustered over the headphones. "I owe this little girl everything."

Trinity stared at the screen, tears welling in her eyes. All this time she'd assumed her guardian had been too wrapped up in his own fantasy world to recognize any of the work she'd put in behind the scenes. But he'd noticed. He'd been paying attention all along. A choking sound escaped her throat.

"I love you, Grandpa," she whispered, then repeated it louder so he could hear.

"I love you too, sweetheart," he said. "And I'm not going to let anyone touch a hair on your pretty little head." He huffed. "I am Stegg the Barbarian after all!" His character beat his chest and roared.

She laughed. "Yes. Very frightening." Then she sobered. "So what's the deal, Connor? You still haven't told us what you plan to do."

She heard his deep sigh over the headphones. "I honestly don't know," he said. "The thought of allowing dragons to exist in the world terrifies me more than you could ever know. But at the same time, how can I go and mercilessly cut someone down in cold blood who has done nothing wrong?" He paused, then added, "And not just someone. *You*."

His breath hitched and Trinity felt her heart beat a little faster. She suddenly wished she wasn't in the game but right in front of Connor in real life, so she could look into his eyes and see the truth that she so desperately wanted to see.

"I always prided myself on following orders," he continued in a rush, "never questioning what they told me to do. But what if they were wrong? What if there is another way? Should I blindly stumble on because some people from an alternate future once told me to?" He cleared his throat. "I can't. I just can't. Maybe that makes me a terrible soldier. Maybe they should have never sent me here in the first place. But I'm here now. And I think it's time to start making my own rules. Find a way to make this all work—where no one innocent has to die."

His words were passionate, his tone fierce, sending chills down Trinity's spine. Did he really mean what he said? Could they really have a chance? "What about Emmy?"

"Well, I'm not likely to let her sleep at the foot of my bed or lick my face anytime soon," he said dryly, "but I'm willing to give her a chance. Most historians claim it was the hybrids that caused all the trouble. If this is true, then it should be okay for Emmy to exist—as long as we can get her away from the Dracken."

"But wait," Trinity hesitated. "Can't the Dracken help us? They've got everything you'd need to raise a dragon here, not to mention a good hiding spot."

Silence fell over her headphones. "What?" she demanded, a cold chill rising inside of her. "What aren't you telling me?"

"Trinity, honey," Grandpa interjected at last, "the Dracken tried to kill me."

She froze, staring at the screen in horror. She suddenly realized that in her joy of seeing her grandpa still alive, she'd neglected to connect the dots in her mind. Darius must have doctored that newspaper, assuming the deed had already been done. And worse, he'd tried to pin the whole thing on Connor to make sure she'd never trust him again.

He'd been so sympathetic. So willing to comfort her when she'd fallen into his arms. Ready to hold a memorial service even—to honor a man he himself had ordered killed. She squeezed her hands into fists. "God, I should have had Emmy flambé that bastard when I had the chance."

Connor's knight put a comforting hand on her character's shoulder. "While I'd definitely be the first to toast marshmallows on *that* bonfire," he assured her, "there's no time for that now. I had to trick my poor brother so I could get inside and give you the laptop. It won't take him long to figure out what I did and return. We can't be here when he does."

Trinity's heart squeezed as she thought of Caleb. "He isn't…" she started, then trailed off. "I mean, he's not like…"

"He didn't know about your grandfather," Connor told her gently, "which means he wasn't in on Darius's plans."

Trin let out a sigh of relief. That was something at least. "I'm pretty sure the rest of the kids here—the Potentials—aren't either. They're so nice. They truly believe they've been brought here to save the world." Her heart ached at the thought.

"We'll figure out what to do about them later," Connor said. "First we need to find a way to get out of here. I could walk right in, pretending to be my brother. But I can't exactly waltz you and Emmy out the front door."

"No, but we can take the back," Trinity broke in excitedly. "There are back passageways that run along the entire mall. The Dracken had them all sealed off—I don't think many people here even know they exist. But I was able to find a door in the west courtyard that leads to a parking garage underground where an elevator can take us outside." She paused. "In fact, I was about to head down there and make my escape when you showed up."

"You were?" Connor's character face-palmed. "And here I thought I was your knight in shining armor coming to your aid."

She smirked. "Please. This princess can save herself," she declared. She paused, then added, "But I am glad you're here all the same."

Chapter Thirty-Five

The door to the parking garage should be right around here somewhere," Trinity whispered, consulting her blueprints before beckoning for Connor to follow her down the long, dark hallway that wound parallel to the mall. Emmy flapped along behind them, her eyes darting to every corner, her ears pricked for signs of trouble. The passageways hadn't been used for some time, judging from the dust and cobwebs, and it was all Trin could do to keep from sneezing and giving their position away. The walls were so thin that at times they could hear muffled conversations going on behind them, and Trin realized it would take only the slightest noise for the Dracken to discover that they had rats in their walls.

The passageway rounded a corner and the three of them stopped to take a peek. Sure enough, as the blueprints had indicated, the corridor dead-ended in a set of tall double doors rising before them, banded with iron. What the blueprints hadn't been able to tell them, however, was that these particular doors were guarded by two armed men. Trinity's heart fluttered with apprehension as she exchanged a look with Connor. What were they doing here? The Dracken must have left another entrance open when they did their remodel.

But why? Was there something hidden behind these doors besides freedom? Something worth guarding?

She looked down at the blueprints, searching for another way out. But this was it—the only way into the underground parking garage and their only hope for escape. They'd have to take out the guards somehow—quickly, quietly, as to not alert anyone on the other side of the walls. At least from the blueprints, she knew the store behind them was being used as unoccupied storage space, so it was unlikely anyone was in close proximity, but a gunshot would definitely be heard throughout the mall. There had to be another way. But how? Walk up to the guards and ask nicely?

You're going to have to push them, Connor told her silently. *I'd help you, but it took all the spark I had left just to get inside and get you that laptop. I'm completely drained.*

She let out a slow breath, thinking back to the cop she'd unknowingly pushed on Christmas morning. It had practically killed her. But what choice did she have? They had to get past the guards somehow.

Emmy can help you, Connor added, *if you combine your spark.*

Right. She nodded. That was one of the things they'd been working on during training—pooling their energies to become twice as strong. But still, practice was one thing. Two heavily armed real-life men was quite another. If she failed...

Connor reached out, squeezing her hand in his and giving her an encouraging look. *You can do this,* he assured her. *You're the Fire Kissed, after all.*

She rolled her eyes. *Oh God, don't you start all that too,* she moaned. But inside she was secretly pleased. Connor believed in her. He trusted her with his life. She wasn't about to let him down.

Okay, she declared. *Here goes nothing. You ready, Emmy?*

She reached out to her dragon, finding her with her mind. Emmy responded immediately, melding her spark with her mistress's. Soon the whirling ball of their combined energy spun and sparkled at the front of them, seeming as big as a planet. Trin grinned at the dragon, her confidence rising.

Oh yeah, baby. We gotz mad skillz. Just try to resist us!

Connor gave her a dry look. *Um, let's not overdo it.*

Quiet, peanut gallery, she scolded. *Just count us down.*

In three…two…one…

She pushed. *Let us in. Let us in. LET US IN.*

The all-too-familiar nausea washed over her like a tidal wave. Trin winced, closing her eyes until the initial feeling passed. Forcing in a shaky breath, she looked up at Connor in question. *Did it work?*

Only one way to find out. Connor motioned for her to stay put as he rounded the corner.

"Hey, guys!" he greeted the guards casually. "How's it going? I've got some business behind these doors. Do you mind letting me in?"

The guards looked at him, then at each other. "Sorry," the first one said. "Darius left specific instructions that no one is allowed to pass through these doors."

Connor rolled his eyes in a perfect mimic of his brother. "Darius was the one who told me to come here in the first place. So how about it? *Will you let me in?*" He said the words slowly, so Trinity could repeat them with another push.

Let us in. Let us in. Let us in.

The effort almost knocked her off her feet. Yet the guards' expressions didn't change. They didn't step aside. Trinity bit her lower lip, glancing up at Emmy nervously. Why wasn't it working? The strength of their combined push should have had the guards falling over one another trying to be the first to let Connor through. Instead, they seemed completely unmoved.

"Maybe we should give Darius a call," the second guard said, "just to make sure."

Connor snorted. "Yeah, good luck with that," he replied. "I mean, personally I'd rather wake a sleeping bear, but maybe that's just me." His tone was casual and confident, but Trin caught a thread of fear winding through his voice. He obviously knew something was wrong. But what was it?

She searched the guards' faces, praying for even a hint of doubt somewhere in the depths of their eyes. It was then that she realized how young they were. Under their imposing uniforms, they were merely teenage boys, unlike the other guards she'd seen milling about the place. The mercenaries the Dracken had hired were all ex-military—burly and beefy and scarred. These boys were skinny and fresh-faced and...

...not guards at all.

The realization hit her with the force of a ten-ton truck. These weren't guards. They were Potentials. Whatever was behind the door was evidently too secret for mere mercenaries to be entrusted with guarding. Instead, the Dracken had manned it with those who would be resistant to mind manipulation.

Those who could read minds on their own.

Connor, we need to get out of here! she sent. *This isn't going to work.*

If the Potentials read Connor's mind, they would realize everything. They'd sound the alarm. They'd stop their escape. She and Emmy would be captured. Connor would be killed.

She couldn't let that happen.

She squeezed her eyes shut, trying one more time. *Let us go, let us go, LET US GO!*

Icy pain stabbed at her like a thousand icicles boring into her brain. Her legs gave out from under her and she fell to the ground with a crash. But the Potentials remained unaffected, the first one making a move for his transcriber.

"You know what?" Connor broke in with a barking laugh. "Maybe I made a mistake. Maybe I'm at the wrong door." He hastily began to back away. But before he could break free, the second Potential grabbed him by his collar, yanking him toward him, then shoving him face-first into the cement wall. Trin let out a squeak of horror as she caught the blood trickling down Connor's jaw as he staggered, dazed from the blow to his head.

"You aren't going anywhere," the Potential growled. "Not until we check your story out." He pinned Connor to the wall by his neck, then turned to his friend. "Call Darius," he commanded. "Inform him we've got a situation."

The Potential palmed his transcriber, ready to make the call. Trinity's fear threatened to throttle her and she grappled for a solution. In seconds it would all be over—any chance they had to escape gone for good. Desperate, she reached out to her dragon one final time.

Emmy—help!

She meant help with another push, but Emmy evidently had other ideas. The dragon took flight, diving into the room, facing down the Potentials with a fierce, furious expression on her reptilian face. The two men stared up at her, their faces draining of color.

"Oh hell," one of them cried. "It's the dragon."

"Let's get out of here!"

They turned to run, fighting one another to be first out of the room. In their haste, one of them bowled straight into Trinity, knocking her over. As she stumbled, her head slammed against the cement post and she cried out in pain.

Emmy reacted instantly, spinning around, diving after the boys, effectively blocking their paths. Black smoke billowed from her nostrils. Sparks danced on her tongue. The Potentials tried to scramble away but there was no place left to go.

I won't let you hurt her! the dragon roared in Trinity's ears. *I won't let you take her away!*

"No, Emmy!" Trinity croaked.

But it was too late. The beast drew back her head, opened her mouth, and released her flames.

The fire hit them straight on, engulfing them completely before they even had a chance to scream. They fell to the ground, convulsing, writhing—their clothing consumed, their skin blackening to a charred crisp. Black smoke filled the room and the smell of burning flesh permeated the air.

"Oh God," Trin whispered, horrified but unable to look away. "Oh God, no."

But Emmy wasn't done, swooping down on the boys again and again, clawing out their eyes, ripping away swaths of blackened flesh. Trin reached out with her mind, trying desperately to soothe her dragon's frenzy. But Emmy's consciousness was too hot to touch, the rage gripping the creature's mind and refusing to let go.

"Please, Emmy..." she begged, staggering to her feet. "It's okay. You can stop. Please stop."

Vaguely, she realized Connor had ripped off his pack, yanking out his coat. He threw it over the burning boys in an attempt to smother the flames. Sweat dripped down his face as he pulled it away, then brought it down again. Over and over. Again and again—until he finally managed to extinguish the blaze. Breathing heavily, he dropped the coat over the corpses, then leaned against the wall, his face ashen and his expression grim.

Thankfully, Emmy's own internal fire seemed likewise extinguished. The little dragon abandoned her victims and flew back to Trinity, giving her an excited look, as if waiting for congratulations for a job well done. Her claws were caked in flesh and her mouth was dripping with blood. Tears streamed down Trinity's cheeks and the dragon's face clouded with confusion. She looked at her mistress, her big, blue eyes filled with hurt.

Didn't I do good?

Trinity's gaze fell to Emmy's handiwork. Then she leaned over and threw up. Emmy let out a whimper of dismay, then left Trinity, flying back up toward the ceiling, looking down on her with sad, uncomprehending eyes. As if to say, *What did I do wrong?*

"Yeah, sure, dragons aren't dangerous at all," Connor muttered under his breath as he reached down to hook the first corpse's shoulders under his arms. He started dragging it down the hall. "Let's go ahead and unleash them on the world. What could possibly go wrong?"

Chapter Thirty-Six

After hiding the bodies as best they could, they hurried through the double doors, closing and barricading them before rushing down the stairs. The Potentials' deaths had been shockingly quiet considering the level of violence—their throats literally melted before any screams could escape—but neither of them wanted to take any chances that someone had overheard the struggle. The sooner they found the elevator and left the building the better.

Tears pricked at Trin's eyes as she forced her feet to take step after step, her mind relentlessly replaying the nightmare they'd just witnessed. Her supposedly gentle dragon raging completely out of control, tearing through two human lives as if they were tissue paper. She tried to remind herself that the dragon had only been trying to protect her, that she had probably saved their lives. But the fear and horror refused to loosen their grip as she relived the scene of smoke and fire and blackened flesh over and over again. Those two boys weren't evil monsters—they were orphans who had come here to help save the world. And yet they'd died horribly for it instead. What would the others think if they knew what her dragon had done? She imagined the revulsion on Malia's gentle face. The fear in Aiko's eyes. They'd think she was a monster. And maybe they wouldn't be wrong.

And then there was Connor. She glanced at his grim face as he took the stairs two at a time. She'd promised him she could control Emmy. That their shared bond meant the dragon would do as she said. But it was as if Emmy couldn't even hear her when she flew into her protective rage. Was Connor, even now, reconsidering his decision to allow her dragon to live?

To allow *her* to live?

She looked up at Emmy, who was still following though at a slight distance. The dragon had licked the blood and gore clean from her body and once again appeared to be her sweet old self. But when Trin had tried to reach out to her, the dragon refused to answer. She was still hurt by her mistress's obvious disapproval, and try as Trin might to explain what had made her upset, the dragon seemed not to understand. In her mind it was simple: the Fire Kissed had been in trouble. She'd saved her life. How could that possibly be wrong?

After what seemed an eternity, the stairs ended, splitting into three hallways. After consulting the blueprints, Trinity selected the middle one, which was supposed to lead to the parking garage and elevator. They were getting close, she realized with growing excitement. They were almost free.

"We're not out yet," Connor said flatly, as if reading her thoughts. "Let's keep moving."

They crossed the parking lot as quickly as possible, feeling vulnerable and exposed in all the open space. But the place was deserted, and soon they spotted the rickety looking elevator, just as the plans had mapped out. Trin sent up a quick prayer of thanks as she reached out to press the red button embedded in the wall. She heard a rumbling from behind the doors and a moment later they groaned open, revealing the elevator's interior.

"Come on!" she cried excitedly. "Let's get out of here." She waited for Connor and Emmy to enter, then stepped onto the elevator herself. But just as she was about to press the up arrow, a strange trilling sound reverberated through the parking lot.

"What was that?" she asked, looking around uneasily, her skin prickling with goose bumps at the high-pitched sound. It died out for a moment, then came again. Louder this time, bouncing off the walls and repeating back again.

"Forget it," Connor said. "Let's just go."

She heartily agreed, pressing the up arrow and waiting for the doors to close. But just as they were about to slide shut, Emmy shot back out into the parking garage.

"Emmy!" Trin hissed, appalled. "Get back here!"

But, once again, the dragon seemed not to hear her. Instead, she bolted across the empty space in the opposite direction.

"Hell," Trin swore. She dove out of the elevator. She couldn't leave the dragon behind. "Emmy, get back here!"

"Trin! Wait!" Connor tried. She whirled around only to find the elevator doors sliding shut behind her, with Connor still inside. She pressed the red button frantically, but to no avail.

"Connor!" she cried. But the elevator was already shooting upward, sending him to the surface to where her grandpa would be waiting, leaving her behind.

She gritted her teeth. *No big deal*, she tried to tell herself. She'd go grab Emmy and by the time she got back, the elevator would have returned. *Wait for me up top,* she sent to Connor.

I'll be there in a minute. Sighing, she plodded through the parking lot, calling out to her dragon as she went.

Emmy, where are you?

Soon she found herself back where they'd started—at the bottom of the stairs and facing the three identical passage-ways. Her eyes caught a fluttering down the hall to the right and she shook her head as she headed after her errant dragon.

Come on, she scolded Emmy as she raced down the hall to catch up with her. *You can be mad at me later. Right now we have to get out of here.*

She caught up to the dragon at the end of the hall. Emmy was pacing back and forth—her eyes wide and her ears flat-tened against her skull. When she saw Trinity, she gave her a grateful look and took flight, landing on her shoulder, claws digging painfully into her skin.

I guess this means I'm forgiven, Trinity thought wryly.

"What's wrong with you?" she asked, starting to get a little worried. An angry and annoyed Emmy she could deal with. Scared-half-to-death Emmy scared her as well.

Then she heard it—the strange trilling—sounding as if it were coming from behind the wall.

I want to leave, Emmy told her. *I want to go now.* Trin realized the little dragon was literally shaking with fright.

"Why? What do you feel?" she asked, curiosity getting the best of her. "Is there something down here?" She thought back to the two Potentials guarding the door. Was this what the Dracken didn't want anyone to see?

Let's go now, Trin. Let's get out of here.

Trinity was tempted to comply. Connor was waiting—they were this close to a perfect escape. And yet, something compelled her to stay. If the Dracken were up to something, she needed to know what it was. Otherwise, how would they ever be able to stop them from doing it?

"We need to figure out what's making that noise," she told the dragon firmly. "Then we can leave." She walked over and put her ear up against the wall. The noise came again, causing Emmy to squawk in alarm. Trin knocked on the wall with her fist and realized it was hollow.

"There's something behind here." Her fingers danced across the wall, feeling for some kind of handhold or crack. "Give me a little light," she commanded the dragon. Emmy blew out a puff of fire, illuminating the dark corridor. Just for a moment, but it was enough for Trin to locate a lever hidden in the shadows. She wrapped her hand around it and pushed down. There was a groaning sound as the wall sank into the earth, revealing a dark passageway beyond.

"Come on," Trin instructed Emmy with growing excitement. "Let's go."

Emmy hovered at the doorway, shaking her head vehemently. Trin rolled her eyes. "You know, for a fire-breathing killer dragon, you're kind of a scaredy-cat."

But Emmy only plopped down onto the ground, crossing her wings over her chest. Trin gave up. "Have it your way," she told the dragon. "But I'm going in."

She stepped into the passageway. The noises grew louder, the trilling sound now accompanied by pitiful squeaks and moans and cries. Her heart thumped in her chest as she pressed onward, no idea what she was about to uncover. Whatever it was, the Dracken definitely didn't want anyone to see it.

The passage wasn't long, dead-ending at a small wooden

door. Reaching down, she wrapped her hands around its handle and pulled it open. As she stepped into the darkened room, a sharp pain dug into her ankle, like a needle piercing the skin, and the door slammed shut behind her. She screamed, stumbling off balance and crashing into a nearby wall, springing a switch in the process. The room burst into light.

She looked around, her eyes widening, her mouth falling open in shock. Her knees buckled, threatening to give out from under her.

"Oh God," she whispered. "It can't be!"

But it could it be. And it was.

Dragons. Sick, mutated, diseased-looking baby dragons, some three times the size of Emmy, stacked in cages from floor to ceiling on every possible wall. Some sported three eyes; others, a fifth leg or a stump where their leg should be. Some had no legs at all—flapping their misshapen wings against the wire cages, looking at Trin with hollow, desperate eyes. A few had broken free of their confines and were tottering across the floor on skinny, malformed legs. The ankle biter looked up at her, opening his mouth and revealing a single gleaming, bucktooth fang.

Trin's stomach clenched. It was all she could do to not run screaming from the room. Instead, she stood, frozen in place, trying to digest what she was seeing, trying to understand how it could be possible. Her brain told her it was too horrible to be real, that her eyes must be playing tricks. But when she closed them and opened them again, the dragons remained. Somehow, some way, they were really here.

Emmy? she managed to send in a shaky voice. *You need to see this.*

But before the dragon could reply, Connor's voice slammed into her consciousness. Urgent and afraid.

Someone's coming down the elevator, he rasped. *Wherever you are, get out of there. Fast!*

Chapter Thirty-Seven

Trinity froze, Connor's warning echoing through her head, as her ears caught voices down the hall, confirming his words. Her gaze darted around the room, searching for an escape, but there was only one way in and one way out. And the voices were getting closer.

"What are you doing all the way down here, little one?"

Trin flinched. The voice was unmistakably Darius's, and she realized he must have found Emmy. In another moment, he'd open the door and head in her direction. Frantic, she hit the light switch and dove behind the dragon cages. She could feel Emmy's growing alarm ringing through her head while the dragon croaked weakly back at the Dracken master.

"Unbelievable!" another voice, heavily accented, rang through the hall. Trin furrowed her brow, trying to place it. It didn't sound like any of the Dracken or their mercenaries—at least none she'd met. "A dragon!" the voice continued in hushed awe. "A real-life dragon, just as you said!"

"I told you, didn't I?" Darius proclaimed, his voice rich with pride. "Now come with me and I'll show you the rest."

Footsteps approached and Trin crouched deeper into her hiding spot. A moment later, the door squeaked open and the light switched on again. From her vantage point, she could just make out Darius, dressed in a dapper black suit, leading a distinguished, forty-something-year-old dark-haired man into the room. As he entered, the foreigner gave a low whistle.

"Amazing! Simply amazing!"

"Didn't I tell you? It's quite a sight to be seen," Darius replied, reaching into a drawer and pulling out a metal band. He slipped it over Emmy's mouth, effectively muzzling her. Guess he wasn't about to take his chances with dragon fire. When Emmy struggled in protest, he dug a firm thumb into a spot under her wing. The dragon whimpered but meekly quieted down. He opened up an empty cage and shoved her inside, closing and locking it behind him.

"I have to confess, I didn't really believe you," the man exclaimed, his eyes darting from cage to cage. "It just seemed too fantastical to be real."

"Oh, they're real all right," Darius assured him. "All with perfect pedigrees. The ones you see here are approximately one year of age. Soon each will be paired with a Guardian to begin their training."

Trinity squinted at the men, trying to figure out what was going on. Why hadn't anyone told her there were more dragons in the mall? She'd been led to believe Emmy was the last of her kind. But that was clearly untrue. Did the other Potentials know their dragons had already been born? They couldn't have; they wouldn't have been so excited to see Emmy.

But why keep the rest of them a secret? And what was wrong with them, for that matter? Why were they so deformed looking? She turned back to the conversation, hoping for answers.

"When will they be ready for delivery?" the man was asking, poking a finger into one of the cages. The dragon inside hissed angrily and he pulled his finger away with a nervous laugh.

"Each dragon will complete its training at five years of age," the Dracken Master replied smoothly. "At which time we will deliver both dragon and Guardian to your people, yours to do with as you wish." He gave a smug smile. "Dragons have many gifts, after all: curing disease, sniffing out natural resources, finding water in the—"

The man waved him off. "Yes, yes," he said impatiently. "But can they fight?"

Trinity held her breath, praying for Darius to scold him for the idea. To tell him these creatures were made for saving the world, not destroying it.

But the leader's lips only curled cruelly. "Your enemies will be annihilated before they even know what hit them."

She collapsed against the wall, her heart sinking in despair. Connor had been right all along. Caleb had been completely deceived. The Dracken were never interested in using dragons to help mankind. They were nothing more than time-traveling arms dealers.

And the Potentials! They would be sold off along with their dragons. Made into slaves. Forced to go into battle. No wonder the Dracken took only those with no family. That way there was no one left to rescue them—no one to care—when they found out the truth.

"These dragons," the foreigner remarked, his eyes scanning the cages again, "they don't look like the other one." He gestured to Emmy. "Is something wrong with them? I don't want defective merchandise."

Darius looked uncomfortable. "We had some…issues… with the original batch of eggs," he admitted, wiping a sheen of sweat from his brow. Trin stole another peek at the mutated dragons and wondered again what could have happened to them. Maybe something about being brought back through time? Maybe the process had corrupted their DNA somehow? It made sense now why they were so eager to get their hands on Emmy. She was perfect.

She realized Darius was still talking. "But purchase these now and you'll get first pick of the next hatchlings. The ones born from our queen." He gestured to Emmy, who was clawing at the inside of her cage, looking terrified. "Through her, the line will grow and strengthen, providing you with a never-ending supply of the strongest, most powerful, fire-breathing beasts the world has ever seen."

Emmy let out a horrified squawk, now thrashing wildly in her cage. Trin tried to send soothing thoughts to calm her down.

I won't let them do that to you, she promised. *No matter what.* Though, she had to admit, that was easier said than done. She turned back to the Dracken and his customer.

"So do we have a deal?" Darius asked, clamping his hand on the man's shoulder. "I must have your commitment now. We have many potential buyers waiting in the wings. It would be a shame to allow your enemy to buy your dragons and use them against you."

Don't let him! Emmy begged. *Stop him now!*

The man opened his mouth to speak. Trin gulped down her fear. In a moment, the deal would be done. It would be too late to do anything to stop it.

You don't want any dragons, she pushed, on sudden impulse.

She didn't know if it would work, but it was worth a try—if only to calm Emmy down. *You want to leave. Now.*

She opened her eyes, focusing back on the man in question, whose face had clouded with sudden hesitation. Trinity grinned, realizing she'd managed to reach him in time. Totally worth the headache now stabbing at her skull.

Sorry, Darius. No sale.

"My apologies," he said to the Dracken leader in a voice wrought with confusion. "I don't think I want any dragons. In fact, I'd like to leave. Now."

Trinity waited, breath firmly lodged in her throat, as a shadow crossed Darius's smooth face. For a moment he did nothing, said nothing, only stared at the man with growing realization. Then, without warning, he reached into his suit pocket and pulled out a gun, shooting the man square in the chest. The foreigner fell to the ground. Dead.

"You can come out now," Darius announced, scanning the room. When Trin didn't move, the Dracken leader sighed deeply, then marched over to her hiding spot, grabbing her by the neck and yanking her out into the open. She yelped as his jagged nails dug into her skin.

"Very clever," he sneered. "Though very stupid. Had you kept quiet I might not have known you were here." He tsked. "Very stupid indeed."

"Why would you do this?" she demanded, fighting to free herself but to no avail. "Why would you try to sell dragons to that guy? You're going to end up destroying the world all over again!"

"Actually," he corrected, "we're going to save it."

"What?" She stopped fighting, staring at him, confusion

mixing with fury. "What are you talking about? You put drag-ons in the hands of these people—who want to wipe each other out—what do you think is going to happen?"

"I think the fire will burn and the world will be purged," he replied simply. When she gave him an uncomprehending look, he continued, "Don't you see, Trinity? This is why we came back here in the first place—the Dracken have been chosen to do God's work."

"What are you talking about?" she stammered, not sure she really wanted to hear.

"It's simple, really. Just as once upon a time the Almighty washed away the world's evil by sending a mighty flood, so now we have a chance to cleanse it again—this time with flame." He looked down at her, his eyes shining. "God's word is clear. Only through destruction can we have any hope of salvation."

Holy crap. She stared at him, heart beating wildly in her chest. He was totally looney tunes! Could this really be the true reason the Dracken had come back in time? On some kind of insane religious crusade?

"You can't be serious!" she cried, though the look in his eyes told her otherwise. "You'd really burn down the world on purpose? Let millions of innocent people die?"

"Innocent?" Darius repeated incredulously, for the first time losing his cool. "Innocent? Please. Have you watched your local newscasts lately? Spent any time on your Internet?" He loomed over her, his eyes darkening to angry thunder-clouds. "Not a day goes by when there isn't a bombing or a shooting or a kidnapping. Rape, torture, or war. Child abuse, drug abuse, not to mention a complete disregard for the environment." He shook his head. "Just like Sodom and Gomorrah, the world has become a filthy, corrupt place—far beyond the point of redemption. And it only gets worse in the future." He drew in a breath, as if trying to regain control of his emotions. "We are left with no choice but to raze the whole thing to the ground and then rise again, like a phoenix from the ashes. Except this time," he added with a triumphant smile, "it will be on the backs of dragons."

Trinity shrank back, unable to speak as the enormity of what he was saying sunk in. Sure the world had its problems, she wanted to protest, but there were good people here too. People worth saving.

"We never lied to you, Trinity," Darius continued. "We told you from the very start we planned to use dragons to save the world. And that's what we're doing: saving the world from itself." His gaze bore down on her. "You should feel honored," he added. "You have been chosen out of millions as a pure soul, worthy of becoming part of our brave new world. You and the other Potentials—our own little Noah's Ark."

Trin nodded grimly, everything sliding into a sick sort of place. That's why they'd gathered representatives from every country. Just like Noah saved each species of animal. Her stomach churned and she suddenly knew what she had to do.

Sorry, Emmy. But we have no choice.

"You're sick!" she declared, drawing up all the courage she had left inside of her. "Not to mention totally insane. And if you think for one second I'm going to play your little reindeer games, you've got another thing coming." She crossed her arms over her chest and looked up at him with defiant eyes. "You might as well go ahead and do it. Kill me now and get it over with. Because I'll never join you—no matter what you try to do."

She held her breath, her heart pounding in her chest, praying the Dracken leader would take the bait.

Sacrifice one to save the world. Turned out it'd been *her* mission all along.

Darius looked at her for a moment, then he burst out laughing. "Do you think I'm stupid?" he demanded. "Do you think I don't know that Emmy's life force is entwined with your own? If I kill you, she dies. Unless…" His lips curled into a smirk. "I de-bond you and bring in the backup." He nodded slowly, as if coming to some sort of conclusion. "Yes, I think that's the only thing to do at this point, seeing as you're so unwilling to see the light."

Trinity froze. "Backup?" she repeated doubtfully.

"My dear girl, do you think we came all this way without a plan B?" Darius asked in an incredulous voice. "Of course we kept a spare around, in case this kind of thing was to happen."

"You're telling me you have a spare Fire Kissed just sitting on ice?" she shot back. The idea was ridiculous. But something in Darius's eyes told her it was also somehow unfortunately true.

"But of course. There's usually one in every generation. And it can often be hereditary."

She gasped, what he was saying suddenly making perfect sense. "You mean my grandpa!" she breathed. Thank goodness Connor had him under his protection. She prayed he was far, far away and out of the Dracken's reach.

Darius raised an eyebrow. "No, no," he corrected, giving her a cold, hard look. "I mean your mother."

Chapter Thirty-Eight

Trinity stared at him, her mind reeling at his pronounce-
ment. "That's impossible," she protested. "My mother
is dead."

"On the contrary," Darius replied smoothly, "she's very
much alive. Would you like to see for yourself?"

Trin nodded dumbly—what else could she do? She tried
to tell herself it was some kind of sick joke, a trick Darius
had concocted to screw with her head. Because her mother
couldn't be alive. Trinity had seen her body, her head blown to
smithereens. Her beloved bunny slippers still on her feet. The
emerald ring still on her finger.

She twisted the ring in question almost violently, her stomach flip-flopping madly, this close to throwing up. How could
she be alive? There was no way. No way on Earth.

Except, what if there was?

Giving one last longing look at Emmy, still stuck in her
cage, she allowed Darius to escort her back to the staircase
with the three hallways, this time taking the one to the left.
The only one she hadn't been down. She followed the light
from the Dracken leader's industrial-strength flashlight, her
pulse pounding out her fear as she forced her feet to step, one

foot in front of the other, down the featureless hallway. She wondered dully if she should try to escape. To overpower him and make a run for the elevator where Connor was probably still waiting. But Emmy was locked in a cage, and now more than ever, she couldn't leave her behind. Not now that she knew what the Dracken were planning to do with her. She couldn't even dare risk sending a message to Connor to let him know what had happened for fear Darius would intercept it and learn of his location.

And then there was her mother. If she was really here somehow—really alive—there was no way Trin could just walk away. Not without knowing for sure.

They stopped in front of a door at the far end of the hall—a simple door made of wood with no fancy locks to keep it secured or closed. Darius wrapped his hands around the knob and pulled it open, gesturing for Trinity to enter. She did, stepping into a small bedroom.

It was stark and barren, with none of the luxuries of her own room upstairs. A plain twin bed, lodged up against one wall, fitted with crisp, hospital-cornered sheets. A washbasin and toilet sat against the other, simple but recently cleaned.

But it was the back of the room that pulled Trinity's gaze. A lone figure, silhouetted in the darkness, rocking slowly in a small wooden chair. From here, Trin could just make out the woman's long, stringy black hair and emaciated frame, a dingy white tunic dress hanging from her shrunken flesh.

She stepped closer to get a better look, her mind a crazy tangle of hope and fear. She wanted it to be a lie but she wanted it to be the truth all the same. As she approached, Darius flipped a switch and light flooded the room.

Trin gasped, staggering from the shock. It couldn't be.
But it was.

"Mom?" she whispered

The woman in the chair—her mother—did not respond.
Instead, she continued to rock herself slowly, as her vacant
black eyes stared into space. Trinity ran to her, dropping to
her knees, peering up at her, waving her hands in her face. But
it did no good. Her mother did not respond.

"What's wrong with her?" she demanded, turning back to
Darius. He shrugged.

"She's in the Nether," he said simply. "It's where she pre-
fers to spend all her time these days. It's more pleasant in
there, I suppose, than her everyday reality."

Looking around the room, Trinity couldn't blame her.
Slowly she rose to her feet. "She was dead," she protested
weakly. "I saw her body. And the coroner confirmed it.
Fingerprints, DNA. It all checked out."

"All bought and paid for," Darius replied. "You'd be
amazed at how little the coroner charged us for the false iden-
tification. He had no idea how valuable she really was."

"But why?" she asked, staring down at her mother, feeling
out of body and disconcerted. The last two years she'd had
to deal with the horror of walking in on her mother's corpse.
Only to find out now that it belonged to someone else entirely.
"I mean, why go through all that trouble to fake her death?"

"The space-time continuum is a fragile thing," Darius
explained. "Your mother did die the first time around—she
accidentally mixed up some pills and took too many of the
wrong kind—the day after spending Christmas with you.
Because of this, you were sent to live with your grandfather,

where you bonded with the egg. We still needed that to happen, but we wanted to save your mother's life this time around, just in case. So we went in a day early and replaced her with one our own—a Dracken woman who didn't survive the trip back in time. We simply dressed her in your mother's clothes and used her as a stand-in. Thus, the important threads of the timeline remained largely unchanged. We did unfortunately have to change the cause of death, seeing as keeping her face intact would have given the game away. But with her history of mental illness, it didn't seem too farfetched to have her blow her head off."

And Trinity had believed it. Believed her mother to be capable of such a horrible thing without even questioning it. What kind of daughter did that make her?

"Oh, Mom," she whispered, reaching down to embrace the woman who'd given her life. She was cold and stiff, but Trinity clung to her all the same as tears streamed down her cheeks. "I'm so sorry. I didn't know. I didn't have any idea!"

She thought back to all the resentment she'd allowed to build up inside of her over the last two years. Believing her mother had broken her promise. Had abandoned her on Christmas Eve forever.

But that had never been her mother's intention. The Dracken had stolen the last day of her life. Ripping her from reality and imprisoning her all alone, in a dark lonely room—as backup in case her daughter didn't meet their expectations. It was all too horrible, too much to even contemplate, and she felt guilty as hell for every bad thought she'd had over the last two years.

"I'm so sorry, Mom," she babbled, burying her face in

her mother's lap, sobbing uncontrollably. "I'm so sorry I ever accused you of letting me down."

But her mother did not answer. And soon the guards arrived to take Trinity away.

PART 5:

BURN

Chapter Thirty-Nine

Caleb trudged down the mall corridor toward his bedroom, his heart heavy and his legs feeling like lead. He'd been a total duffer to believe his brother. He should've known better than to leave the headquarters on a wild chase for a dead man. But the idea—the slightest possibility—that Trin's grandfather wasn't actually dead was too much to pass up. If he'd been able to find him, to bring him back, he would have finally proven himself worthy of her.

Instead, he had only proven himself pathetic.

He was so wrapped up in his own misery, he scarcely noticed at first all the shouting and banging coming toward him in the opposite direction. Finally it registered and he looked up to see what all the commotion was about. To his shock, his eyes fell upon none other than Trinity herself, being dragged roughly by two Dracken guards. She was struggling and fighting with all of her might but they refused to let her go. Furious, Caleb stepped into their path.

"Have you gone mad?" he demanded. "How dare you treat her like this? She's the Fire Kissed."

"Not anymore," the first guard said with a smirk. "Now step aside and let us through."

"No. You release her now. Or Darius will hear of this."

"Darius was the one who ordered it," jeered the second guard. "Go talk to him if you have a problem with it."

His heart stuttered. "He wouldn't do that!" he protested. But something in their mannerisms told him he was wrong. He shot an anguished look at Trinity, taking in her bruised eyes and scraped face.

"Trin!" he cried, rushing to her, not caring what the guards would do. Before he could reach her, the first guard shoved him back with the butt of his gun, sending him sprawling into a wall. For a moment he was too dazed to move, the wind knocked from his lungs. The guards regarded him with satisfaction before continuing their march down the hall.

"Trin!" he repeated, desperate and afraid. Ignoring the pain in his head, he dashed forward again, grabbing her this time before they could stop him, squeezing her hand with all he had. *Send!* he begged her. *Send it all!*

And so she did.

Caleb staggered, dropping her hand and hitting the ground hard, stunned and dazed by what she'd sent him. Their touch had only lasted a second, but it had been enough—enough to see the mutated dragons. The seedy arms dealer looking over the merchandise. Darius—his beloved mentor, Darius!— informing her of the Dracken's true intentions.

"No," Caleb whispered, rocking on his knees. "It can't be."

Darius had saved him. He'd rescued him from a life of crime and impending imprisonment. He'd promised Caleb a chance to become a hero. A chance to save the world. And yet all along, he'd been plotting to destroy it.

Somehow Caleb forced himself to stagger to his feet.

While he could no longer hear Trinity's whimpers of pain, they ravaged through his head all the same. He'd brought her here. He'd promised her peace and safety and a place to raise her dragon. Instead he'd put them both in danger.

"Caleb, there you are."

He whirled around to find Darius walking slowly toward him, his lips curled into a self-satisfied smile. It was all Caleb could do not to smack it off his face.

"What's…what's going on?" he demanded, barely able to speak past his horror.

Darius gave him a pitying look. "There has been a complication," he said, reaching Caleb and placing a fatherly hand on his arm. Caleb bit his lower lip hard, forcing himself not to jerk away from his touch. "The Fire Kissed's mind, it seems, has been unable to accept the dragon's bond." He shook his head slowly. "We knew it was a possibility from the start. But we had hoped…" He trailed off.

What are you talking about? Caleb wanted to scream. *You're the one who's been selling dragons as weapons. The one with the sick plan to burn down the world.* How many people were in on this? All of the other Dracken? Had they known all along? Had they been laughing at him behind his back this whole time? Stupid, gullible Caleb, so desperate for someone to love him, he'll believe anything you tell him—do anything you ask.

Gritting his teeth, he forced the thoughts from his mind. He couldn't risk Darius overhearing them. "What did she do?" he asked instead.

The Dracken leader sighed deeply. "She tried to escape, ordering her dragon to slaughter two of our most promising Potentials in the process. Burning them alive simply for doing their jobs." His face twisted into a self-righteous scowl. "Can you believe it? After all we did for her. Rescuing her from the Hunter, taking her in, clothing her, feeding her. Treating her like an honored guest…"

The indignation in his voice, along with the smooth lies rolling off his tongue, filled Caleb with rage. How many other lies had he willingly swallowed from this man over the last few years? Believing Darius when he told him he was special, that he had a gift? Yet all along, he'd been nothing more than a Dracken lap dragon, following orders without ever questioning them.

It took everything inside of him not to slam his fist into his former mentor's face. To make him feel even half the pain that Caleb felt. Half the betrayal burning within him. Instead, he swallowed his anger down and forced his face to remain slack. Subservient. This wasn't the time to act. It would only land him in the same prison Trin was headed for. And then there would be no one left to save her. To save Emmy.

To save the world.

"I've failed you," he said, bowing his head in front of the Master, looking as contrite as possible. "I did everything I could to win her to our side. Obviously it wasn't enough. I'm sorry. You believed in me and I let you down. I don't deserve to call myself a Dracken."

Darius's face softened. "Don't blame yourself," he said, patting him gently on the back. "I know you did all you could. I don't blame you in the least."

"Thank you," Caleb said in his most earnest voice. "I promise, I won't let you down again." He looked up at the Master. "So what happens next? Do we just kill her and move on?"

"I am scheduling a de-bonding ceremony for three days from now," Darius said, "to give Mara enough time to prepare. We'll do it publicly, with all the Potentials in attendance. After all, it was their brothers the traitor slaughtered so mercilessly. We'll break the bond between the dragon and the Fire Kissed and then give Emberlyn to the other. Hopefully she will prove more worthy of the privilege."

Caleb swallowed hard. "And what will happen to the traitor?" he asked, daring to meet his former mentor's eyes with his own. "Will we keep her in custody? It would seem risky to let her go…"

"She's not going anywhere," Darius assured him. "No human has ever survived a de-bonding. Before the ceremony is even over, she will already be dead."

Chapter Forty

Creak!

Trinity looked up blearily as she heard the turning of a lock outside her makeshift cell. They'd been keeping her in a wildly painted former Hot Topic dressing room, reinforced with steel bars. The room was small—too small to lie down in—and so she'd contented herself to pull her knees to her chest and lay her head on top of them in a desperate attempt to get comfortable. She had no idea how long she'd been there at this point—the blows the guards had delivered to her head had been sending her in and out of consciousness for some time, and she half wondered if she'd suffered a concussion. At least she knew they wouldn't allow her to die—well, until they'd severed the bond between she and Emmy that was. After that, all bets were off.

Emmy. She reached out again, trying desperately to find her dragon to make sure she was okay. But, try as she might, she couldn't lock onto the creature's spark. She wondered if maybe they'd drugged her. Emmy had to be going insane without her mistress nearby, and no one wanted an insane dragon on their hands. At least she knew they wouldn't hurt her. They needed her now more than ever. But the thought wasn't as comforting as it should have been.

The door opened and light spilled into the room. Trin looked up to find a dark shadow, standing in the doorway. For a split second, she wildly thought it could be Connor, come back to rescue her somehow. But that was ridiculous. He was long gone. And it was Caleb standing there, flanked by two guards.

"Well, well, there she is," Caleb said, his voice cutting and cold. "Our little traitor."

Trin looked up at him in horror. All this time she'd been secretly praying that he'd received her desperate send when he'd grabbed her hand in the hallway. That he'd seen all the atrocities going on below the mall—the mutated dragons, the Dracken's true plan. But maybe it hadn't worked. Maybe he had no idea what the Dracken were really up to. Or maybe...Her heart skittered at the thought. Maybe he'd known all along.

"Caleb," she tried, but her lips were so dry and cracked she found she couldn't get the words out. Not that she had any idea what she really wanted to say. He shook his head at her, then grabbed her by the hair, yanking her out of the fitting room and dumping her onto the floor of the empty store. She hit the ground hard and cried out in pain as her knee wrenched from under her.

"How could you do this?" he demanded, glaring down at her. "How could you go and betray the Dracken?"

"I—I..." she tried to say, but a sudden voice in her head silenced her.

Trinity, listen to me.

She startled, confused. With her mind still hazy, it took her a moment to realize what he had said—and, more importantly, how he had said it. He flashed her a warning look, then glanced back at the two guards. *Don't let them know.*

"Those boys were innocent," he continued. "And yet you let your dragon murder them."

I'm so sorry. I would have never brought you here if I had known. I thought it would be safe.

Somehow Trin found her voice. "I didn't ask Emmy to kill them. She was trying to protect me."

Caleb, it's not your fault. They lied to everyone. You, me, the Potentials . . .

"And what about the wireless laptop we found in your room?" he sneered. "Who were you talking to?"

"I was just playing a video game. *Fields of Fantasy.* It's my favorite."

You have to get us out of here, Caleb. Before they break me and Emmy's bond.

"A video game? Please. Do you think we're stupid? You were contacting someone. I want to know who."

I know—but how? There's too many of them. We'd need a flecking army to even stand a chance.

She frowned. *Well, I'm sorry. I don't have a spare army in my—*

Trinity stopped short. Wait a second. Maybe she did.

What about your friends who broke into the museum? The government guys. They're probably still out looking for the egg. If they found out it was here, they could raid the place. And in all the confusion we could escape.

Caleb seemed to consider this for a moment. *It's not a bad idea,* he relented. *But how can we let them know? Darius has the place on lockdown now, thanks to your little escape attempt. And there's no phone or Internet.*

"Um, is everything okay, sir?" asked the guard behind Caleb, looking at the two of them suspiciously. Trinity cringed, realizing they'd gone too long staring at one another without talking out loud. In desperation, she managed to scramble to her knees before Caleb, holding out her hands, as if in prayer.

"Please," she begged. "Just let me go. I've learned my lesson. I'll be good. I won't try to escape again. Just don't de-bond me from my dragon. I can't live without her."

What about Connor? Can you reach him through the Nether? He could pretend to be you and put in a call.

Caleb sneered. "Can't live?" he spit out. "Funny, that's kind of the whole idea."

No, Trin. We can't trust my brother. We both know what he was sent here to do. And now that Emmy's hatched . . .

Trinity fell back, burying her face in her hands. "Please. I'm begging you! I don't want to die."

We don't have a choice. He's the only one left. And he promised not to hurt me or Emmy. We have to believe him.

I don't know, Trin. If something happened to you—

Something will happen if you don't get us out of here. Connor's our only hope.

Caleb turned to the guards. "Throw the traitor back into her cell," he commanded. "I can't stand to look at her pointy little face anymore."

All right. I'll try to contact him. But, Trin—if he even looks at you sideways, I promise you now, I'm going to shoot first and ask questions later.

The guards sprang into action, grabbing her by the arms

and dragging her back to her cell. She fought and clawed at them like an alley cat, her eyes locking onto Caleb. "Screw you, you bastard!" she screamed. "Go back to the Nether with your little sluts. That's all you're good for! I never want to see you again!"

A ghost of a smile flickered on Caleb's face before he quickly masked it again. He turned away, heading out of the Hot Topic, leaving the guards to deal with Trinity on their own. But just as they were about to throw her back into her cell, she caught his whisper echoing through her mind.

Oh and for the record? I never took anyone else to the Nether. He paused, then added, *No one but you.*

Chapter Forty-One

*C*ome on, Connor. We're running out of time.

Trinity winced as the guards yanked her roughly down the corridor, on their way to the de-bonding ceremony. It had been three days since Caleb had promised to contact his brother through the Nether to see if he could help rally the troops. But whether Connor had answered his brother's request or was able to get the government on board, she had no idea. Caleb had never returned to her cell to let her know what had happened—probably too worried that Darius might notice too many visits to his prisoner.

The Dracken had gathered in the main ceremonial chamber and the de-bonding ceremony was about to begin. In just moments, she realized, she and Emmy would be torn from one another and she would be put out of her misery. She tried to console herself with the fact that at least the dragon herself would live on, but the thought wasn't very comforting. While Emmy wouldn't be physically harmed, she was doomed to a life of captivity as a backyard breeder of biological weapons of mass destruction. Stuck in a cage, never seeing the sun, never allowed to spread her wings and fly. It was a fate worse than death for a dragon.

And then there was her mother. Her poor, sweet, innocent mother who'd been locked in a dark cage of her own for the last two years, her mind lost and her body atrophying. Would she even have the strength to bond with Emmy and help her lay her eggs? And what would happen to her if she didn't?

The ceremonial chamber was adorned much like the birthing room, a former anchor store now bathed in silver runes, a high balcony circling the perimeter. The senior members of the Dracken had gathered at the bottom level, while the Potentials had camped out above. In the center of the room stood a tall pole, which uncomfortably resembled a funeral pyre. Trinity guessed that was for her.

As the guards dragged her over to the pole, tying her hands and feet with thick rope and gagging her mouth, her eyes lifted to those watching from above. The faces she found—once happy and welcoming—were now solemn and disapproving, the judgment rich in their eyes. If only she could tell them the truth. On impulse, she tried to send to them but was quickly shot down. They'd all blockaded their minds against her. She imagined Darius instructing them to do so, so they wouldn't find themselves lured in by her lies.

Her eyes fell to Caleb, who stood among his Dracken brothers, helping them at their tasks. He caught her look and glared back at her with cold eyes until she dropped her gaze. She knew it was only an act, but his expression and his garb managed to chill her all the same.

An angry squawk resounded through the chamber and she looked over to see Emmy being wheeled through the room, encased in a golden cage. The dragon was putting up quite the fight, hissing and spitting fire at her handlers.

But the cage had some kind of force field around it and the dragon's efforts proved ineffectual. Emmy had grown since the last time Trin had seen her, now about the size of a small cocker spaniel. Soon she'd be big enough to ride. Trinity felt tears spring to her eyes as she remembered her own amazing dragon ride through the Nether. Would she ever be able to feel so free again?

Come on, Connor. Are you out there, somewhere?

A hush fell over the room as Darius entered, stepping to the center of the stage. The Dracken had dressed in special ceremonial robes for the occasion—fitting attire for a crazy cult leader, Trin noted bitterly. As he turned to her, his eyes gleamed eagerly and his mouth twisted. She shivered under his gaze.

"Say good-bye to your precious dragon," he hissed, so low that no one else could hear. Then he turned to the crowd.

"Brothers and sisters of the Dracken," he pronounced in a grand voice, "I thank you for meeting me here today. A time of sadness for all those of us who believe in our fight. For, it seems, one of our own—nay, not just one but the founder herself—has chosen to betray us. Conspiring with dragon hunters to send the world's only hope spiraling into extinction."

The crowd let out a collective condemnation and Trinity could feel their anger and judgment rain down on her below. She wanted to shout to them—to tell them of Darius's true intentions—but, of course, she was gagged and their mind blocks seemed impenetrable.

"Trinity Foxx, standing before you, was born with the gift and chosen by our own Emberlyn to be her Fire Kissed,"

Darius continued in his grand voice. "And yet she has chosen to turn her back on her gift—to turn her back on her own dragon. And so, as guardians of the dragon race, we are left with no choice. We must begin the de-bonding procedure."

The crowd erupted in murmurs, looking both excited and disturbed as they gazed down upon her. Darius, having concluded his grand speech, motioned to Mara. Evidently the birthing maiden could sever bonds as well as create them.

Mara stepped over to Trinity, solemnly placing a plastic cap threaded with wires over her head. Trin struggled as best she could, hoping to buy Connor more time, but two guards soon stepped in to hold her down as Mara did her work. Out of the corner of her eye, she could see Emmy dancing anxiously in her cage and Trin sent the little dragon as many comforting thoughts as she could. But she was admittedly more than a little low on hope right about then. If Connor didn't come—which was seeming more and more likely as the clock ticked on—it would soon all be over. And there would be nothing either of them could do.

Her eyes sought Caleb's, but he had disappeared from the group of Dracken standing nearby. She prayed he wouldn't try to act alone and get himself killed in the process. Knowing at least he would still be here, an undercover agent for good who could make things more pleasant for Emmy and her mother, gave her a small bit of comfort. And she didn't want anything to happen to him.

I never took anyone else to the Nether, he'd told her. *No one but you.*

"The time has come," Darius, ever the showman, announced, interrupting her wistful thoughts, "when our traitor will get what she so richly deserves." He gestured to Mara who headed over to a nearby instrument panel, readying it for action. Trinity's stomach sank as her last remaining hope left the building. It was too late. The end was here. There would be no rescue. No happily ever after for her. She turned to Emmy, gazing at her with wistful eyes.

Take good care of my mother and Caleb, she sent to her dragon. *They need you now more than ever.*

No! Emmy's panicked voice rang through her head. *Don't leave me, Trin. Don't leave me here alone!*

Stay strong, Emmy. For me, promise me you'll stay strong.

She closed her eyes, unable to bear the dragon's bereft face. She'd promised Emmy the world, that she'd never let her fall. She promised that she'd never leave her alone, like her mother had before her. And now she was breaking those promises— and all the others she'd made as well. She could only hope the dragon would understand somehow. That she would know it was the last thing Trin wanted to do.

Tears splashed down her cheeks as she waited for the switch to be thrown. The moment seemed to stretch into eternity.

I'm so sorry, Emmy. I'm so sorry I couldn't protect you.

Suddenly sirens blared through the chamber, warning lights flashing at every corner. Trinity looked up, heart in her throat, as the spectators erupted in panic. A moment later a voice came over the loudspeaker, cutting through the sounds of confusion.

"The mall has been breached!" the man's panicked voice cried. "We're being invaded."

Connor! Trinity's heart surged with hope.

The room broke into chaos, the ceremony all but forgotten

as the Dracken, the Potentials, and armed guards alike scurried in every direction. Only Darius, along with Mara, still stood on the stage. The Dracken's face twisted in fury. "Do it!" he cried to Mara. "Throw the switch! Now!"

Looking frightened, Mara made a move to do as he asked. But before she could reach the panel, Caleb dove in—seemingly out of nowhere—tackling her and throwing her to the ground. He had shed his other clothes and was now dressed like a soldier. Reaching out, he grabbed a piece of heavy equipment and brought it down on Mara's head, knocking her out cold. Then he shot Trinity an excited look.

My hero, she sent. *Now get Emmy!*

Darius screamed in rage, launching himself at the instrument panel. But Caleb was too quick, reaching Emmy's cage and releasing her into the wild. The dragon let loose a stream of fire, melting the panel before the Dracken leader could activate it, leaving nothing useable behind.

Darius glared at the dragon, hatred clear in his eyes, but hesitated, unsure what to do. Obviously he couldn't hurt Emmy. But he couldn't just let her go off and flambé his friends either. The dragon leveled her eyes on him, opening her mouth, ready to end this game once and for all.

But before Emmy could fire, the doors around them burst open, armed men swarming the chamber. The cavalry had arrived.

Emmy, hide! Trin sent. *Whatever you do, don't let them see you!*

The dragon huffed, shooting a look of annoyance at Trin for letting her prey escape, but obediently flew up toward the rafters and out of sight before anyone realized she was there.

In the meantime, Caleb had scrambled to his feet. He

looked at the men, then pointed at Darius. "Seize this terrorist," he cried.

Darius's face drained of color as the men flew into action. He turned and started to run but soon found himself surrounded. Trinity grinned. *Sorry, Darius.* She watched as they approached the Dracken leader, guns drawn, half hoping he'd do something stupid and force them to shoot him where he stood. Instead, he allowed himself to be handcuffed and led away. *Wuss.* But at least he was out of the picture for now. Hopefully, when they discovered what he'd been planning, they'd lock him up tight and throw away the key.

Trinity turned back to the remaining soldiers, her triumphant smile fading as two men in black suits pushed through the crowd, making their way to center stage where she stood. Two unfortunately very familiar-looking men in black suits.

Oh, crap.

"Miss Foxx, you are under arrest," the first one declared, pulling a set of handcuffs from his pocket, "for obstruction of justice; assault against two officers of the law; not to mention…"

Suddenly Trinity caught a flash of movement from the balcony above. Her eyes widened as she realized it was none other than Connor himself, trying to get her attention. He gave her a knowing smile, then reached into his bag, casually flipping a silver disc over the railing.

Trinity's heart leapt. The Bouncer! She caught Caleb's smirk out of the corner of her eye.

Hope you're not still afraid of heights, princess.

The silver disc skittered, Connor's aim perfect, coming in for a landing not two feet in front of her. She grinned, giving the agents a small wave, then hopped onto the disc, flying high into the air, as graceful as a bird—or maybe a dragon—as the agents and operatives watched in dumb disbelief down below. When she'd reached full altitude, she threw herself forward, stretching her arms out to grab the railing looming in front of her. Connor was able to yank her over the balcony before anyone could even think of firing shots in her direction.

She scrambled to her feet. "You, my friend," she declared, "have impeccable timing."

He flashed her a grin. "I aim to please. Now come on. My brother tells me you have a mother in need of rescuing."

"I do indeed," she agreed. "Let's go.

They ran through the mall, fast as they could, heading toward the west wing courtyard and the entrance Emmy had made in the wall. Trin hoped no one had discovered the secret passageway behind the tapestry in the last couple of days—the last thing she needed was for it to be blocked up again. After all, it was the only way she knew to get to Mom—and later to freedom.

As they burst into the courtyard, they stopped short, realizing it wasn't as empty as they'd assumed. In fact, the place was packed full—with dozens of Potentials, some wounded, some huddled in corners, their eyes wide with fright. They must have been trained to regroup here, Trin realized, if any security was breached.

Heart pounding, she scanned the room, taking in all the faces. Had they always looked so young? So innocent? So scared? Her heart lurched. If only there was a way to take them all with her, to free them from this psychotic prison. At the very least, she determined, she could finally tell them the truth.

But Connor had other ideas. "Come on," he urged, grabbing her arm. "We need to go!"

She shook him off. "Wait," she said. Then she turned to the Potentials, who were watching her with wary eyes. She drew in a breath. Here went nothing. "Listen to me," she said, clearing her throat. "The Dracken are not who they say they are. They're not out to save the world. They're using dragons to burn it all down and they need your help to do it." Her gaze darted from one unbelieving face to another. "There's a door behind this curtain. It leads to a set of stairs and a passageway to a parking garage. You can escape through that. You can all be free."

"Liar!"

Trinity startled as a girl shot up from the back of the group. Rashida, she realized in dismay. "No," she forced herself to continue. "The Dracken are the liars, not me. They've been lying to you since day one. They—"

"Come on, Trin," Connor urged, looking more and more worried. "Let's go."

But Trin found she couldn't move.

"Who do you think you are?" Rashida demanded, pushing her way through the frightened crowd. "We welcomed you into our family. We tried to be your friend. And in return you killed our brothers." Her eyes flashed fire. "And then you invited our enemies into the one place that was supposed to be safe."

She waved a hand to the other side of the room where a small, bloodied figure lay prostate on the ground. Trinity gasped as she realized it was Malia. Sweet, gamer girl Malia.

"They shot her," Rashida informed her coldly. "She was

trying to run, scared for her life, and your soldiers shot her in the back."

Oh God.

"Before you came, we were safe. We were cared for. We were protected. Now our world has been torn apart. Our sisters and brothers are dead. You're the one who deserves to be shot," she declared. "And a lot worse than that too."

The room erupted in murmurs of assent, the crowd rising to their feet, their fear now masked with burning hate. Connor grabbed Trinity by the arm.

We have to get out of here, he told her. *Now!*

Trinity forced a nod, still staring at Malia's limp frame, tears streaming down her cheeks. This was not how it was supposed to go! She swallowed back the lump in her throat and met Rashida's eyes. "I'm sorry," she said. "I'm so, so sorry."

"Get her!" Rashida commanded the Potentials. "Destroy her!"

The crowd surged, unarmed but frightening in their sheer numbers and rage. Trinity and Connor tried to dash for the hidden door, but the mob blocked their path. Two girls grabbed Trin by her hair, yanking her backward, catching her off balance. As she tumbled to the ground, the mob surrounded her, kicking her and punching her as hard as they could.

Her head swam. Her vision blurred. She fought back best she could, slamming her foot down on one Potential's ankle while elbowing another in the ribs. At one point, she managed to roll herself over and leap back to her feet, lashing out at any one who came near. But it was only a temporary escape and soon her arms were grabbed and yanked behind her, locking her into submission. A warmth dripped down her face and a copper taste filled her mouth.

Across the room, Connor wasn't doing much better. They'd pinned him to the ground, a foot securely placed on his throat, preventing any movement. He screamed in rage and fought ferociously, but there were just too many of them to have an effect.

In fact, there was only one thing that could possibly stop them now, she realized.

Emmy! To me!

It was the last thing she wanted to do. They were innocent kids—lied to, deceived, given false hope, with no comprehension of who their leaders really were. But what choice did she have? They would kill her if she didn't do something soon, leaving the entire world in jeopardy.

Sacrifice one to save the world. It wasn't at all how she'd imagined it'd go.

"Get out of my way," she dimly heard a voice at the back of the crowd. She looked up, through blurry eyes, to see Rashida striding toward her. "She's mine."

The crowd parted, much as they had that first day at the mall, allowing Rashida through. But this time it wasn't a friendly hug or a welcome home that the Potential hoped to deliver. Rather a kiss of death. Trin watched as the Indian girl grew closer, her face and hands smeared with blood. Malia's blood, she realized, her stomach swimming with nausea. And soon hers as well.

Hurry, Emmy.

Rashida stepped up to her, staring at her with eyes filled with venom. "Just tell me one thing," she hissed, her voice cracking around the edges. "Why?"

"Because," Trinity croaked, "the world still deserves a chance."

Rashida slammed her fist into her face, busting Trin's nose with the impact. Blood splashed onto the Potential's already bloodied white shirt but she paid it no mind. "That's for Malia," she spit out. "And this is for…"

The Potential trailed off, freezing as a shadow crossed over her, hovering just above her head. Slowly, she looked up, finding herself face to face with a small, green, very angry-looking dragon.

"Oh hell," she muttered.

Trinity squeezed her eyes shut, not wanting to see, not wanting to witness what she knew had to come. She knew it was necessary. But she also knew it was awful and terrible and cruel. And if she opened her eyes now, she'd never be able to close them again without seeing fire and death beneath her lids.

And so, she waited, like a coward, eyes shutting out a reality she couldn't bear to face. The sounds of shouting and scrambling erupted all around her, her hands falling free as her captors fled.

Yet strangely, she heard no fire. Felt no heat. Smelled no smoke.

Open your eyes, Trinity.

And so, heart in her throat, she did. Only to find, to her utter astonishment, the room completely empty, save for Connor and Emmy looking at her impatiently.

"What happened?" she whispered, her voice hoarse and confused.

Connor shrugged. "Guess they had a change of heart."

"But…Rashida!" Her eyes darted around the room, searching for some kind of blackened lump where her former friend had once stood.

"It seems Emmy had a change of heart as well," Connor informed her in a solemn voice. He looked up at the dragon with something akin to respect. "She withheld her fire. Just scared them a little instead. Seemed to do the trick."

Trinity couldn't believe it. Her mind flashed back to the last time. When just a simple knock to her head had thrown the dragon into an uncontrollable rage. This time she'd clearly been at death's door with a real threat standing in front of her. And yet the dragon had held back her fire. She stared up at Emmy, her eyes filled with questions.

"You didn't hurt her?" she whispered.

You didn't want me to, Emmy said with a shrug of her tiny shoulders. *So I found another way.*

Trinity didn't know what to say. "Thank you," was all she could manage. The words seemed so inadequate, but she hoped her dragon understood just the same.

"Come on," Connor urged. "We've wasted too much time already."

Trinity shook herself, flashing her dragon a grateful look, then ran after him, through the hidden door, down the hall, to the staircase leading to the parking garage. Finally they reached her mother's chamber and she pushed through the door.

"Mom!" she cried, dropping to her knees in front of her. "We're here to rescue you! Come on! Get up!" She tugged at her mother's hand.

But her mother just stared into space, unmoving.

"She's stuck in the Nether," Trinity explained to Connor. "She's been there almost two years, according to Darius."

Connor frowned. "Then it's going to be nearly impossible

to get her out," he told her. "Once you've spent enough time there, your mind starts losing touch with reality. You probably won't be able to wake her."

Trinity frowned. "Well, I'm not leaving her here." She tried to lift her mother from her chair, but the woman fought her, thrashing blindly until Trin was forced to give up. She bit her lower lip, her mind racing with solutions. "I'll have to go in there after her," she concluded. "Talk her into coming out."

"We don't have time for that," Connor said, glancing at the door. "They're going to figure out where we went and come after us. We need to get Emmy out of here before it's too late."

She crossed her arms over her chest. "I'm not leaving without her."

"Well, I'm not leaving without you."

Their eyes met, pinning one another in a strange déjà vu. She remembered how beautiful she thought his eyes were on that first day, as if they would glow in the dark. They still glowed, she realized. But that wasn't what she liked most about him now.

Just like last time, he gave in first, rolling his eyes and shaking his head. "Did anyone tell you you're the most stubborn girl in the world?" he muttered, reaching into his pocket and tossing her a ruby.

She grinned. "Maybe once or twice." Then she turned to Emmy. "Go find Caleb. Make sure he's okay. Connor, you guard the door. Don't let anyone through until I'm back."

Chapter Forty-Two

The blackened landscape stretched out before Trinity, smothered under a blood-red sky. The smell of sulfur burned through the air and a mournful wailing assaulted her ears. Only one path stretched out before her, winding across the desolate landscape to meet tall, gray mountains on the other side. But it was narrow and steep and strangled by thorns, all but impassable to someone on foot.

"Mom?" Trinity cried out, surveying the scene with an encroaching fear. She had known it would be bad here, inside her mom's self-imposed prison. But she had no idea it would be like this. So black. So dark. So dead. "Are you there?"

The hungry wind devoured her words as soon as she spoke them and returned no reply. But what had she expected? Her mother clearly didn't want to be found. Straining, she freed her mind, sending it out into the Nether, seeking to pinpoint some hint of her mother's spark, deeply rooted in this nightmare world. She knew, after two long years, it would be faint at best. At worst, gone entirely.

No, Trin told herself. *She lives. She breathes. She has to be here somewhere. And I will find her. I have to find her.*

Suddenly, out of nowhere, she felt it: a strange, whirling

vibration, fluttering far off in the distance. She squinted her eyes, scanning the horizon, catching the faintest glimmer of light—as dim as a star from another universe, flickering among the mountains' dark shadows.

"Mom!" she cried, excitement welling up inside of her. "I'm coming! Stay right there! I'm on my way."

But even as she spoke the words, doubt assaulted her. How would she reach the mountains in time? They had to be fifty miles away and she was on foot. There was no way she'd reach them—

Unless…

She bit her lower lip, considering her options. Caleb had always manifested whatever he needed from the Nether. Could she do something like that herself? But what would she create that would help her? A car? It'd never make the trip up the mountains. An airplane? She'd have no idea how to get it off the ground, never mind land.

Then it came to her. She was in the Nether. A world created by dragons. She drew in a quick, sharp breath and sent out her cry.

"Um, hello? Dragons of the Nether?" she called out, feeling a little silly. "Are you there? I could really use some help!"

At first, there was no reply. So she sent out her plea a second time. Then a third—but still she got no answer. Her heart sank. Could the dragons not hear her? Or were they just unwilling to help?

"Guess I'll be hoofing it after all," she muttered, readying herself for that all-important first step. "Hang on, Mom. This could take a while."

Suddenly, the sky darkened, the air filling with thunder.

Trinity looked up, jaw dropping as her eyes fell upon dragons—dozens of dragons—raining down in front of her. Big ones, small ones, red ones, green ones. Every size and every color of the rainbow, all descending before her and landing at her feet. She took a hesitant step backward, swallowing hard as she felt a hundred pairs of eyes look at her with expectancy.

"Um, I didn't actually need all of you," she stammered, looking from dragon to dragon. "Wow, there's quite a few of you here, aren't there?" she added, not sure what to say.

There was a brief shuffling as the beasts parted down the middle, clearing a pathway for a large, green dragon with golden wings to step through. The dragon walked slowly, deliberately, stopping in front of Trinity and gazing at her with dark blue eyes. Trinity forced down her fear and met her gaze, surprised to realize the dragon looked strangely familiar, though she had no idea why.

"Um, hi," she managed to spit out. "Thanks for coming. I'm Trinity Foxx. Do you happen to know my friend Emmy? Green dragon, about this high? Has a thing for bloody carcasses?"

The dragon dipped her massive head. *I am Lyria. And we all know who you are, Fire Kissed.*

Lyria. Trinity scrunched her face. Where had she heard that name before?

And then it hit her.

"You're Emmy's mother!" she gasped. No wonder the dragon looked so familiar. She'd seen her during Emmy's vision. She frowned as she remembered the mother dragon unfurling her massive wings and flying away, abandoning her own child without even saying good-bye.

But then, she reminded herself, she had thought that about

her own mother as well once upon a time. And things had not been as they seemed. She needed to give the dragon the benefit of the doubt.

Emberlyn was indeed born of my blood, the dragon before her admitted. *But I cannot call myself her mother. I allowed fear to steal that right from me on a day long ago. A day I have regretted ever since.* Her eyes leveled on Trinity. *I hope you will not make the same mistake as I did.*

Trinity shook her head fiercely, thinking back to her tiny dragon, resting on her shoulders, chirping in her ears. Her heart filled with love. With a protectiveness that shot straight to her core. "I won't leave Emmy behind," she promised the mother dragon. "No matter what happens. We're a team. And we'll take on the entire world if we have to."

Then you *are her true mother now.*

Trinity felt a warm glow at the dragon's words, knowing how difficult it must have been for her to say them. Behind her, the other dragons snorted and grunted their agreement.

"Thank you," she said simply, not sure what else to say. "I'll take good care of your daughter. I promise. And any other dragons I come across in the meantime." She thought about the mutated dragons from the Dracken's lab. Those poor souls. Somehow she needed to save them too.

We will be watching you, Fire Kissed, Lyria continued. *The fate of the entire dragon race is in your hands.*

Wow. Talk about putting on the pressure. Half of her wanted to protest—to say it was too much for one girl. But as her gaze roamed over their hopeful faces, their beseeching eyes, she realized she couldn't disappoint them. They believed in her. It was time she started believing in herself as well.

She forced a smile to her lips. "You can count on me," she declared. Then she squared her shoulders. "But first I have a favor to ask."

Chapter Forty-Three

Just do it. Do it now and be done with it.

Connor stared down at Trinity's limp body, unguarded and completely helpless as she traversed the Nether. He toed her lightly with his boot, but she didn't move. Whatever was happening in there, she was obviously in deep—so deep she probably wouldn't even wake up. It would be over in a second. Quick and painless. She'd never know he'd done it. And the world would finally be free.

Come on, you coward. This is what you trained for!

It was his father's voice he heard jeering in his head—taunting him, torturing him, reminding him of how far he'd strayed from his mission. He'd come here to save the world, his father reminded him. So why had he just gone and saved the one girl who was destined to destroy it instead?

She's not like that. She wouldn't do it. She doesn't deserve to die.

Are you so sure about that? his father demanded. *Are you willing to bet the world on it? 'Cause that's what you're doing by allowing her and her dragon to live: risking millions of lives. My life. You already killed me once, Connor. Are you prepared to make that same mistake again?*

Connor hung his head as memories of that day swam

through his mind—the dragon blasting his father; his father falling to the ground, engulfed in flames; the realization that it was all his fault.

He'd promised Trinity he'd find another way. But that was before he'd seen how easily things could spiral out of control. If he hadn't gotten there in time today—if he hadn't been able to rally the troops to raid—Emmy would now be in the hands of the Dracken and Trinity would be dead anyway. And once again, it would be his fault.

He could do it now and no one would know it was him. They'd assume it was one of the Dracken. Or one of the soldiers. And the world would be safe forever.

Sacrifice one to save the world. It had been his mission from the start.

He stared down at Trinity's unconscious body, her mouth set in a determined frown, as if daring him to do the deed. She was so stubborn. Even at the edge of death she was so damned stubborn and strong—not to mention selfless. Back in the courtyard she could have easily run by the Potentials, left them to their delusions. But she'd tried to help them instead. Tried to get them to see the truth—to save their lives—and it had almost cost her her own life.

But it hadn't. Because Emmy had come. The violent, rage-filled creature who should have acted on character, letting loose a mighty holocaust across the entire hall, had somehow, some way resisted millions of years of instinct. She'd acted rationally. Peacefully. Almost human in her analysis of the situation. She'd taken what had happened the last time and used it to guide her actions this time around.

Which meant she could be taught. She could be trained.

But was it worth the risk?

"It's worth it. And she's worth it too."

Connor whirled around to find his brother had silently stepped into the room. Caleb didn't appear armed, but the look on his face told Connor he was ready for a fight. Of course that wouldn't stop the Hunter from pulling the trigger first. All along he'd known there was the possibility he'd have to give his own life to the cause. That didn't scare him.

But, he realized, glancing over at the Fire Kissed, a world without Trinity did.

"Don't worry, I can't do it," he said with a long, slow sigh, partially to her, partially to his brother, but mostly to himself. "Even if I wanted to. Even if I knew for sure that the apocalypse would come." He dropped his gun to the ground, then sank to his knees, scrubbing his face with his hands. "I'm sorry, Dad. Once again I've let you down."

Caleb stared down at the gun, then over at his brother, an unreadable look on his face. He reached for the weapon, wrapping his fingers around the hilt. Connor gritted his teeth, readying himself for the pain that he knew would come. He only prayed his brother would act quickly, cleanly, and not make him suffer.

Instead, his brother stuffed the gun into the waistband of his pants. "Did you ever go back and read the autopsy report?" he asked slowly, surprising Connor with the question. "The one they did on the dragon that killed our father?"

What? What did that have to do with anything? Connor shook his head, puzzled. "No. Uh, why, did you?" What was his brother trying to get at?

"I did. Two years ago. Just before I agreed to go back in

time with the Dracken. The Council keeps detailed reports on every kill, you know, and it's all public record, not that many people bother to check them out." He paused, then added, "I don't know why I did it. Maybe I was trying to talk myself out of going. To convince myself that you were doing the right thing by destroying the egg. That dragons actually were evil and that I shouldn't try to stop you from wiping them out."

"So what did it say?" Connor asked, curious despite himself. "What could it have possibly said to convince you that dragons were worth saving?"

"That she was pregnant."

"Wait, what?" Connor shook his head. "No. That's impossible. If she was pregnant, she would have been nesting. She wouldn't have been flying over the Strata in the first place."

"She wasn't. At least not until Dad drew her out with his Hunter's song. He was a very powerful Hunter, as you know. He pushed her, convinced her to leave the safety of her nest—all so he could kill her."

"But that's illegal," Connor protested weakly, feeling as if his world was sliding out from under him. His father—his hero father—why would he do such a thing? It was Dragon Hunting 101; you never lured a dragon into a populated area on purpose. It was far too risky. "Why would Dad do that?"

"He needed the silver," Caleb replied. "Our family was hungry. Mom was sick."

"So he was trying to protect his children then."

"Just as the dragon was trying to protect hers," Caleb concluded. His eyes pierced his brother's. "So now, Connor, tell me this. Was the dragon who killed our father an evil creature consumed by blood lust? Or a desperate mother, doing whatever she could to save her babies from an evil man who was trying to kill them?"

Connor hung his head. "I don't know," he said quietly. "I just don't know anymore." He stared down at his hands, thoughts whirling madly.

"In any case," Caleb declared after a moment, "you can relax. I'm not going to kill you." He glanced over at Trinity. "For one thing, she wouldn't want me to."

Connor looked up. "She should," he said with a grimace. "She'd be safer if I were gone."

His twin shrugged. "She sees good in you," he said simply. "And judging from the fact that you didn't kill her when you had the chance makes me think she might be right." He gave his brother a rueful look. "I should have listened to you about the Dracken," he admitted. "Deep down, I suppose, I always knew they were too good to be true." He sighed. "I guess I just wanted a chance to be noticed for once. To be a hero." He rolled his eyes. "What a duffer, right?"

"No." Connor shook his head. "You fought for what you believed in—risked your life for it, even. And the fact that the people you trusted didn't prove worthy of that trust doesn't take away from what you tried to do." He gave his brother a crooked smile. "I guess in a way we both came back in time on the same mission, you know? To save the world. Sadly, neither one of us had any real idea how to do it."

Caleb seemed to consider this. "Maybe we've been thinking too big," he declared after a pause. "Maybe instead of saving the world, we should just concentrate on saving one girl. And one dragon, of course." He grinned. "What do you think? Think we can manage something like that between the two of us?"

Connor laughed despite himself. "Why not?" he said. "I mean, two of us, two of them? How hard could it be?"

Chapter Forty-Four

Lyria sank to a quiet landing on the side of the cliff, lowering her wing and allowing Trinity to slide off her back and onto the ground. She nodded her head in the direction of a small cave, cut into the side of the cliff. *You will find your mother there*, she said in a throaty voice. *I hope she can give you the answers you're looking for.*

Trinity reached out, her heart overflowing as she stroked the dragon's nose. "How can I ever thank you?" she asked. "I never would have made it without you."

Actually… Lyria started, then trailed off. *There is one thing…*

"What is it? What can I do?"

Let Emberlyn know how sorry I am. And that I hope one day she can forgive me.

The mighty dragon looked down at Trinity with huge baleful eyes, overflowing with sorrow. Trin gave her a rueful smile, then reached out, wrapping her arms around the beast's thick neck. "I'm sure she will," she promised the dragon. "Someday you guys will be reunited again. Just like me and my mom."

Lyria nodded, then nudged Trinity softly with her snout before unfurling her wings and lifting back into the sky. Trinity watched her go, feeling both wistful and hopeful. If

Emmy and her mom could find peace, maybe there was hope for her as well. She turned to the cave.

"Here goes nothing." And she dove in.

The light from outside dimmed and the walls started closing in as Trinity pushed deeper and deeper into the cave. Soon it was so tight she had to drop to her hands and knees and crawl her way through. A horrifying claustrophobia pressed at her chest, but still she pushed forward. She couldn't stop. Not now. Not when she'd come so far. Instead, she concentrated on her mother's spark, just up ahead, and crawled on. She was almost there.

After what seemed an eternity, the narrow passageway finally opened up into a clearing, allowing her to straighten to full height. Relieved, she pulled herself to her feet, sucking in a long, hard breath and looking around, her jaw dropping as she recognized where she was.

Home. Not her grandpa's home but her mother's home—the house they'd shared just before that fateful Christmas Eve. The same blue shutters. The same red mailbox. The same bushes sparkling with the same Christmas lights.

She was home. Really, truly home.

Unnerved, she forced herself up the steps and through the front door, déjà vu hitting her hard and fast. When she pushed open the door, she half expected to stumble upon the nightmare all over again. A bloodied corpse. A shotgun by its side.

But that didn't really happen, she reminded herself. *That wasn't Mom.*

And so she dared to step over the threshold, trying to prepare herself for anything.

"Trinity! You're home!"

She looked up, her eyes widening as none other than her mother herself stepped out from the kitchen, carrying a plate of freshly baked cookies. She was dressed in a red velvet dress, a checkered apron tied to her waist. Her hair was pulled up into her familiar ponytail and she even wore some makeup on her face. She looked fresh and healthy and happy. And not the least bit insane. As she walked over to her daughter, as if she'd seen her just a few hours before, she held out the plate.

"You must be starving!" she said. "Dinner will be here soon. In the meantime, a few cookies won't ruin your appetite, right?"

Trinity slowly reached out, feeling half in a daze as she took a cookie from the plate and put it to her lips. It was sweet and buttery, just like a cookie should be, and she bit back a groan of delight.

"Good, right?" her mother asked.

"Amazing," she concurred. But she wasn't just talking about the baked goods.

After taking another bite, she looked around the room, trying to sort things through. It was all there, identical to how it had been—the same simple furnishings, the same cheery Christmas tree. The only difference was the presents underneath weren't stained with blood as they had been the first time around. And there was no body sprawled out in the middle of the floor, no head blown to smithereens.

She turned to her mother. She had a million things she wanted to say. Instead, "I thought you were dead!" was all that came from her lips.

Her mother gave a shrill laugh. "Dead? Please. Can a dead

woman dance like this?" She flittered around the room, using the plate of cookies as her dance partner. Trinity watched her, tears misting her eyes as she remembered all the dance parties they'd had over the years. Whirling around the room until they collapsed in dizzy glee.

"Oh, Mom," she whispered. "I've missed you so much."

Her mother stopped dancing, her eyes twinkling merrily. "If you're buttering me up for Chinese food, you needn't bother. I've already placed the order and your grandpa's picking it up on his way over here. Extra duck sauce, just as you like it." She clapped her hands in excitement, bouncing up and down. "Oh, Trinity, this is going to be the best Christmas ever!"

Just like she'd promised.

This was how it was supposed to be, Trinity realized suddenly, things finally sliding into place. *This was the Christmas Eve I was supposed to have.*

She sank down onto the couch, watching her mother rummage through the presents under the tree. She realized she'd never unwrapped a single one the first time around—she'd been too traumatized and they had eventually donated everything to Goodwill instead. Meaning she had no idea what her mother had picked out for her.

She was about to find out.

Mom crowed triumphantly as she found the present she'd been looking for. Lifting it from the pile, she set it on Trinity's lap, her face shining as she looked from the gift to her daughter. "Here you go, honey," she said. "You can open this one early. Just don't tell your grandpa. He thinks everyone should wait till Christmas morning."

Trin drew in a breath, bit her lower lip, then carefully undid the wrapping. She knew she should be hurrying—they were running out of time in the real world—but it was so nice to be here—to finally be allowed to live through that stolen day—she couldn't help but drag out the moment a little longer. Pulling off the paper, she gasped as she found an ornate golden music box inside. Lifting the lid revealed a small princess, pirouetting to a simple tune.

She looked up. "Oh, Mom, it's your music box!"

She'd wondered where the box had disappeared to when they'd come back to clean out the house. She never would have guessed her mom had wrapped it and put it under the tree. It must have gone to charity, along with the rest of the presents.

Her mother smiled, her eyes misting with tears. "Your father gave me this," she told Trinity. "He told me when you were old enough that I should give it to you."

Her father. Trinity turned to her mother, realizing this might be her one and only opportunity to know. "What happened to my father?" she asked in barely a whisper.

But before her mother could answer, the room started to shake. The walls began to buckle and a long crack ripped down the ceiling. Trinity grabbed on to her mother, her eyes darting around the room, terror gripping her like a vise.

"Mom, we have to go!" she cried. "We can't be here anymore!" The dream world was collapsing. They didn't have much time.

"But your grandpa's coming over," her mom protested. "We're about to celebrate Christmas."

Trinity shook her head. "Mom, this never happened. It's all

in your mind, holding you trapped here. It's time to wake up so we can escape!"

Her mother's face crumbled. "No," she whispered. "I don't want to go back."

"Mom, you have to. You can't stay here! You don't know what they plan to do!"

Her mom broke away, her face white and her eyes terrified. "Do you think I don't know?" she whispered hoarsely. "I've always known. Your father told me. And I was going to tell you. They took me away before I could!"

Trinity had no idea what her mother was talking about, but it didn't matter now. The carefully constructed dream world was collapsing out from under them and if they didn't leave now, they would be trapped here forever.

"Please, Mom!" she begged, tears running down her face. "Come with me!"

But her mother only reached out, swiping away Trin's tears with careful fingers. She looked at her daughter with fondness in her eyes as she slowly shook her head. "I was waiting to give you your Christmas," she told her gently. "To keep the promise I made. Now I have. And I'm free to go. Now I can finally say good-bye." She leaned forward to press a kiss on Trinity's forehead. "I love you, baby girl. Merry Christmas."

Trinity closed her eyes, trying to memorize the moment as best she could. A single, perfect moment to relive over and over again for the rest of her life.

"I love you too, Mom," she whispered. "Merry Christmas at last."

Chapter Forty-Five

Trinity burst from the Nether, the gem's dust seeping through her hands. She looked up to find Connor and Caleb watching her with strained faces. She turned to look at her mother. Her eyes had closed. Her face relaxed. Her mouth turned up at the corners in a serene-looking smile. Free at last, just as she'd wanted.

Two years ago, her mother had promised her a real Christmas in a real home. A family Christmas, just as Trin had always begged for. And so she'd held on, all this time, waiting patiently in the Nether for her daughter to finally come home. So she could keep her promise at last.

"Good-bye, Mom," Trinity whispered, reaching out to trace a cold cheek with her fingers. She wanted to cry, but the tears wouldn't come. The woman had clung to life two years longer than the universe had intended her to; now it was time to let her go. Trin smiled down at her mother, then pulled the emerald ring from her finger and slipped it into her hand.

I'm a lot like Mom, she said to herself. And the thought made her smile.

"Come on," Connor urged, interrupting. "We have to get out of here. Now!"

Trin nodded, forcing her mind back to the present. But as she rose to her feet, something fell from her lap. She looked down, shocked to find the music box her mother had given her while in the Nether now lying at her feet. How did she bring it back with her? That should have been impossible…

"Come on, Trin!" Caleb urged. "Let's go!"

She grabbed the box and ran, deciding to puzzle it out later, following the two boys out of the room and down the dark hallway. Emmy met them at the split, her eyes anxious and her expression grim.

They're coming! she cried. *Hurry!*

"Wait!" Trinity protested. "What about the other dragons?"

Caleb shook his head. "There's nothing left," he told her. "The other Dracken must have come by and taken the healthy ones with them, then burned the rest so the government couldn't extract their DNA. There's just ashes down there. Nothing left to save."

Trinity could feel Emmy's horror rising within her and tried to send comforting thoughts to her dragon to ease her distress. The last thing she needed was for Emmy to lose control now. But deep inside, she couldn't help but worry. Darius had been captured, but the other Dracken were still at large. And they had dragons at their disposal—maybe not the healthiest of dragons, but dragons all the same.

This is not over, she realized, a cold chill creeping into her bones. *Not by a long shot.*

But for now, there was nothing they could do. And so they raced through the parking garage, toward the elevator, getting on board and shooting up to the world above. When the doors slid open, they tumbled out the back of the mall. The sun was so bright Trinity was forced to squint. It had been so long she'd almost forgotten what it looked like.

"Come on," Connor urged, grabbing her hand. "This way!"

She followed him to a black van parked nearby. He yanked open the door, then ushered her inside. She crawled in, her eyes widening as she realized who was driving their getaway vehicle.

"Grandpa!" she cried, throwing her arms around him and squeezing him tight—the real-life hug a thousand times better than the *Fields of Fantasy* one had been. She breathed in deep, rejoicing in the faint scent of tobacco clinging to his shirt. She'd have to scold him about smoking later. Right now she was just too happy to see him.

"Welcome home, kiddo!" he said with a grin.

Trinity laughed. "There's no place like it," she declared. And this time, she meant it.

Grandpa chuckled, then turned the key in the ignition. The van roared to life and they pulled out of the parking lot and into the night. Soon they were speeding down the highway, the mall and all its horrors fading into the distance. Emmy settled comfortably on Trin's shoulder, resting her head against the backseat, purring happily. As if to tell her, *my home is wherever you are.*

Trinity watched the mall disappear out the back window until she could see it no more. Then she turned to the boys.

"So now what?" she asked. "Got any ideas of what we should do next?"

The boys looked at one another and smiled, as if sharing a secret joke.

"Now we raise a dragon," Connor replied.

"And," Caleb added, "make sure she doesn't destroy the world."

Acknowledgments

To my editor Leah Hultenschmidt, who shouted, "I want this book!" after only a one-sentence pitch, then helped me shape it into what it is today. Brainstorming sessions have never been so much fun! And to the entire Sourcebooks team—your enthusiasm and support is invaluable to me and I'm thrilled to be part of the family.

To my agent Kristin Nelson, for reading many, many early versions of this book until we found one that worked. And for understanding why this story was so important to me and needed to be told.

To my husband Jacob, for all the tireless conversations and charts on time-travel paradoxes. Not to mention all the delicious dinners on deadline and all-encompassing support. Seriously—best husband ever.

To Diana Peterfreund—author, friend, and beta reader—who insisted a dragon book can never have too many dragons. And to blogger Donna @ Bites—the toughest beta reader you will ever love and my sister in Lost Boys fandom. And to my Werearmadillo writing group—for all their encouragement and support when things got tough. Not to mention my Austin SCBWI and RWA friends who make Texas a great place to live.

And, lastly, to author Robin McKinley, who introduced me to the awesomeness of dragons when I was young with her amazing book, *The Hero and the Crown*. As writers, we don't always know who we have touched with our words. So I tell you now, I would not be who I am today without your stories.

About the Author

Mari Mancusi always wanted a dragon as a pet. Unfortunately, the fire insurance premiums proved a bit too large and her house a bit too small—so she chose to write about them instead. Today she works as an award-winning young adult author and freelance television producer, for which she has won two Emmys. When not writing about fanciful creatures of myth and legend, Mari enjoys goth clubbing, cosplay, watching cheesy (and scary) horror movies, and her favorite guilty pleasure—playing video games. A graduate of Boston University, she lives in Austin, Texas, with her husband Jacob, daughter Avalon, and their dog Mesquite.